D0827543

THE TRAVELLER'S TALE

TALES OF DARKWOOD BOOK 1

STACEY UPTON BRACEY

EWP PUBLICATIONS

EWP PUBLICATIONS

Copyright ©2022 by EWP Publications

All rights reserved.

No portion of this book may be reproduced in any form without written permission
from the publisher or author, except as permitted by U.S. copyright law.

Cover Art by www.allaboutbookcovers.com

FOREWORD

The book you are about to read has a companion, *Witch of Darkwood*, which you can get for free and sign up for my newsletter, too. It's Henna's origin story, and intersects neatly with this one. It was fun to write the reverse viewpoint and see Bella from a fresh pair of eyes. You can find it here: https://www.subscribepage.com/m2f4a3

The Darkwood has proved to be rich territory, and there are more books coming to continue the story of Bella and her family. The next one is a twist on Hansel and Gretel, a low fantasy dark adventure called *The Twins of Darkwood*. https://www.amazon.com/dp/B09NH45625 I've put an excerpt in the back of this book for you.

There are for sure three, maybe four books to follow in The Tales of Darkwood Series. I hereby make a solemn vow to you, dear reader, to have them all done and available for you to devour in a timely manner. I hate waiting for sequels, too.

And finally... tread lightly through these pages. They contain depictions of witch prosecution, medieval torture, and loss.

CONTENTS

PROLOGUE

B urgermeister Strom supped alone. Except for the servants, of course, but they were beneath his notice. Strom savored his swan with stewed plums in his richly appointed dining hall filled with gifts given to buy his favor. All of them paled in comparison to the gift that was rolling towards the gates of the city. He'd waited fourteen years for a particular gypsy witch to float within his reach.

Now she was coming. The witch and her motley clan of Travellers were finally coming to profit from a Saint's day in his town. Did she know it was the working of his curse that had guided her to return? The strength of his will? No matter if she knew or not, he thought, spearing a bite of swan breast. The witch was nigh, bringing with her the prize he would soon possess. Her daughter. The witch owed him a wife and a life after all; it was only fitting that her daughter be the sacrifice.

Delicately holding his satin-lined sleeve aside, he plucked up a plum from the platter before him. His ruby ring flashed in the firelight as he brought the fruit to his fulsome lips. He'd let the witch and her clan come into his town as if by their own free will. They'd sell their wares and perform their show today. He'd lull them. On the morrow, he'd have the lot of them arrested, perhaps play with them a bit in the dungeons before taking what he was owed. The life of the mother first. Then he'd make a new wife of her daughter, just come into her flowering. Exquisite.

He bit the plum, let the juices flow down his lips and throat, and thought of blood.

CHAPTER ONE

Saints, she was late! Bella ran, clutching a tiny orange kitten. She nimbly dodged people right and left, her dark hair threaded through with scarlet, blue, and green ribbons flying behind her. Her bare feet pounded on the cobblestone streets while her leather knapsack with the baby's cleaned diapers banged against her leg with every other stride.

She pinched her nostrils together to keep the stench from gagging her as she ran up the steep street. This part of the city nearest the river docks stank. Besides the tannery and the slaughterhouse, the elders of the town, in all their wisdom, had placed the charnel house here as well. Even breathing through her mouth barely lessened the smell of the dead wafting from the place. No wonder they'd placed it downwind from the town. Speeding by, she noted the cart for the dead placed just beside the charnel house. It was so big! How many people must die a night for them to need such a thing? The jail was placed here as well. How awful for the prisoners to smell that as they waited for the executioner, she thought. As if being shut up inside never seeing the sun wasn't bad enough.

Bella ran on. Buildings of wattle and daub and stone and timber rose high around her. Two stories tall in the outer circle of the city to three stories and more as she neared the middle of the town. She avoided the center of the street where the night water, trash, and offal flowed down to the river. The outermost stalls of the folk in for the festival lined the first square she passed through. Wares were called out by the vendors in sing-song patter. Everything from weapons and suits of armor to everyday dishes to toys and trinkets, there was a myriad of goods and treasures to choose from.

Her side ached, but she kept moving. She'd spent too long watching the clouds float by, laying on the grassy riverbank. The little orange kitten had wandered by and cuddled next to her. The purring of the kitten, the sparkle of the sun on the river, the peaceful sound of its flow, and the deliciousness of being on her own for an hour had lulled her. Her errand had been to wash out the disgusting cloths they used for the new baby in their tribe. Why did they poop in vivid yellow, anyway? Bella was resolved never to have babies. They started out as crying lumps and only got worse as they got older and learned to talk. Her aunt Kezia had been burdened with four of the things, all of them completely annoying at any age as far as she was concerned, especially her pouty cousin Rose. Rose would be supremely irritated if she had to go up and dance in her stead.

Bella wove through the outer food vendor section of the holiday market. Fried doughnuts sizzled as they were dipped in hot honey and handed out as fast as they were made. Wafts from roasting meats made her belly growl, but there was no time to stop for food or even steal an apple as she dashed toward the performance area in the center of the town. It was wonderful to finally be here, in this town that her parents had avoided for so long. Especially her mother. It had been like moving heaven and earth to make her come here. Bella was happy she'd finally nagged them into coming here for the biggest festival in the area.

A pack of small boys pushed past her. They ignored the calls of their parents to slow down. Bella saw men put wary hands on their coin purses as the boys brushed by them. In crowds like these, the thieves would circulate, eager to prey on the careless. The crowd packed together as they entered the giant square. Bella jumped to see over the throng. Maybe her father hadn't taken the stage yet. Her heart sank as she heard the first beats of his drum. The drum she was supposed to be dancing to. Saints! Why wasn't there a side alley to dash through when she needed one?

CHAPTER TWO

The Traveller's stage had a place of honor opposite the church. Bright banners flanked each side, and a large patchwork curtain hung at the back. Older boys clambered onto the fountain, which stood in the middle of the square, to try for a good view. Smaller boys pushed and elbowed their way through the crowd to reach the edge of the makeshift wooden platform that had been erected the night before. They wedged themselves into a raucous group of young men, who stank of drinking too much ale too quickly.

As the rings of the noon bell faded, a broad-shouldered man parted the curtain with a flourish and stepped forward onto the stage. The storyteller wore black knee-length pantaloons like a pirate, and a scarlet vest that only covered part of his massive, deeply tanned chest. His thick, dark brown hair was pulled back in a long tail tied with a ribbon. He tossed back rakish bangs with a gleaming smile. Young women nudged each other at the sight of him and vied with the children to get closer to the stage.

The storyteller grinned, and with a flourish beat the bohdran drum that hung around his neck with his strong, deeply tanned hands. He let the drum bid all who heard it's song to come near. He turned in a merry dance as he did so, his bare feet shaking dust from the boards, powerful leg muscles flexing. A bright clash of cymbals on a tambourine joined the drumming as a pretty young woman stepped out from behind their curtain, dressed in a blue and green dancing gown with generous skirts. She shook the instrument merrily in a wide circle, flashed a smile, then paused and looked at the man with the drum expectantly.

He turned to the crowd and waved a hand towards the girl. "Can I get a cheer for my lovely niece Rose, who is to dance for you?" The crowd cheered obligingly, and several of the young men hooted and whistled. The man acknowledged her with a small bow. "Are you ready, Rose?"

Rose knew how to play the crowd, even though she wasn't fond of performing. She pretended to think about it, putting her hand to her chin, letting the masses of curly red hair fall to one side, turning in a small circle, swiveling her hips enticingly. Rose rolled her eyes at him as her back turned to the audience. She then whipped front to make the skirts fly, curtsied to her uncle, and nodded. "Yes, Uncle Ebbe, I'm quite ready!" Rose picked up her hem with a flourish, flashing a bit of leg to keep the menfolk in the crowd engaged. After all, they were the ones holding the purses.

Rose pranced up and down the stage, smiling as broadly as she could through gritted teeth. It was supposed to be her cousin Bella's turn to dance the crowd to the stage, not hers. That Belladonna was always haring off somewhere, doing something she shouldn't, leaving all the work to her. Still, it wouldn't do to let the crowd see any annoyance. After all, the Travellers stuck together through thick and thin. She shook her bright red hair back, letting the ribbons twisted in her long locks dance to the beat of her Uncle Ebbe's drum.

The crowd grew larger, as it always did. With a final flourish of drum and tambourine, Ebbe and Rose stopped in unison. With a nod to the audience, Rose stepped back behind the curtain, leaving Ebbe alone in the center of the platform. An expectant thrum filled the air as the crowd murmured and shifted to get a better view. A few babies cried and were hushed. Above them, the pennants of the town hung in celebration of the Saint's Day snapped in the wind.

Ebbe raised both of his hands to the sky and swept them in a wide arc, bringing all who could see him into his circle. He eyed the crowd, and with a flash of white teeth in his tanned face, bowed to them. Ebbe reached back and pulled the ribbon from his hair, then tossed his head back so the hair cascaded off his brawny shoulders, tumbling wantonly. There was a collective sigh from the women in the crowd. As always.

"Who's ready for a Traveller's Tale?" Ebbe cried out.

"I am! Me! Me!" the children in the crowd called out in an excited cacophony. Quite a few adult voices cried out to begin as well, for who didn't love a well-told story?

"Today's tale is that of The Sleeping Beauty!" Ebbe's rich baritone voice rolled over them. It was his gift. It easily reached the far corners of the city square. He could transform both it and his body to take on the character of a prince or an old witch, a bewitched princess, or an enchanted frog.

Behind the stage, his wife Vadoma smiled as she limped away from the prop table and stood to the side of the curtain of many colors that hung behind Ebbe. She'd stitched and added to it hundreds of times over the course of their years together. She never tired of watching her husband tell a tale, although this particular story of a cursed princess made her uneasy. As always, Ebbe began by setting the story in a town that just happened to match the landscape of whatever town they occupied.

"Once upon a time, in a land filled with green forests, rushing rivers filled with fish, golden fields of oats, and distant mountains that glistened silver and white when the sun hit them just so, there was a fine town filled with stone houses, some of which were five stories high! There were large squares with fountains that handsome young men could climb!" The boys perched on the fountain cheered. Ebbe laughed with the crowd. Then he continued. "And in the finest house of all, facing that magnificent square, there lived a handsome prince."

Ebbe paused and shifted his stance, leaning towards the little faces at the edge of the stage. "And tell me, fine lads and lasses, what color hair did this prince have?"

"Yellow! Black! Red!" the children yelled out their answers.

"Yellow! Yes, he had golden yellow hair and green eyes—or were they brown?" Ebbe knew how much the children loved helping to create the tale. He smiled to see the excitement on their faces.

"Green, yes, green!"

"You're right! Let me see if I have this straight and true. The handsome prince had green hair and yellow eyes, and—"

"No! No! You've got it backwards!"

Vadoma watched the parents smile, heard their chuckling and murmuring as their laughing children delighted in correcting the storyteller. Ebbe cocked his head in that endearing way he had, an exaggerated, puzzled frown creasing his face while his long brown hair lopped over to one side.

As usual, other comments filtered up from the crowd. Mean, petty comments. No matter how much their stories and songs were loved, the Travellers themselves were held in contempt. The hateful words threaded through, louder and more frequent when the crowds grew in size. People were always bolder in the anonymity of a throng.

"Of course he got it wrong, he's nothing but a stupid Traveller." "Can't even tell a story right, the dirty gypsy."

Ebbe let his voice soar above the crowd, ignoring the taunts that floated out from it. He continued the tale. "And do you know something else? This handsome, yellow-haired, green-eyed prince had an OGRE for a mother! Rawrrrrrr!"

Delighted squeals erupted from the crowd as Ebbe reached up with hands outstretched, and stomped around like an ogre, pretending to swipe at the children at the edge of the stage. Just as quickly, he transformed into his storyteller persona again and continued the tale.

"This is the story of how that prince awakened an exceptionally beautiful princess who had been cursed and had been sleeping for a hundred years. Do you know how he did that?"

"Nooo," came most of the response, with a few bright "I know how!" scattered among them.

"With a kiss!" Ebbe made the longest kissing sound he could, making the crowd laugh.

Shaking her head at how quickly her husband could have the audience in the palm of his hand, Vadoma turned to make sure all was ready for the second part of their show. She was in charge of the sound effects as the tale rolled on.

Rose stood in front of the lines they used to hang up pieces of costuming. The girl folded her arms across her narrow chest. "Aunt Vadoma, your selfish daughter was to sing and dance for the crowd today. This was to be my day off. Where is she?"

"If you keep frowning like that, your mouth will get stuck and you'll never be able to smile again," Vadoma replied mildly. "As for Bella, she was sent to wash your baby brother's soiled diapers. Perhaps you'd rather have done that?"

"Maybe I would have!" Rose retorted. "I hate having the boys at the edge of the stage try to look up my skirts!" Her cheeks flared pink. "I suppose I'll have to do the gypsy dance as well if she's not back. Now I won't have time to shop for myself!" She pursed her lips and stomped her foot.

"Step on a few fingers if they get too close," suggested Vadoma. She opted to keep her temper, as her niece had made several good points. "Remember," she continued before Rose could interrupt her again, "the money we make here is what will tide us through the winter. We all pull together."

Rose puffed out a sigh and turned away to add bells to her ankles and tie ribbons to her wrists. "We might all pull together, but that Bella only pulls for herself. She's worse than ever lately!"

Vadoma patted the flustered girl on the shoulder as she passed by, ready to rattle the sheet of tin they used for the thunder effects. She picked up the sheet with both hands and prepared to give it several good shakes. The sound was timed to the entrance of the evil fairy in the tale Ebbe was telling. She would shake it again when the fairy cursed the little princess to a hundred years of sleep when she pricked her finger on a spindle.

A shiver crept down her back as she readied herself. This story struck close to the bone, to the terrible secret only she knew. That she had brought an actual curse into their family. Their only child, Belladonna, had been cursed, just like the princess in the story, moments after she was born. A curse bound by air, earth, and blood. Unbreakable. Payment for the two deaths she'd allowed. Two scapegoats had been picked to carry that blame and the burden of the hateful words. Herself and her daughter. Worse, Vadoma worried that the time was coming for the full power of the curse to strike and bring horrible consequences to those she loved most. For the hundredth time, she wondered how she'd let herself be talked into returning to this terrible town.

CHAPTER THREE

B ella squeezed closer to one side of the stage. She could hear her father had already reached the part of the story when the Prince woke the Princess with a kiss. Grimacing, she tucked the kitten more securely under her arm and shoved impatiently through the cloaked people. At least she could do the final dance of the show. Rose was terrible at getting the crowd to pay their coins for good entertainment. One older woman smacked her with her cane as she passed and made a show of grabbing her coin purse out of the way.

"Disgusting thieves, all of them," the old lady sniffed to her plump male companion. "Shouldn't allow them into the town at all, if you ask me."

"Yes, Aunt Bettina, all of them are rotten thieves to be sure." The lazy words dripped from the man's mouth with a sneer. He looked like a grumpy owl, with tufts of brown hair sprouting out of his ears. His purse was also fat and dangled by his side. *Easy pickings if I did have a mind to take it,* Bella thought as she moved past him.

Bella was nearly to the platform, but a clump of young men who had ranged themselves at the corner edge of the stage blocked it. Wealthy young men from the looks of their clothes, the kind that thought they were better than anyone else. She'd seen their like in dozens of cities, thinking themselves smart that they were positioned to look up the skirts of the dancers on the stage. The only way past them was straight through. Bella moved quickly, but the boys were ready for sport. They grabbed at her, laughing as she tried to shove past them.

"Here's a fine fish, hey, does the little wiggly fish want some of my wood?" A big boy with jug ears tried to put his hand into her bodice. He leaned in close, his breath smelled of rotting fish and bad wine. She moved her head aside, avoiding his attempted kiss. Bella yanked hard on one of his ears and made him let go with a howl. The other boys laughed and shoved him back towards her as he clutched his ear. His face was red now, his leer turned into a snarl.

Bella saw her father take notice. His voice got louder. The last thing she wanted was for her father to wade in and rescue her and interrupt the story. Bella tried a new tactic and dropped to the ground, out of his circling arms. With a quick crawl and wiggle, she was nearly past the last of the pack, but one of them caught her around her waist, yanked her up towards him, and tried to kiss her. She yearned to give him a sharp slap but knew better than to strike him. That would just get her arrested and her family driven from the town.

She snapped her teeth at him and snarled. Alarmed, he let go. "Watch yerself, you stinking gypsy!"

"We're Travellers! Not gypsies!" She retorted over her shoulder as she slid behind the curtain, out of breath. Her mother waited there, hands on her hips. Her mother always looked twice as big as she normally did when she was angry. And the line down the middle of her forehead got deeper, too. Rose stood next to her, her nose in the air and her arms crossed.

"Sure, and you've missed the performance," Vadoma said in a harsh whisper. "And what is that creature you are carrying?"

"I had to go on in your place," added Rose in her insipid voice. "You owe me."

Bella ignored Rose, brushing by her to her mother. "It's a kitten. I've named her Selena. She'll help keep away the vermin in our wagon. I'll take care of it. Here are Pattin's nappies, cleaned and nearly dry." Bella spoke in low tones. She handed over the baby's wraps one-handed from the bundle she carried. She hoped that the job well done would mollify her mother, but as usual, Vadoma kept on scolding. All she ever did was find fault with her only daughter.

"Bella, you know your uncle cannot abide cats. Put that thing back outside. And these are not nearly dry enough," Vadoma sniffed. "And now what do you think you're doing?"

Bella had already plopped the kitten down on the table, stripped off her dull brown overskirt, and pulled on her favorite red dancing skirt over her linen underdress. She reached for her metal finger cymbals. "Getting ready to go on stage for the last dance, of course. Rose doesn't know how to keep the crowd like I do." She flashed a smile at her mother and swished her skirts.

"That's not true!" Rose's whisper was vicious. "And it's my turn to wear the red!" Rose yanked at the skirt, pulling it partway off.

Bella slapped away Rose's hands and tugged the skirt back up. "Then you should've put it on when you had the chance. Anyway, I look better in the red than you do, Rose. It clashes with that brassy hair of yours."

"Girls!" Vadoma broke in, separating them as they both tugged at the costume. "There is a show going on. Bella, you're too late, and you'll pay for it by doing both Rose's chores and your own for the rest of the week."

"Ha, serves you right!" Rose danced out of the way of the sharp kick Bella aimed at her.

Vadoma glared at both of them. "Rose, it's nearly time for the dance. Put on the yellow skirt, it looks beautiful on you. Bella, just get out and take that kitten with you. Go to the stall and help Kezia with the boys so she can sell our goods in peace. And tie your shawl on as well. No need to be flashing all the townsfolk if you're not on stage."

"But Ma!" Bella's voice raised. "I'm a better dancer than Miss No-chest over there! Miss empty-headed no-chest who can't dance a lick!" Bella spat out the comment. Rose's mouth dropped open. Bella could see that she was straining to come up with a retort. Bella laughed when all Rose could produce was sticking her tongue out at her.

"Shush, child! No buts. You had plenty of time to do this chore and get back here. Now go help your aunt at the stall. And mind, you keep your distance from those town boys as you do so. Tie up that shawl!" Vadoma's long green eyes sparkled dangerously, daring Bella to argue.

Bella felt her anger rise quickly. It was so unfair. "I always have to do everything! And I'm not a child, *Vadoma*!" Bella emphasized her mother's name, knowing full well she hated it when Bella used her name rather than calling her Mother. Well, too bad, so sad. Flinging the finger cymbals onto the table they used for props during their shows, she left her brown overskirt where she'd dropped it and flounced away. She kept the red dancing skirt on, tying it firmly. Rose would not have it today. After all, scarlet was her favorite color, and she looked good in it.

She snatched the hated shawl out of Vadoma's hands. She had to get out now; her mother was stifling her. "Take care of little Selena for me," she said saucily, nodding towards the kitten, which had cleverly found its way to the bit of cheese Vadoma had put out for lunch. Before her mother could respond, she darted out behind their stage on the opposite side from where the gang of boys sat. She glanced over as she heard the jingle of Rose's ankle bells and saw that she'd been right. Two of them were already stretched flat onto the stage itself, trying to peek under Rose's skirts. If Bella had been up there, she'd have the sense to accidentally stomp on them early on during her dance.

Or kick them in the face during the fast part of it. That always worked. Still fuming, Bella left the shawl dangling on the side of their tent poles. It was a warm day. There was no need for that thing at all. If people wanted to look at her, they could do so. She took a full, deep breath, glad to be away from her mother once more.

On side streets leading to the square, and all along edges of it, wheeled carts had been brought in for the festival. Some were more elaborate than others. Those were usually the ones run by local merchants. Stalls like her family kept were more makeshift, as they took them down and put them up in every village and town they came to on their yearly route. Moving through the crowd, Bella noticed that, as was usual, the townsfolk preferred to shop with their own people, and not the Travellers. You needed something special to lure them to buy if you were a Traveller. Easing through the crowd she overheard snippets of conversations about trade, card games, and errant husbands. Each small group was wrapped up in their own drama. Bella felt superior to them and held her head high. She had no worries such as these. Sure as sure could be, if she had a husband, she'd keep him.

Bella's thoughts wandered to what she might do to keep a husband. She wasn't a stranger to what men and women did when they were married. The camps they stayed in were full of couples and there was little privacy to be found. It was only recently that she had paid them any more mind than she did the horses or goats that walked the long trail with them. There were young men in the groups that their family group merged with during the spring and summer. In their winter camp, there were even more. It was only in the past few months that Bella had really seen the boys, the way their hair curled, lips curved, or their muscles bulged as they picked things up. One boy in particular had stood out from the rest, but she didn't want to tell anyone about it. It was her secret. And her puzzle, as this boy had been a childhood friend for years. What had changed? Over the past few months, it seemed she spent all her waking moments thinking of him, of his full lips and warm eyes—

"Watch yerself!" Bella startled as a woman with more rolls of fat than she'd ever seen before huffed indignantly at her. "Yer in my way, aren't you, you dirty trash!"

Widening her eyes, Bella moved an exaggerated step back. "A thousand pardons, madam," she replied clearly. "I've just never had to give so much room to someone before!"

Bella ducked away through the crowd before the outraged woman could strike her. Making her way past stalls selling carved wooden goods, pottery, and woolens, she stopped at the one selling exotic spices. It was one of her favorite stalls, run by a dark-skinned woman named Aisha and her son Malik. They originally hailed from further south and east than her clan had ever travelled. Bella wished she could go with them when they followed the spice road across the ocean. She yearned to see new things, experience a new land. Every third year, the pair made the long journey, taking tin goods and furs to trade. They'd return with silk, pepper, ginger, cinnamon, and other spices. The cloth that covered the top poles of the spice stall was a weathered canvass, like most of the Travellers used. What made it special were the strips of vibrant yellow silk fluttering in the corners.

Bella reached up and fingered the cloth, wondering, as she always did, how such a light, strong thing could exist. Malik had told her it was woven from a material that worms spat from their butts, but she knew that couldn't be true. There was more of the stuff, in beautiful greens and reds, in the back of the stall, giving a backdrop to the potions Aisha sold alongside simple spices. Potions for illness, for love, for sleep. Bella knew there were other potions too, not displayed, ones that helped women with their monthlies, ones that caused illness rather than curing it.

There was a dark, secretive side to Aisha and her potions. Bella thought it was best not to delve too deep.

Moving in front of the stall, she bent close to the small dish holding powdered cloves in olive oil and inhaled the intoxicating scent. Making sure that Aisha wasn't looking, she moved to dip a finger in the oil.

"Dipping your finger in the dish, why should today be different, *amira*?" Bella snatched back her hand, abashed. Aisha was giving her a side-long glance and wasn't smiling. Even though she and her family had worked the trade routes up and down the country with Aisha and her son Malik for many years, Bella always found her mysterious and a little frightening. She was one of the most exotic women Bella had ever seen, with her ebony skin, high cheekbones and close-cropped scalp. Bands of black tattoos in odd patterns circled both of the woman's arms. She was taller than most men and Bella knew she carried sharp blades on both her arms and calves. Bella was jealous of the shortened split skirts of green serge Aisha wore. They seemed to be so much easier to move around in than the heavy womanly skirts Vadoma made her wear in all seasons. Her mother made her cover up more than any of the other Traveller women. One more spiteful thing she did to make her life a misery.

Aisha gave her a stern look. "There's no stopping what's been started. I see your fingers are glistening with the oil, don't try to hide them." Bella had been too slow to tuck them behind her back. Aisha relented. "Go ahead and have a sample, but be sure to tell people why you smell so good and send them my way." Aisha waved a graceful, long-fingered hand at the clove oil.

Bella daubed the sweet fragrance behind her ears and on her wrists, inhaling deeply. The scent made her think of castles, elaborate pavilions, and banners waving under a crimson sky. Like being wrapped in a story. "Thank you, Mistress Aisha. Is Malik around?"

Aisha flashed a white smile and gave Bella a knowing glance. She claimed her beautiful teeth resulted from chewing on cinnamon sticks, and it gave her sweet breath as well. "No, my *alhabib* is out working the crowd."

It surprised Bella how disappointed she felt. He was just a friend, after all. Pushing down the irrational feeling, she raised her eyebrows and leaned in close, beckoning to Aisha. "I spotted a fat pigeon who doesn't have proper care for his purse. He looks like a fat, grumpy owl, and squires an elderly woman with a cane."

Aisha gave her a measuring look, then nodded her head. "I'll let him know. Here's a bit of cinnamon to chew on." Aisha then looked at a customer lingering behind Bella in expectation. Bella moved away as she knew the woman wanted her to. While brief conversations were fine, it was an unwritten rule to never interfere with another's trade on market days.

Bella knew she couldn't drag out her journey to help her aunt much longer. Chewing on the cinnamon that tasted exactly like a person would expect the rusty brown color to taste, she breathed in the air and commotion of the street fair. Dust and body odor fought with the smells of food aromas, a heady combination that never failed to put a smile on her face. These large market days were worth the tedious journeys in between cities.

Bella reached the next square over. This one also had stalls, but they were further apart, and the crowds fewer. She could hear the animal bellows from the slaughterhouse nearby. This was the section reserved for most of the travelling folk to display their wares. Only the truly exotic sellers with oddities from far away, like Aisha's spice stall, got to be in the main square. Common Travellers with the usual goods on offer would get a fair amount of buyers because of the size of the festival crowd, but it grated on Bella that they were always pushed into the meaner areas.

Hearing a pinging sound of metal on metal, she moved towards it and saw her uncle by his small forge, doing a bit of repair on a rich person's brass ewer. As usual, the patron was standing by, keeping a sharp eye out while her uncle did his work. Tinkers were trusted by no one.

"Hey-ah, Uncle Timbo!" she called out as she got closer.

The man raised his shaggy head and gave her a half-smile with the part of his face that worked. The other half slumped downward and didn't move, the skin hanging in folds like clay pushed down too hard by the potter. It had been that way since he had taken a horrific beating in another town they'd never returned to. He wiped the drool from the slack side of his face.

"Hey-ah, Belladonna." Uncle Timbo always called her by her complete name. The only time she heard it from others was when she was in deep trouble. "Kezia's over there." He indicated with his shoulder, the only part of that arm that still worked. Bella was always struck by how Timbo was able to move around his frozen left side. She paused, wondering if she should talk to him about the kitten she'd found, but he was deep in his work. He could be irritable at odd times, so maybe now was not the right time.

She headed to the far side of the square. She heard the squalling long before she reached her aunt. The baby Pattin was forever crying, and young Timbo, two years older, was yelling right next to him.

"Praise be!" her aunt had a grim look. Her long green eyes veined with red revealed her weariness. "Nary a customer will come near with these two crying a river of tears."

Bella looked at the table, which seemed just as full as when they had set out the pretty hair ribbons and beaded earrings that morning. Then she looked at the snot running out of young Timbo's nose, and the red, screwed-up face of baby Pattin, who was winding up to give another scream. *No way am I getting saddled taking care of those two*, she thought.

"Maybe they're just hungry. I bet you are too, Aunty Kezia. I can mind the stall while you find yourselves something to eat and drink," she said helpfully. She gave her aunt her best beaming smile.

"Hmph." Kezia was a tough woman to fool. She considered, then blew the wisping strands of red hair out of her face. "Mayhap you have the way of it. All right, pray to the gods I won't be long." With that, she picked up both boys, one under each arm, and marched away with them. The boys stopped their howling, taken by surprise when she snatched them up, but quickly resumed as she marched away.

"Take as long as you need!" Bella called out to her aunt. She didn't mind doing the selling of their pretties; it was like performing in a way. She straightened out a few pairs of the earrings and picked up a pair of green dangles to put in her own ears. Bella moved in front of the stall, swished her skirts, and raised her arms, tossing her hair so the earrings sparkled in the midday sun.

"Pretties for sale, pretties for you!" she called, the singsong patter their family had used for as long as could remember. "Bright beads, bright ribbons, Pretties for sale!" She kept going, drowning out the old woman a few stalls down who was trying to sell her own ribbons and earbobs. She swished her red skirts, and smiled nicely as a few sets of shoppers turned her way.

Stepping back behind the bench where they had their wares laid out, she sat down on the three-legged stool. It didn't do to be intimidating once customers were in front of you. Many people in the towns thought it was ill luck to hold the gaze of a Traveller. To busy herself and make it easy for customers to shop without accidentally catching her eye, she picked up the needle and green thread that they used to embroider shamrocks on the ends of their ribbons, and set to work sewing as a pinch-faced, thin mother with two young girls approached. Behind them, a servant held a baby over her shoulder. *Rich people* thought Bella.

"Good day, missus," she said politely. "And young misses," she added when the older of the two little girls peeped her head around her mother's skirts, clearly taken by the bright ribbons on display.

"Allo," the little girl said brightly.

"Carlotta! We don't speak to gypsies!" Her mother yanked her backward. "Nor should they speak to you." She arrowed her gaze at Bella, who cast her eyes downwards and restrained herself from retorting that they were not gypsies.

"Mama, I like the red ones, like the ones she has in her hair!" Carlotta said, an imperious note of command in her voice for one so young. "Mama, look, they have green plants on them."

"Those be shamrocks fer luck," said Bella to no one in particular. She'd found the best way to communicate with townsfolk was to speak to the air when they were close up. That way, they could choose to hear her or not.

"Hm. The stitching could be better," the woman sniffed. "But, yes, I'll take the red ones. Bettina, what color would you like? Yellow?" The other little girl nodded, her thumb in the way of words.

"Mama, baby Rue needs some too! Blue ones!" Carlotta piped up, again using a demanding tone.

Bettina took her thumb out of her mouth and said, "Blue for Rue!" and giggled at her rhyme. Bella smiled at her, and the little girl grinned back.

"I suppose you'll have me buying ribbons for Cook next," the woman replied. "And don't ask me to get anything for Dagmar. She's been very naughty," the mother said to Carlotta.

"Mama, Dagmar would like the green ones." Carlotta looked at her mother, her little hands fisted on her hips. Bella couldn't help but raise her eyebrows in surprise. She'd never speak to her mother that way, no matter how much she wanted something.

The mother turned back to Bella. "Very well, we'll take one each of the red, the blue, the yellow, and yes, all right, Carlotta, the green too. And I won't pay more than a copper for each."

"Yes, ma'am." Bella hid her smile as she handed the ribbons over. It was usually two pfennig for three ribbons, so she'd made a good bargain already. "Thank ye for stopping, an' ye may want to see the dancin' show on t'other side of the square. Or the second story. It's sure t'have princesses in it." Bella mimicked the local accent when making sales. It was fun, and good practice for blending in if there would be a need to do so.

As the group turned away, Bettina looked back at Bella and smiled again. Bella gave her a wave of her fingers in secret. She heard Carlotta proclaim to her mother just as they went out of earshot, "Mama, we will go hear the princess story." Maybe not all children were so bad, she thought, as she put two pfennig in one pocket, and the extra one in another. After all, she was the one who had made the sale. It wasn't like she was stealing; she was just taking her commission. She patted the pocket.

"Boo!" Bella startled as a lean black shadow detached itself from the space behind her stall. Malik stepped into the partial shade of the booth and smiled down at her. "Gotcha," he said. He grinned, his teeth just as white and whole as his mother's.

"I saw you there the whole time." No way was she going to let Malik know he'd made her jump.

"Ah, yes, all the girls jump an inch off the ground when they hear me speak." Malik had a way of lolling his words so that you hung on them without meaning to. "Got anything to eat?"

"No, do ribbons and earrings look like food to you? Do you not have something hidden in one of your many pockets?"

"I might." Malik pulled a braided loaf of bread out from under his grey cloak and handed it to her with a flourish. "Thought I'd come share, since your pigeon paid for it. Your description of him as a fat, grumpy owl was perfect. Thanks for the tip."

Bella stopped before her first bite was complete. "I just told your mother about him a few minutes ago, how—"

Malik grinned. "You didn't see me then, either. I was just behind Mother, in the corner of our stall." He leaned over and sniffed the place where she had placed the clove scent. "It smells good on you."

Bella felt the hairs on her neck stand on end as his warm breath caressed her skin. She pushed him away. "Must be nice to be so dark you can be part of the shadows and unseen."

Malik broke off a hunk of the bread and chewed it thoughtfully as he handed her back the loaf. "It's nice sometimes, but most of the time it's twice the trouble to be dark than light. We are always the first to be looked at when someone's purse goes missing. Even before any other Travellers."

"And here I am, helping you eat the evidence," said Bella dryly.

"Ah, but that bread was properly paid for. After all, the purse became mine the moment it was no longer his, and I paid for this bread with that good coin." Malik leaned over and fished a different pair of earrings off the table. "These red ones would look the best on you." His gaze took her in, and Bella felt her belly flip. Really, it was silly. She and Malik had been friends during the travelling season for years. It was only this past year that he had grown taller than her and gotten all those muscles.

Bella tossed her head and turned away from him, hoping he couldn't hear how fast her heart was beating. "I'm already wearing earbobs, thank you."

"Are you?" With a flourish and a laugh, he turned her to face him. Malik opened his fist, the dark fingers unfurling, revealing the light pink of his palm and something else besides. Lying on his palm were the green earrings she'd chosen to wear but a few minutes before. Her fingers flew up to her ears, and she gasped when she realized he had somehow whisked them off her without her feeling anything.

"Malik!" It wasn't rage she felt, but she thought it would be a good idea to act like she was angry.

"Here, I'll put them in for you, *jameela*." Bella's breath caught in place as Malik leaned into her and, with the briefest of touches, tucked the red earrings into first one ear, and then the other. She knew *jameela* meant beautiful girl in his language. Her eyes met his and everything in the world went still, filled only with the sound of her beating heart. His hands gently brushed her cheeks. His lips were so full, just inches from hers. When he breathed, she could smell the cinnamon bark on it. She was fiercely glad that she had also chewed some of the bark.

"Bella, your eyes, they are the most beautiful, golden…" Malik whispered. He leaned closer, so that she saw nothing but him, felt nothing but him. The sounds of the market faded away and time stretched out to an infinite slowness. Bella shut her eyes. The air surrounding them felt so close, so heated. Just for the briefest moment, she could feel his breath upon her lips. Any moment now she would feel the press of his warm lips on hers—

"Whoa! I am so telling your Ma!" The gleeful voice cracked on the last word, moving from a man's voice to that of a boy.

Time sped back up again to a gallop. Bella jumped away from Malik. She whirled to see the bane of her existence standing in front of the stall, arms folded, stocky legs firmly planted, his shock of rust-red hair tumbling across his forehead.

"Stefan! There's nothing to tell, you little noodle head. We were just practicing." Bella wanted to punch him right in his smug face, especially when her cousin nodded his head and widened his eyes like he'd just heard a joke rather than a perfectly good explanation.

"Practicing for what? Parenthood?" Stefan cracked up at his own joke as he pushed his hair back and then gleefully rubbed his hands together. "Malik and Bella, well, well, well. Bella, your Ma's going to have a conniption after I tell her what I just saw. You'll be scrubbing all the pots through next year." He grinned.

Bella grimaced. The last thing she needed was to give her mother more things to yell at her about. Stefan was right. She'd be scrubbing pots and pans nightly if her mother found out. Probably emptying the nightsoil buckets as well.

"Come now, Stefan. As Bella said, we were practicing for a new story to perform for the crowd." Malik stepped up next to Bella and looped his arm around her waist, where it burned like fire. Bella didn't know if she wanted to snug in closer to him or fling him off.

Malik continued in his smooth voice that had just the slightest accent to it. "It's about a robber bridegroom who steals girls away with a kiss and slays any annoying cousins who get in the way." He smiled pleasantly at Stefan, but the smile had an edge to it. "We'd love for you to be a part of our stage story. You're perfect for the part. How would you like to die on stage? Sword? Knife? A twist of the neck? Shall we practice now?"

Stefan shifted his feet uneasily and backed up as Malik swung around the edge of the stall. Malik moved closer until they were almost nose to nose.

"Back off, Malik, you never know how to take a joke!" His voice cracked again, and Stefan blushed a deep red that spread over his entire face and spread down his neck to cover his chest. He shoved Malik back a foot and raised his chin defiantly, even though Bella could see it was quivering.

"Angling for a fight, are you?" Malik's voice remained pleasant, but the tone shifted to something more threatening.

"If you want one!" Stefan's voice rose and his flush took on a darker hue. He planted his feet firmly, raising his fists.

Bella breathed in through her nose sharply. Oh no. People near them were turning to look. A young girl tugged on her mother's skirts, pointing at the two young men squaring off. The potter who had the stall next door glared at the three of them and moved a fancy pot away from that side of his stall. The tension in the air felt just like a pot getting ready to boil. If she didn't do something now, it would turn into something awful.

Bella forced herself to laugh, the tinkling laugh she used to call attention to herself when she was getting ready to dance for a crowd. "Boys, boys, stop this silliness." Plastering a smile on her face, she moved between Malik and Stefan, swishing her hips to create more space between them. She lightly put a hand on each of their chests and kept her smile in place, willing it to cool the passion that was flowing between the two. She noticed Malik's chest was much higher than Stefan's and she felt a wave of compassion for her younger cousin. He was still a boy, after all, barely twelve years old. And he was her cousin. Even if he was a cocky annoyance most of the time.

"We have customers to attract, and not with a fight. Malik, we'll just have to practice at another time." She gave him a little push with her hand, and met with solid, firm resistance. When had his chest filled out so?

Malik's nostrils flared. Bella got an icy shiver up her spine as he resisted her for a moment longer, looking past her to pin Stefan with a baleful look. Then he looked down at her, and his gaze softened. "I'll take you up on that practicing later, Bella." He stroked her arm, and then disappeared into the crowd like a wraith.

Bella moved past her cousin, giving him a hard glare as she did so. She raised her arms in the air and sang out. "Pretties for sale, pretties for you! Bright beads, bright ribbons, Pretties for sale!" The crowd that had started to clump and stare broke up like leaves scattering, the spell of a near-fight broken. Blowing out a breath, Bella kicked her cousin in the back of his knee so that he broke his defiant stance. She hissed at him through her teeth as she moved to help the trio of customers that her call had attracted.

As the young women buzzed about earrings, holding them up so their friends could help them choose, Stefan approached from behind her. "I came to help you with the boys. I was being nice." He spat out the last word, but had the sense to keep the conversation low so that it didn't distract the buyers.

Bella slanted her eyes towards him quickly. It was never good to take your eyes completely off the goods when customers were standing there. It was too easy to pocket their baubles without paying for them. Stefan was still angry about the confrontation. He'd been shamed by Malik, no question, and had probably gotten his feelings hurt. Stefan could hold a grudge for a long time. Bella knew this firsthand. He'd waited nearly a year to get her back from smearing his bread with mud and telling him it was "special jam." She could still taste the metallic tang of blood from the "special red sauce" he'd put on her corn fritters one night in revenge.

"We really were just practicing, cousin," she said. "I don't know why that turned into such a fuss."

"I say that's a lie," he retorted as he slunk away. "I know courting when I see it."

Bella wanted to go after him, calm him down, talk him into keeping his peace about what he had seen. But one of the women at the stall chose that exact moment to hand a jet-black pair of earrings to Bella. "I'll take these." Bella looked up and saw a pretty face with a healthy peach glow. These town people all looked healthy and well-fed. Bella squashed her concern over Stefan and nodded. "Sure an' these will look well on ye, miss." She looked critically at the girl, then picked up another pair, with blue beads in with the black. "Ye might like these as a bargain. We have a special; one pair for four black pfennig, or two pair for six."

The girls whispered among themselves. "All right, I'll take both." The girl fished in her bodice and pulled the pennies from her purse. There was a flash of real silver in the purse as well, and Bella thought she might have gotten more, but double their normal asking was still a good transaction. She put away in her right pocket the proper amount for her aunt and uncle, and transferred the extra to her left pocket. She'd earned it, after all.

Her conscience gave a hard twinge, but she ignored it. She turned a bright face towards the milling crowd, but inside, her guts were churning. What would Stefan do with his information? And what should she do about Malik and his almost kiss? She put a hand on her heart to calm it and realized what she wanted from Malik was a kiss in full.

CHAPTER FOUR

"**I** dance well! I don't know why we didn't earn more, and those boys down in front were awful. I had to keep over on one side of the stage to avoid them." Rose pouted as she handed the collection basket over to Vadoma behind the stage.

"No one is complaining, Rose." Vadoma barely contained the sigh she wanted to let loose. Her sister's oldest child was about to indulge in a full-on sulk. The day had turned sour, and Vadoma's throat felt tight. Worry was chewing on her insides. Rose's stomping around wasn't helping.

Rose yanked off her finger cymbals and untied her dancing skirts. Irritation buzzed off her like a midge fly. "Just because I don't wiggle my *assets* the way Bella does hers is the problem, isn't it? You might as well admit it, Aunty. Mine is the more proper dance! I do it the proper way, the way you showed us. Not all that waggling around. She jiggles on purpose."

Vadoma nodded her head, trying to keep her temper in check. This display had more to do with Rose's ongoing rivalry with Belladonna than it did her wanting to earn for the clan. Time to give sugar to the fly and help it fly away. She forced a kind smile. "You did fine, Rosy, dear. Why don't you take this coin for yourself and get a treat?"

Rose pushed her nose up in the air, pretending to consider the offer. She caught sight of the little orange kitten, now curled up and napping in one of Ebbe's shoes. "If Bella keeps that kitten, then I get to have a pet, too. But I want a bird that will sing for us. Much better than a cat, don't you agree?" Without waiting for a reply, the girl snatched the proffered coin and flounced away.

Vadoma loosed the sigh she'd kept locked in her throat. It was just like Rose to want a caged bird that sang. She sat on their little three-legged stool and rubbed her bad leg. It was nice to sit in the cool darkness alone, if even for a minute. Yes, she would take a moment and try to relax. They were just at a festival, like hundreds of others. Nothing to worry about. She breathed in for a few heartbeats and out the same number several times. It didn't work. She stood up again. She saw the remains of the cheese the kitten had consumed. Sighing yet again, she fetched more from the shopping basket. Seeing how empty it was reminded her she had yet to do the marketing to restock their wagon for the next journey up through the Darkwood three days hence.

Her thumbs were pricking as she placed a new hunk of cheese near the ale Ebbe used to keep his voice from getting hoarse. Uneasily, she thought of the old rhyme of pricking thumbs and wickedness approaching. With a shake, she forced herself to do the chores that needed doing before their next show that afternoon. She picked up the yellow skirt Rose had carelessly tossed aside in her pique. Brushing it, she remembered the times she herself had worn this skirt to dance for the crowd when she was a young woman. She examined it carefully to see if any holes needed to be mended. They were running low on both yellow and the scarlet threads. Perhaps she should get some in the market. And some remnants of cloth too, to make more ribbons for their next stop on the travelling route. Any task to push back against the darkness that seemed to be circling was welcome.

She gathered her shopping basket and tied on the stiff leather shoes she preferred to wear in town. There was a rustling sound as Ebbe came into the backstage area carrying his drum. Ebbe put down his bodhran and picked up the ale she had ready for him. He downed the whole thing in one long swallow, his bronzed throat tilted back to get every drop. Wiping his mouth with his hand, he shook his head. "Tale telling's thirsty work, I'm bound to say."

"And say it you do, every time," Vadoma replied.

"Ah well, it's kept us in luck, hasn't it?" Ebbe carefully untied his sleeve ribbons, smoothing them as he did so. He was a tidy man and liked to have everything in its place.

"You and your luck and your signs." Vadoma waved an impatient hand at him. She knew she was feeling prickly and forced her tone to remain light. "It's our route that's brought us luck this year. And the weather. We might make it all the way up to Saxony if it holds."

Ebbe looked at her steadily, the crinkles in the corners of his eyes and lips that appeared whenever he looked at her deepening as he smiled. It was one of his best qualities, she thought, the way that man made a person feel seen and appreciated. "You could be right at that."

Vadoma felt some of her tension melt away. She smiled and gave him a peck on the cheek. "I suppose you'll consult the birds later."

"I might. And take a wander into the forest to see what the trees have to say about it in the long talk."

"You just don't like cities," she retorted, snuggling under his arm. She liked the way her head fit perfectly in the hollow of his shoulder. "We'd be forever in the woods if you had your way."

"Aye, you are right again, my love." They stood and swayed together in the dimness of the curtained off stage.

This was what she was most happy for, thought Vadoma as she twined her hands in Ebbe's, admiring the strength and beauty of his tapered fingers. Fifteen years after being handfasted at thirteen, they still took joy with each other and had never looked away to other people. If only the Saints had blessed them with more than one child. Ebbe liked to say that they'd simply gotten it right the first time around, but she knew he'd wanted many children, as had she. Their Belladonna was beautiful, talented, and utterly wayward. More trouble than a pack of boys would have been, thought Vadoma.

"Where's our beautiful Bella?" asked Ebbe. After so long married, it no longer surprised her that he seemed to read her mind. "She was supposed to be our dance performer today. I thought you wanted to keep her close."

Vadoma felt a shadow fall over her heart. Yes, she had wanted to keep Bella close in this town, above all others. If she could have her way, she'd have packed Bella in a cask and kept her hidden for the entire weekend. For a moment, she considered telling Ebbe the truth, finally. Explain to him why she'd tried to convince him to avoid this particular town again this season, even though it was a place many said brought rich hauls, one they'd not returned to in fourteen seasons. If she told him now, though, after all the years of dissembling, what would he say? Would it be a crack in their relationship that would never mend?

She chewed on her lip as she looked at her husband. She'd taken too long to respond to him. He'd turned slightly away from her, his head tilted to one side, his eyes unfocused, his skin strangely slack. He seemed to listen to something far out of the ordinary range. Gently, so as not to break the connection she'd come to understand was a strange gift he had no control over, Vadoma touched his arm. He closed his fingers on hers, tension quivering through them.

"Trouble is coming," he said at last. "Trouble and pain."

Vadoma felt her throat go dry. "For one of us?"

Ebbe nodded slowly. "Yes, one or perhaps more of our clan. I cannot tell who. But something comes, something long in the making."

"Something coming due." Vadoma finished the thought in a frightened whisper. Her entire being felt weighted down with stones. As if she'd been cast into a cold pond to drown as a witch. "We should all go. The entire clan. Right now. Just pack up and go. As we did before from this cursed town." Taking quick breaths, she forced herself to stay in the present, to do what needed to be done. Quick! She darted to a wooden chest and started folding costumes into it.

Her husband came up behind her. He wrapped his arms around her to stop the frantic folding. Vadoma held herself rigid, trying not to let a sob escape her. She clamped her mouth shut and closed her eyes to focus. She would not burden her husband with her fear—no, it was her knowledge—that it was Bella, their beloved child who was in trouble. In a moment of terrible, piercing clarity, she knew this was her personal problem to deal with. One way or another. Ebbe would not know of the curse.

"Beloved," he said gently into her ear. "You fear this place. You've held your own counsel as to the reason and I've never questioned you as to the why of it. Whatever this is, we'll survive it together. As we've always done."

He gathered her close, and Vadoma let herself sink into him, finding comfort in the familiar fold of his arms. She nodded her head to placate him, and to hopefully confound his eternal curiosity. She would not tell him why she so feared this particular town, and most particularly the mayor of it. Burgermeister Strom. The betrayal of trust she'd just committed would bring its own consequences. Right now it was her task, her burden, to confront that formidable man who'd cursed their child. She'd beg him to rescind the geas on Bella, give her all the blame and whatever punishment that meant.

Inwardly, she quailed at the thought of facing Strom again. A dim, small part of her cried out that she was making a mistake. That there was more to him than people chose to see. The

Burgermeister held a dark power beyond that of simply being the mayor. She was sure of it. She breathed in and gathered her courage. It didn't matter, what needed to be done would be done.

Vadoma turned to Ebbe. She wanted to remember him this way, the way the love for her shone in his eyes. If she survived the confrontation and its outcome, then she could deal with the pain of trying to reconcile with her husband. She had to trust that in this too, they would find their way.

Ebbe cocked his head, no doubt trying to read her mind. Vadoma stood fast. Then he put on his rolling stage voice. "Beloved, why dost thou look so fraught? Have I becom'st a weak man in the last few hours, unable to protect what is thine and mine?"

Vadoma poked him in the stomach, forced a light chuckle. "Stop quoting lines from your stories at me. You should rest, *beloved,* I'm off to get us what we need for the next part of our journey. I hear the roast turkey legs four stalls down are excellent if you're hungry for more than cheese." Vadoma took a moment to bundle her wild black curls into a nondescript kerchief, then let down the plain homespun brown skirts she had tied up to move about backstage more easily. "Oh, and Bella found an orange kitten. It's over there, in your shoe. She's already named it."

"We can't keep it. You know how Timbo gets with his coughing around cats."

"Aye, I know. Leave it to Bella to try and finagle a way to get what she should not have." Turning to her husband, Vadoma hunched over a bit and hobbled a few steps, exaggerating her limp. "Well, will I pass as a simple servant woman on a market day?" she asked him.

"They see what they wish to see," said Ebbe. "I only ever see the beauty I married."

His easy, trusting smile pricked Vadoma's conscience fiercely. But she managed to smile in return as if all were well, picked up her basket, and limped through the draperies into the bright sun on the square. It might be her imagination, but the leg she had broken so many years ago felt even weaker today. She worried it would fail her.

Banishing visions of crumpling to the flagstones unable to rise again, she angled across the busy Marktplatz. Vadoma behaved as if she were subservient to all, giving way to any whose path she might cross with a small polite bob of the knee. It was better to pretend to be a lowly servant than a Traveller in the larger towns. Especially on market days, when the ale and brandy were guzzled with abandon. She could smell the stink of alcohol on many of the well-dressed men she bent her neck to as she drifted through the crowd, even though the noon hour had barely passed. It would only get worse as the day wore on.

If a thing must be done, it best be done quickly. The old moral beat through Vadoma's brain as she edged past stalls and into the next square. Ahead, she could hear Belladonna singing out the family wares, her beautiful clear voice rising above the others. Blessed with the ability to make her voice travel, just like her father. Vadoma's heart swelled within her, and she found herself blinking back tears. Whatever it took, she would protect their daughter. She made sure to stay out of Bella's sight as she ducked down another street, one well-known to her. It was the street that led into the very oldest and finest neighborhood in town.

The houses grew taller and more grand, timbered homes giving way to stone. A completely residential neighborhood, without shops on the lower floors. These were people who could afford servants who would make the journey to acquire the daily needs of their households. The long, straight street's cobbles were all intact and clean of the usual grime and offal. It was usually quiet in these streets, and today even more so, with most out at the market or dancing around maypoles in the outer fields. Turning a final corner, Vadoma didn't let herself think of anything but keeping her feet moving as she mounted the six steep steps to the sturdy front door of Burgermeister Strom's house. She took a deep breath before picking up the eagle-head knocker on the dark green door. She must do this quickly, or she would lose her nerve. Her hand seemed to reach up of its own volition to the knocker, as part of her screamed to run away. She knocked sharply three times on the mayor's door. The mayor whose infant son and wife she had killed fourteen years ago.

CHAPTER FIVE

T he door opened a few inches. A cross-looking man who was nearly as wide as he was tall scrutinized Vadoma through the opening. He sniffed and said in a haughty tone, "Tradespeople and servants to the back." His fat jowls jiggled as he swung the door to close it.

Vadoma felt her anger rise and take over her fear. She stepped up and stopped the door with a firm hand before it could shut. "I'm here on important personal business with the Burgermeister." She met the man's imperious gaze full on, as they were nearly of a height. He had some crumbs from his breakfast stuck in his tiny beard. Somehow, that gave her a boost of confidence. The people in this house were simply people, not servants of some dark force.

"The Burgermeister does not have personal business with servants," the man replied, his voice growing even more annoyed. "Nor would anything someone of your ilk had to say be of any importance to anyone in this house, let alone the master himself. At any rate, Burgermeister is not home at present." The man seemed pleased with his little speech and started to close the door again.

Again Vadoma blocked him from doing so. "It concerns his wife and his son."

The man laughed at her. "I have no desire to bandy words with an ignorant guttersnipe. Our most esteemed Burgermeister has no wife or child." His breath smelled of garlic.

"I know. I need to speak to him about that."

"Do you plan to become his wife, perhaps? You must be mad or drunk, woman. Now be off before I call our Roundhats on you." The little man waved his hands to shoo her away. Vadoma squelched a mad desire to step through the door and shake him.

"Can you at least tell me if he is at the festival today?"

"I wouldn't tell you if he was on fire and needed putting out! Now leave!" Planting his stout legs, the man shoved her back with the flat of his hand, and then put his shoulder to the door, slamming it in Vadoma's face. She heard the inner bolt shoot home for good measure.

Vadoma slumped to the stairs, her heart beating far too quickly. Counting bricks on the building across the street, she forced herself into a calmer state. Maybe this was a sign. Could be she was worried over nothing. Perhaps the man's curses on herself and her daughter had been simple grieving words, with no dreadful magic or power behind them. Her stomach did a flip at the thought. Unbidden, her mind flashed to that terrible night, fourteen years ago. She could hear the weeping of the maid, see the streaks of blood on her hands and arms, the way the blood mixed with slick sweat covered the sheets, darkening them to a near-black color. The agonized slow rocking of the woman on the bed before her.

She smelled the metallic tang. It permeated the air. The woman was bleeding too much and could not birth the child. Perhaps if she had some yarrow, or witch hazel, she could staunch the flow, but she was without the supplies she normally used. Vadoma raked her memory for a solution, something that would save at least one of them. She'd seen babes cut from their mother's stomachs before, but she had no tools and doubted her abilities. Even that measure had no guarantee, especially when the mother was exhausted already, as this woman clearly was. The maid attending her had said in halting tones the woman had been in labor for over three days, and that the town doctor had thrown his hands up in despair and left.

The maid had stayed with Vadoma throughout the night, but the strain was telling on the teen, who wrung her hands in distress and hovered near the fire, afraid to get close to the blood and looming death bedside. More to help the girl over her fear than for any true need, she turned to her. "More hot water and cloths, if you please." Vadoma was surprised at how steady and sure her voice sounded. It surely was no match for how she felt on the inside.

A sharp pain from her own gut drew the breath away from her, the band of tightness around her belly clutching so fiercely that she had to grab the edge of the bed to stay upright. Saints, why had she answered this call? Her own time to give birth was near. But she hadn't had a choice, not really. The Burgermeister's men had come down to the river to the space allotted for the Travellers, shouting for an herbalist to come attend their master's wife in childbirth. As a healer, she was bound to answer if called. Both Aisha and she had answered the call, and the uniformed men had rejected Aisha for the color of her skin. More fools them, she thought. Aisha might have had the herbs and experience to make this birth a happy and successful one.

Another band of pain followed on the heels of her first one. With a moan that matched the woman's gasps in the bed she had been tending for the full night, Vadoma bent her knees. She felt a gushing of warm fluid and another spike of pain. She cried out, unable to stop herself.

The woman on the bed turned her head, her hair soaked in sweat, stringing in long strands across her face, clinging like dead seaweed around her throat. It nearly obscured the large, square-cut emerald the woman wore as a necklace; one she had touched repeatedly during her agony, as if it gave her aid. The woman clutched the green gem and moaned. She reached out her free hand to Vadoma. They clasped hands, breathed through their birthing pains. Their eyes met, and Vadoma saw compassion there, one woman to another, as well as the flicker of darkness and despair. The woman's neck stiffened and her hand spasmed in Vadoma's. She took one final deep gasp of air and then collapsed. Her final breath rolled from her lungs in a sigh.

"No! Gods above and below, no!" Vadoma massaged the woman's heart, which remained still, then her belly, trying her best to get the child out. If she could just get the child out, perhaps it would live. She could see the crown, perhaps if she could just turn it within the chilling womb, then pull the feet, she could save the babe. Frantic, puffing air out past her own contractions, Vadoma bent to the task.

Just then, the maid burst in, followed directly by Burgermeister Strom himself. He shoved the little girl out of the way. "I'll not be kept out of my own bed chamber any longer!" The man was dressed in sumptuous robes of crimson edged with gold, as if he'd been entertaining dignitaries. Not the dress of a man who'd been awaiting the birth of his first child for days. His presence overwhelmed the room. Taking two large strides to the bed, he took in the blood, his unmoving wife. He stopped, his bluster turning to horror.

"Esmeralda! No!" His voice broke. "My love." He stroked back his wife's hair, then turned to Vadoma, who still labored to birth the child.

"Witch, you've killed her, the one thing I have loved!" Strom's voice shook with anger and grew in volume with every word.

Ignoring his wrath, focused on her task, Vadoma delivered the infant with a final pull. It was a boy. Quickly, she cleared the mouth with a cloth-wrapped finger. Rubbed its back, willing it to breathe. Nothing. Held it up by its feet to help dislodge anything that might prevent the child from taking that essential breath of air, rendering it fully into a land creature, not the water creature it had been in its mother's womb. Slapped the baby's back firmly. Pressed on its tiny chest. Nothing.

"Well?" The man's voice grated harshly.

She wept for them. The woman had been only a few years older than herself, and the babe had not lived to draw a single breath. A boy, a sweet boy. She laid the stillborn on his mother's chest gently, taking her limp arm and draping it around her son, and pushed back from the bed.

Gathering her courage, she turned towards the husband, and then shrieked, falling to her knees. A burning agony filled her. She was dimly aware of the maid propping her up as she labored fast and hard. With a final push, Vadoma reached between her own legs, and pulled out her babe. It was a girl, one who started a wonderful, healthy squalling the moment she felt air.

Weeping now with joy as well, Vadoma forgot all as she cleaned her daughter's face with her skirts, marveling at the full head of black curls and the ancient eyes in the red, angry face. The most beautiful thing she had ever seen.

"Angry at leaving your safe place, my darling?" Vadoma whispered.

"You have taken the life of my wife, of my child and given their spirits to strengthen your own spawn!" The spiteful words startled Vadoma back to reality. Strom pointed a finger at her, the ruby ring on his finger catching the firelight. He was a huge man with oversized shoulders and arms that seemed too long for his body. Through her fog, she felt another pang and then her afterbirth passed. She wished she could gather it up and plant it under a rowan tree for luck and protection. But she knew she couldn't linger here. The man's face was growing more and more red, fury filling every part of him. Darkness seemed to swirl around him.

She struggled to her feet, clutching her child to her. The cord snapped as she did so, and with her free hand, she pinched and knotted the tube that had connected her to her child these past months. Dread clutched her heart, all the joy of delivering a living child stripped from her. The powerful man was muttering words she couldn't hear through the buzzing in her head. He had just lost two treasures and was sure she was to blame. It happened all too frequently to midwives and healers, blamed for losses they'd tried hard to prevent. She had to get out of this room, get back to Ebbe, to their clan and safety.

"I grieve for your sorrow," she began. But his eyes, black and reflecting the red dying embers of the fire, fixed on her. His face was an ugly mask of rage. Panic closed her throat, cut off her air. The man's eyes were mesmerizing, and Vadoma realized she couldn't move. This man had a power she had never encountered before. Horrified, she struggled to break free of the hold he had on her. Dimly she heard the maid whimpering behind her.

"By air I curse you." A cold wind whipped through the closed space. Vadoma fought to breathe.

He reached into the fire, grasped a handful of hot ash, and flung it at her. Vadoma stumbled back, twisted to protect the baby, trying to evade the black, burning cloud. "By earth I curse you." Vadoma felt the embers burning her neck and shoulder. Then she felt the grip of his hand in her hair, yanking her upright. She writhed in his grasp. She had to escape, she had to!

Helpless, she watched as Strom placed his hand into the blood on the bed, then raised it wet and dripping in the air before her. "By blood I bind you!" His eyes shifted to blinded white as they rolled back into his head. He filled the room with his cold, black wrath.

"I curse you. I curse this child. I bind you to know fear and loss for the rest of your days. Your child will never love you. By my babe's blood, this child will unleash a chain of hell and death with love's first kiss. Broken, bent, and bound will she be, she and her get. All bound to me, drawn to return to me and pay the final blood price. Nothing breaks this curse but by my will, or my death. By air, by earth, by blood!"

The monstrous words filled Vadoma's ears, although she screamed against them. With a huge effort, she pulled away, leaving a hank of hair and bits of scalp hanging from his hand. His eyes clicked back to black again, focusing all of his ill-will at her.

Vadoma felt the curse strike her heart as surely as if she'd been punched. Staggering away from him, she saw him reach out with the blooded hand to complete the binding. Vadoma twisted away, towards the door and freedom, twisted so he could not touch her baby, could not put his final binding geas on her. It was too late. His hand grasped her upper arm. It burned so! With another scream, she wrenched herself away, keeping her baby from his touch, and dashed out of the door. The baby screamed. She stumbled down the wooden stairs and yanked open the front door.

Fresh sweet air and a rose-pink dawn greeted her. Bells from the churches rang the new day. With a sobbing breath, she clutched her crying child closer, stepped forward. Her foot met air. She stumbled down the steep stone steps, falling hard on one hip to protect her baby. Felt horror as her left leg snapped, breaking down low by her ankle. Pain shot through her. Fueled by fear and using the walls of the houses to support her, she managed to stagger and crawl towards their encampment, her baby clutched to her chest.

She failed to notice the droplets of red blood beaded in her child's hair, where Strom's cursed hand had touched it.

Vadoma's memories had fragmented into tiny swirls after that point, but sometime later she'd awakened to find Aisha bending over her, felt the movement of the cart beneath her. Stray bits of sunshine filtered in through the sides of their wagon, giving the interior a jumbled look as the scattered light moved about. It made her dizzy, and she fought the desire to sink back into the blessed darkness. She had to sit up, find her child, protect her!

"Hush now," Aisha had said, gently pushing her back onto the piles of sacking cushioning her. "We've left the town. All of us. You're safe. I put your leg back together as best I could, but you must not move it."

"My baby!" Vadoma panicked as she looked around.

"Also safe. She'd not stop crying, lying next to you, so Kezia took her. She has milk aplenty with her baby Rose until yours comes in." Aisha had smiled, but there was something tight around her eyes. "What will you name her?"

"Belladonna," The name came to Vadoma instantly. It was a beautiful name. "Belladonna, Belladonna," she repeated quickly. There, the magic of a name three times said.

Aisha had nodded but looked worried. "Are you sure you want to name her after a deadly plant?"

Vadoma had forgotten that detail. Then she understood the name had come from the curse. There could be no changing it now that she'd said it three times. She shut her eyes and wept. The Burgermeister's curse had struck true. Her fault. Her failure to save his wife and son, which had given him cause to curse her child. Her beloved daughter, who would never genuinely love her. Her only child, who was now doomed to unleash death by love's first kiss.

Coming out of her reverie, Vadoma stood up from the cold stone steps with stiff joints. Carefully, she stepped down. Time had moved on while she'd sat there, the sun had moved in the sky, people passed without glancing at her. Six black crows swirled down and pecked at something in the street. She looked at them uneasily. Six crows meant death was near. Time to move away, then. Time to convince Ebbe they had no place in this town, that they needed to leave immediately and never return.

She'd been a right fool to come here, she thought as she started back to their wagon. Perhaps the same man was not even the Burgermeister anymore, or had died. Her own fears had captured her, fears that were not real. Breathing out, she allowed herself the smallest bit of hope. She had time yet. Perhaps she should tell the truth to Ebbe, and together they could find a way to break the spell themselves. Saints knew she'd tried to discover a cure on her own for these many years past. But they'd break it far away from this cursed place. Never again would they come here, she vowed.

Her hope lasted for five more steps. She heard the clanking of metal first and automatically stepped to the side of the street, pressing her back to the wall of the house as was expected of lesser folk. A contingent of armed Roundhats in half-armor strode past her. They surrounded a tall man dressed in rich jewel tones of red and blue, his feet seeming to glide over the stone street in golden shoes. Risking a glance, Vadoma felt her knees go to jelly when she saw the ruby ring glinting on his finger. It was Strom. Still tall, with those overly large shoulders and long arms. It was his face that had Vadoma stifling a moan of fear. It was unchanged, unlined after fourteen years. The same as it had been that terrible night. The only difference was a single streak of white in his dark hair.

She lowered her eyes, wished herself invisible as the group passed. Strom's eyes raked over her, but he didn't pause. She felt oddly compelled to stand still and wait and watch as he climbed the steps of the house she'd just left. The guards waited at the steps as the Burgermeister ascended. He paused at the top and turned, surveying the street. His massive, hunching shoulders twitched. His head swiveled slowly, like an animal scenting prey, nostrils flaring to catch the scent. Vadoma twisted her first two fingers of both hands together, whispering a prayer against evil under her breath.

His black eyes caught on hers. Held. Then, to her horror, Strom grinned.

CHAPTER SIX

B ella popped another two black pfennigs into her private stash as she wished a good day to a young man who'd purchased a betrothal gift for his intended. It had been enjoyable helping him pick out the perfect broach, a piece her uncle had made that featured flowers picked out in amethyst and banded with silver. The customer had been pleased with the price of two fat groshen and a pretty purple ribbon to match it thrown in for free. Bella had been pleased that he'd paid nearly double the asking price. This was her best day selling in a long time, and she'd managed to stitch a few more embroidered ribbons to sell in between customers.

Fisting her hands to the middle of her back, she leaned back into them. She'd been on her feet a long time. The shadows were lengthening from the western side of the square. In just a few more bells, the main bonfires would be lit on the outskirts of town so that feast day dancing and revelry could continue. She smiled. Maybe she could find Malik and a shadowy corner this evening and see if the kiss they'd almost shared would come to pass. Their hands would tangle as one, their bodies would—

"And what has you mooning at the sky?" Her aunt Kezia's sharp voice intruded on Bella's thoughts.

"My own thoughts," replied Bella tartly. She turned away from the front of the stall, being sure to keep her hand on her left pocket so that the coins she'd taken for her own would not jingle. Her gut gave a twist as she did so. She felt irritated and prickly. She knew from her aunt's elevated eyebrows that she'd overreacted to her aunt's teasing question, but now she felt she must stay the course. Either that or apologize, and she just didn't feel like doing that.

Kezia had baby Pattin wrapped in a shawl and tied to her. Her other hand clasped little Timbo's hand. The child looked up at Bella, the pretty golden eyes that were the match to hers rounding as he looked back and forth between herself and his mother. Even he sensed a squabble coming, thought Bella.

Just as Bella expected, Kezia pursed her lips together and knitted her brow. "That means only one thing, that you were mooning about some boy. How many times have your mother and I told you that you are to keep yourself to yourself?"

Bella felt herself flush. Her whole body was hot. She tossed her hair back and raised her chin defiantly. "I'm fourteen years of age, more than a year past the time both you and my mother were betrothed and wed to your own men. I know my own mind, as I am sure you knew yours!"

Kezia's brown eyes hardened. She stepped closer to Bella and took her by the arm. "Do not be wayward about this, Bella. There is more to our keeping you close than you know."

"I know plenty. I know you both want me to stay single, and continue to slave for you, doing your work while you laze and do nothing. Washing your children's soiled undergarments, minding your stall, doing your selling for you, dancing on command. I'm done with it all!"

Bella tried to brush by her, but Kezia's iron grip stopped her. Unwillingly, she looked up at her. Kezia gave her a little shake and her voice grew intense. "You should talk to your mother,

Bella. Make her tell you what she should've told you long ago."
At her side, Timbo gave a little whimper.

Bella squelched her instinct to bend down and comfort the child. She fought to keep her voice even, but lost the fight as she responded. "My mother talks to me daily when she tells me what to do—endlessly. Perhaps you should do some talking to your own eldest daughter and son, and make the topic basic manners. Both of them have been obnoxious and rude to me today. I'm sure neither of them made the coin I made!" Bella fisted up the heavy handful of coins from her right pocket and pushed them at Kezia for emphasis, then pointed at the workbench. "And I made more ribbons as well!"

Kezia huffed in frustration. "This is all well and good, Bella, but you are missing my point—"

"Well and good!" Bella interrupted as she shook her head in disbelief. "Well, a lovely thanks that is for all my work. I'm going." Bella spun away from Kezia. She forgot to hold her pocket still. The coins she'd taken for herself shifted with a distinctive pinging as they fell on one another. Bella winced but kept moving.

"What's in your other pocket?" Kezia's voice was flat and had a harsh undertone. "It looks heavy and sounds like metal."

Bella turned to her aunt. Part of her wanted to confess and beg forgiveness. The other part flared in rebellion. She had worked hard for that coin and hadn't cheated the clan out of any money at all. It was just the extra, after all. Her cut. Her right to take.

Bella's chin jutted out. Her hands fisted, and she felt herself begin to shake. She forced her voice to sound cold and distant. "Why, it's the coin I earned with my body today, Aunt. I lay with multiple men right in this tent all afternoon when custom for ribbons and earbobs slowed." Bella felt a surge of dark satisfaction as she saw her aunt's jaw fell open and face flush red. "So it's mine. Earned fair and square." And with that, Bella strode away.

"Bella!" her aunt called after her. Bella ignored her, even though she could hear the tinge of regret in her aunt's voice. Instead, she picked up her pace, turning the corner at the first street she came to, eager to get out of the Kezia's sight. As soon as she cleared the corner, she picked up her scarlet skirts and ran. The jingling of coin in her pocket seemed to mock her, every step whispering; thief, thief, thief.

She gasped when long, strong arms reached from a doorway shadow. They caught her roughly around the waist, reeling her into the darkened space. She struggled to kick out, but her skirts got in the way. Her anger with her aunt and at herself dissolved into panic.

It was the scent of cinnamon that stopped her from screaming.

"Bella." His voice, barely a breath loud, said her name like it was a gift. Her heart hammered harder, and her breath seemed caught in her throat, neither able to go out nor come in. She was conscious of the hardness of his body, the way it fitted to hers in the small door space he had squeezed them into.

"Malik." She looked up at him, taking in the way his beautiful skin blended with the darkness behind him, almost as if he were made of shadow. Shadow and heat, as the warmth from his body seeped into hers. Bella felt a trickle of sweat pass from under her hair down her neck, past the edge of her bodice. She felt it as it wended its way down her spine to finally stop at the point where her buttocks pushed against the hard stone of the wall behind her.

It was absurd. This was a boy she had known for half her life. She'd fought with him, played with him, they'd bathed in the same cold streams on the road, slept under the same stars at night. They'd exchanged thousands of words, complained about chores given by their respective parents. They'd been hungry together, happy together, had cried together when the baby that would have been her sister died minutes after she was born. They were Travellers of different clans, sometimes taking different paths, brought together seasonally by road and route. Always, of course, glad to see the other again, but never like this.

She felt the space between them melting as their bodies pressed together. His eyes sparkled as she looked into their depths. She watched his full lips curve into a smile, the gleam of white teeth peeking through, and felt her mouth curve up to do the same. Throughout the city, church bells rang the hour, sweet and clear. An oddly cold wind blew by them, circled, making her shiver. An errant plume of dust swirled around them as well. Bella shivered despite the heat between their bodies. Malik reached his arms around her. She matched him.

"Six o'clock and all's well," she said, barely able to push the words past her constricting throat.

"All is well, indeed." The pause after his words seemed to stretch forever. The chilly wind swept around them, binding them more tightly together.

He bent down closer to her, and she inclined her head up to him. There was a buzzing in her ears as blood rushed to her face. They closed the gap and his lips pressed light as air on hers, and then with more pressure. Her lips felt flattened and then yielding to it, to him, she responded. Bella felt her heart thud, then slow as it matched his beat for beat, their breath timed to extend the kiss. Breathing in and out with the boy she'd always known as a friend, transformed now into who she hoped would become her lover, perhaps this very night. Her entire being felt lifted. As the bells chimed and she pressed against Malik, she wondered if she might just be the luckiest girl in the town. She could taste the cinnamon in his mouth, the deeper flavor that was simply Malik beneath it. Kissing him was everything she had always daydreamed a boy's kiss could be.

Later, she would cling to this memory of her first kiss, desperately holding the edge of it like the wisp of a barely remembered dream as proof that she had been happy once.

They separated from each other eventually. Just a few inches back, catching their breath, taking each other in more fully. Bella felt the places where bumps in the stone had pressed into her back ache as she stood more firmly on both feet. She shifted to lean into Malik slightly then lifted her arms up and tucked them around his neck. "Maybe we could take this somewhere less… hard?" She giggled after the question. She wasn't usually a giggler, but the joy just seemed to bubble out of her, taking whatever shape it wanted.

"That could be managed." Malik's eyes flicked back and forth as he looked at her. Bella loved the way he seemed to truly see every bit of her. "But first, I'm a bit short on my day's tally. Come help me."

"You mean your day's thieving." Bella tried to keep her tone light, but also wanted to chastise him for continuing to ply such a dangerous game. What a person could get away with as a young child changed with age. Malik was certainly no child and if he were caught now, it would mean losing a hand at best, or swinging from the gallows at worst.

Malik waved away her remonstrance. "I only take from the very rich and the very slow. And if you're with me, it'll be even easier. We can be a couple. Tell you what, you do the snipping, and if they catch on, you can just say their purse dropped and you're giving it back to them."

"Malik," she began, meaning to give him plenty of good reasons not to go thieving. That it was growing late, and the crowds thinning being the main ones. Not only not enough pigeons to pluck, but also not enough crowd to use as cover if they had to run.

"It'll be like old times." He smiled at her, and she felt her resistance melting. They'd played this game before, she remembered, one summer some years back. She'd gotten a sound beating for it when her mother discovered the stolen purses hidden in the toes of her spare boots. She hadn't been able to sit down for days and Vadoma had made her give away all the coin to beggars as they travelled to the next town. Another overreaction from her mother, Bella thought. Vadoma was always hard on her, always kept an eye out for mistakes. Malik's mother had most likely praised him and bought him a sticky bun as reward. Resentment towards her always-controlling mother swept through her.

"All right, let's do it," she said, feeling a familiar flash of defiance. She took Malik's hand to pull them from the doorway.

He pulled back gently. "We need to leave separately. Come to the fishmonger's two squares over in a few minutes. I'll let you know when I see the right mark and give you a whistle." He grinned at her, gave her a quick kiss on the cheek, and was gone. She felt a thrill of expectation sweep through her. Pressing her hand to her belly, she felt it flop with excitement. Bella smoothed her skirt and wished she were not wearing the scarlet one now. It would be memorable if they had to flee. But there was no time to hurry back to the stage and change into her plain brown ones. Besides, her mother might be there and demand an explanation, or invent yet another chore for her to do. She'd just have to be successful, was all. And just like Malik said, if someone felt her taking their purse, she'd use her sweetest manners and hand it back to them and tell them she'd just seen it fall.

"Like a couple." Bella returned to Malik's words and smiled. How had she been so blind all these years? He was perfect for her. She caught a sudden vision of travelling the spice road with him. Seeing exotic cities on the far southern coasts. Taking a sailing ship to even more foreign lands. She'd always wanted to experience the sea. They'd be happy all the time, make a good living trading, perhaps building a family of their own. Not right away, of course. The last thing Bella wanted was babies getting in the way of her adventures. Adventures with Malik. That had a nice ring to it. She pressed her fingers to her lips where he had kissed her. They felt full and plump, tender to the touch. Like a woman's lips.

After she judged the right amount of time had passed, Bella stepped back into the street and made her way to the next square. The vendors here had closed for the evening. The sun was falling, sending the shadows of the west side of the market crawling up the eastern side. The gloaming had spikes and fingers to it. Even though she knew the shadow fingers were simply the echo of chimneys blocking the fading light, she felt a shiver run up her spine. The feeling persisted. She was being watched.

Bella turned, but saw no one behind her in the square. The few people left were all disappearing into side streets for their evening meal. She felt a crawling sensation on the back of her neck. She looked up and saw him.

The watcher was a tall man on top of the building next to her, the setting sun behind him. His shadow stretched all the way down the house, across the pavers, and lay upon her. His darkness covered her. He had a wooden shingle in one hand, a hammer in the other, paused mid-strike to stare at her. The nails held in his lips for his work looked like fangs to her. His full attention was locked on her body. Bella's breath caught. Her blood ran icy cold, as if she'd suddenly been magicked into prey and the watcher, that he was a wolf perched on high, ready to pounce. With an effort, she forced down the silly feeling, tossed her hair and continued across the empty space. If her steps were quicker than they had been before, then so be it. She was glad to get away from his hungry gaze.

Calming her breathing, she entered the next larger square. This one was still active, with food sellers shouting deals as they tried to empty their carts before day's end. The beer brewer who sold the Maibock made especially for this spring festival had already gathered up his mugs and plugged the casks. No doubt he'd roll them over to where the bonfires would soon be lit and set them up again for the night trade. The fish monger was at the near end, closest to the street which led to the river. Three large barrels filled with water held fresh fish. Eels, of course, as they were always a favorite, sweet when cooked in a pie. From the Bodensee Lake there were fellchen, with their tasty white flesh and few bones. Trout flicked in the third barrel. Huge smoked carp hung on hooks behind the chopping table, ready for slicing. Salted herring was also available, although there was less demand for it now in the spring. It was eaten mostly in the cold winter months when the ice grew too thick to fish.

Malik was nowhere in sight, but she hadn't expected to be able to see him. She lingered, poking at the fish as they flippered in the water. The owner perked up at a possible last sale. "I'll give ye three of any of them for the price of two. Or six for the price of three. Ye cannot beat that, now can you?" He grinned at her, his whiskers bristling outwards.

Bella thought about it. And why shouldn't she buy some fish? Maybe she and Malik could build a fire by the riverbank and cook them tonight, just the two of them. Delighted by the idea, she pulled coins from her pocket. "I'll take six of the Fellchen if you please, sir. Prepped for roasting."

The man dove his deft hands into the water and pulled the fish out one at a time. With a quick flick of his chopper, he beheaded them, and with a second swipe, gutted them. He then wrapped them up in a piece of oilcloth, the whole process taking less than a minute. As he handed her the fish, he said, "Return the cloth tomorrow and I'll give you a piece of the smoked fish for free."

She bobbed a curtsey as thanks and meandered into the square. She was hungry and realized all she'd eaten that day was the bread Malik had brought to her. Well, now she would give him fish. Their very own loaves and fishes. She smiled at the idea. Then sighed. She really was hungry, and no longer wanted to rob anyone, which involved lots of running away. Maybe if she just walked to the river, Malik would follow her, and they could get back to kissing.

A commotion at the far corner of the square caught her attention. The owl-like man she'd told Malik's mother was an easy mark huffed as he attempted to keep up with a contingent of six Roundhats. A tall man with huge shoulders dressed in heavy robes of deep green, his black hair flowing to the nape of his neck, highlighted by one white streak, led them. Authority radiated from him. As she watched, the man pointed to the corner over her shoulder, and sent the armored guards charging forward. They carried pikes with wicked, curving blades on the end. The metal gleamed red in the setting sun.

Bella looked to see who they were pursuing and gasped. Malik ran diagonally across the square. Their eyes met as he looked over his shoulder at his grim pursuers. Usually, Malik delighted in a chase, knowing he could outrun anyone. His normal grin was gone, replaced by panic. He picked up his pace as he headed down a narrow street that led to the river and disappeared from her sight. Bella's stomach lurched.

Malik is in trouble. She couldn't just stand and watch. Bella ran after him. She was on an interception course with the guards. Even though they had a head start, their heavy armor made them slow. She reached the corner just before the guards. Dashing into the narrow street just in front of the men, she undid her package of fresh fish, dumping them on the pavement directly in front of them. She kept running, but then looked over her shoulder when she heard the angry shouting.

The first two guards slipped on the fish and banged into each other in the tight quarters, flailing their arms. Unable to slow their momentum, the men behind them ran into them. As did the men behind them. In moments, all six were on the ground, shouting at one another. Their weapons fell as they jostled to get to their feet.

Bella laughed at the sight, delighted that her outrageous trick had worked. The guards were too preoccupied with straightening themselves out to give her any thought. The same could not be said of the owl man, who entered the narrow street and skidded to a stop at the sight of the floundering guards. His face was bright red in anger. The tall dark man who was with the owl man took in the chaos with cold disdain.

The owl man pointed a finger directly at her. "That girl there! That gypsy girl in the red skirt interfered with the arrest, Burgermeister Strom. I saw her tossing fish!"

The man in black stood coolly to one side, his face unreadable. His calm was otherworldly in the middle of all the chaos. Like an ancient black oak in the middle of a seething storm, unmoving. His keen black eyes took in all the information before him. The flailing men, the irate merchant, the fish, and her. Bella felt her laughter die in her throat when his gaze landed on her. It was like being doused with a bucket of water. Bella shivered, staggered backwards a few steps, and then bolted.

Why, oh why, did I have to wear the red skirt? Her only course of action was to run and change out of it—hide it—as quickly as she could. Malik would be far away and safe by now. That was what really mattered. They could get back to kissing later. Confident that all would be well as soon as she was out of the incriminating clothes, Bella skimmed across the cobblestones, her heart light as she thought of what she and Malik might get up to later tonight in a secluded spot on the riverbank.

CHAPTER SEVEN

She'd hoped the backstage area would be empty, but it was packed with her family. Bella didn't expect to find a scene of despair, either. Ebbe strode up and down, wringing his hands. Aunt Kezia also paced, her face pale. Uncle Timbo sat in the corner, holding his young boys on his broad knees. Rose wept also, theatrically draped across her father's shoulders.

Timbo saw her running towards them first. "Hey-ah, Belladonna," he called, but his voice was despondent.

Bella slowed to a walk, baffled. What in Saint's name was going on? Was this about the kitten? How was she to change out of the red skirt with everyone crowded into the small area? Catching Rose's eye, she frowned at her. Had her cousin built up some wild and untrue story about her again? Everyone always believed that sickeningly sweet Rose. She'd been riled enough this afternoon to do something like that. Yet Rose wasn't acting triumphant. Instead, when she saw Bella, she cried harder, falling into a little heap at her father's feet.

Her aunt Kezia rushed towards her. She shocked Bella by taking her by the shoulders and shaking her. "Where have you been? Why do you smell like fish? We thought you'd been taken as well!" Her aunt crushed Bella to her in a hard hug, and burst into tears herself.

"What is everyone crying about?" Bella untangled herself from Kezia impatiently. "What's happened? Da?"

Ebbe worked his mouth and swallowed. Bella realized he was also choking back tears. Her stoic, always calm father. Alarm crept into her; her chest tightened. She moved to him, took his hands in hers. Searched his face for some sort of clue. His eyes were glazed, and she realized he had retreated far into himself and had no answers for her.

Bella turned around to the rest of the clan. The fear changed into a need for some sort of action, as it always did with her. Her blood was up. "I swear I will hit someone with my shoe if someone doesn't tell me what's going on!"

Kezia moved to her, placed her hands on her shoulders, but then just stood there, not speaking. Bella fought the urge to fling them off and smack her. She could feel her body tremble with the effort it took waiting for her aunt to form words.

Kezia took a deep breath. "Your mother's been arrested. She's being held, in the jail now. The hangman is due to arrive Saturday afternoon, and they have set the executions for Sunday morning. Do you understand? They mean to execute her."

Bella struggled to quelch the sudden wild laughter that wanted to surge out. Surely her aunt was wrong. Bitter words popped out of her mouth instead of the laughter. "What's she done? Been rude to the wrong tradesman?"

Kezia shook her head slowly, disappointment flooding her face. She dropped her hands from Bella. "No, Bella. Nothing as simple as that."

"They arrested your mother for murder." The hollow words came from her father.

Bella gaped at him. "Well, they are clearly wrong!" It was ridiculous. Yes, her mother had a hot temper and a sharp tongue when provoked, but Bella couldn't imagine her mother hurting anyone with intent. No matter what the provocation. She was a trained healer and devoted to doing no harm. "Who is saying such a thing?"

"Burgermeister Strom himself." A new voice spoke. It was Stefan, puffing as he ran the last few steps to join the family group. He turned towards Timbo. "I followed as you asked me to, Papa. I listened to the jailors talking. Strom testified to the writ himself and had his own guards bring her to the jail." Stefan gulped in air, his ruddy face turning pale as he continued. "The worst news is they said Aunt Vadoma has confessed the murder charges to be true."

Bella pictured the jail. That stinking, horrible place next to the charnel house she'd run past earlier in the day. Bella couldn't make that image go together with her freedom-loving mother. The mother who was so annoyingly happy when they were travelling between towns. The answer seemed simple enough to Bella, hardly worth all this drama. "We'll get her out. Bribe or break her out if we have to," she said in what she considered to be her most reasonable tone.

"This isn't the time for reckless actions, Belladonna." The deep, rough voice of her uncle broke into the conversation. "The arrests won't stop with your mother. They never do. They'll want the blood of our entire clan before they're satisfied. That is how it is. We have our children to consider before all else. We will keep them safe first." He lifted his shaggy head, his good eye pinning her. "You well know that the law will not listen to the likes of us."

"We can't just leave Vadoma in there, waiting for the executioner; something has to be done," Bella stated firmly. Talk wasn't what they needed, they just had to fix it.

Kezia went to her husband, her face troubled. "Perhaps if we reasoned with the Burgermeister, after all, it's been fourteen years, surely—" she broke off and looked at Bella.

"Fourteen years since what?" Bella asked. She felt a horrible sinking feeling in her gut. It got worse as she saw her aunt and uncle exchange guilty glances with each other.

"Yes, fourteen years since what?" her father echoed. Surprised that whatever news was about to unfold was unknown to him as well, Bella stood next to him, creating a united front. They looked first to Kezia, who covered her face with her hands and shook her head. This worried Bella even more. Her aunt was usually quick to respond. She never had a lack of incisive words.

It took a long, charged minute of silence before Kezia raised her chin and spoke rapidly. "First, my sister swore me to silence about this, Ebbe. Just over fourteen years ago, here in this very town, Vadoma tried to deliver a baby for Burgermeister Strom. The mother and child both died. It wasn't from lack of her skill or efforts, but that didn't matter to Strom. The husband blamed her for their deaths and had to run to save her life. That night— Saints, this is hard."

Kezia blew out her breath, took in another one. Bella thought she might break in half waiting for the next sentence. She reached down and gripped her father's hand. He was trembling.

Kezia met her eyes, regret etching new lines on her face. "Bella, Strom laid a powerful blood curse on your mother that night, and upon you too, Bella. Bound you to be cursed by air, earth, and blood to a terrible fate. That was the night you were born."

Bella rocked back on her heels. She'd known her mother had delivered her on her own. That she'd broken her leg that same night, which was why she was plagued by a limp. But no one had told her she'd been cursed.

Her father shook free of Bella's grip and stood. He spoke the question that was rising in her own mind. "What was the curse?" His fists clenched; his teeth ground together as he forced out the words. Bella had never seen him so angry. "And why wasn't I told immediately?"

Kezia looked at him with compassion. "She didn't tell me either, not at first. Not for a long time. It was just three winters ago when she was so ill, remember Ebbe? I lost our baby boy to the flux and Vadoma had it too. She thought she would die, and that Bella would need to know."

Bella felt like knocking heads together. "Tell us." She locked her knees and straightened her backbone. *I'm ready for anything,* she thought.

Kezia's voice sank to a low whisper. "You have to know, she's been seeking a way to break it everywhere we go, but she found nothing that would break a blood curse. It can only be broken by death of the one who cast it, or the one who was cursed. Strom put the geas on her that you would never love her, and that she would know terrible pain and loss. That you would unleash a chain of hell and death after love's first kiss, that you'd suffer, be broken, and that you were bound to him."

It seemed as if all the air sucked from the room, taking all sound with it too. Time slowed. Bella stumbled backwards into the table they used for props, sending the finger cymbals and ankle bells flying, along with the pretty wooden bowls carved with vines they used for horse clopping sounds during the telling of the tales. She watched them fall to the floor, saw the kicks of dust they raised in a slow arc when they impacted. She dimly realized she had fallen to the floor as well.

How odd that these visual details in the room were so precise and crystal clear. Others were all too clear as well. The horror on her father's face. Young Timbo and Pattin, their eyes rounded in fear. It seemed that she could even see the individual dust motes still lingering in the air. All coalescing to form one face. Malik's face, the boy she loved. Malik's face as he kissed her.

The sound clashed back in all at once. Everyone was yelling or crying. Bella clapped her hands to her ears. "Stop!" she shouted as she scrambled back to her feet. "Strom cannot rule me. It's a lie, not real."

"Or the curse not completely fulfilled yet." Her father's voice was grim.

"Yes, it's true, your mother always kept you from the boys in the towns," Kezia said. She looked up at her hopefully. "You've stayed away from boys, haven't you, child?"

The simple question hit her hard. Her face felt like it was on fire. She stared at the ground, willing herself to calm down. Part of her simply wanted to scream that she was no longer a child and run away. Not forever, but long enough so she could think of something to do. Now was not the time to admit to anything. She willed her face to only show innocence. Years of being on stage performing were going to pay off.

"Yes, Aunt." The reply felt too short, and Bella saw suspicion cross her aunt's face. Time to add more to the ruse, add a bitter note. "You and mother keep me so busy I never had the time."

Kezia nodded, accepting the lie. "Good, that's good." She turned to her husband. "Timbo, we should get the boys and Rose out of town. You could take them in the wagon up into the Darkwood. It's easy to stay hidden there."

Bella bit her lip as the attention flowed away from her. She needed to get to Malik. Her family would just talk endlessly, but she and Malik together would find a way to get their mother out of jail. She edged towards the side of the tent and ducked behind their costume rack. Stripping off the red skirt, she stuffed it behind the trunk. It would need to stay hidden until they were far away from this town. She changed quickly into plain dark skirts and found a rag to bundle back her hair. It was time to be as anonymous as possible.

Stefan sidled up beside her. She glared at him as she tucked the last of her stray curls into the rag. "And why would you be watching me get changed, cousin?"

Normally embarrassing Stefan was enough to make him back off. Not this time. His face was uncharacteristically somber. He spoke in low tones, so that only she could hear. "I know what I saw today, what's brewing between you and Malik, and it wasn't practice for a play. You should tell them if you've already kissed him."

If he'd been smug or smiling or shown any sign of wanting to get her into trouble, Bella wouldn't have responded. Or would have found a lie that would fit. But as her cousin looked at her with steady eyes, Stefan just looked like he cared.

"I'll think about it," she said reluctantly. "Right now, I want to find Malik. He'll know of a way we can get Ma out of that stinking jail. Or know someone who could help." Bella scrabbled under a bench and pulled out her leather shoes. The streets by the jail were filthy.

Stefan nodded slowly. "All right. I'll keep your secret... for now. But if you two don't come up with a plan before tomorrow, you have to promise me you'll tell them. And if you do come up with a plan, I want in on it!"

Bella finished tying her laces, then grabbed the big laundry sack. She stuffed it with skirts and bits of costuming her father used to change characters on the storytelling stage. It didn't matter if they needed cleaning or not, she just needed a decent reason to get out from under everyone's prying eyes. Including that of her very earnest cousin. Sack full, she turned to him.

"I'm trusting you with this. And yes, if Malik comes up with a plan where we need help, you're the first person we'll come to. But if I find out you've said anything about our 'rehearsal,' I'll wallop you from here to Saint Peter's Gate and back again. And you know I can do it, too."

Stefan grinned. "You used to be able to do it. I'd like to see you try now." He flexed his arms. Bella would never admit it, but he really was developing some muscle there. Instead, Bella squinted and pretended she couldn't see anything. The lighthearted moment was fleeting, as they heard Kezia and her husband start to quarrel.

"I'll not be sent away like a damn cripple!"

"This isn't anything to do with that, Timbo. You're the one best suited to keep the children safe in the forest. You know it's true!" Kezia's voice had a stubborn ring to it.

Bella and Stefan looked at one another, dismayed. "He probably just doesn't want to get stuck with your snot-nosed little brothers," whispered Bella.

Stefan nodded wryly. "Ma will win this one, though."

Bella nodded her agreement as she moved into the main section of the tent. Carrying the sack of laundry, she moved to her father, who sat morosely in the corner. She bent down to him. "Da, I'm doing the laundry quick before the night bell. That way if we want to be leaving, we can."

Ebbe looked up at her, and her heart clenched at the misery she saw there. "Aye beauty, just be well in before the night guard comes around. We don't need another of us locked away." His hand tremored when he patted her absently on the arm.

Bella's mouth dried up, watching that shaking hand. She couldn't remember a time when her powerful father had seemed so lost. She realized suddenly that her mother was like her father's north star. It was in Vadoma that he found all his direction. All her life she'd thought it was her father who had led them and made the decisions to keep them happy and warm and fed. Now she wondered if perhaps it had been Vadoma who was the animating force all along. It was strange to think of her mother in those terms.

"Woman, I'll not be directed by you in this!" her uncle Timbo growled. Bella turned and saw he was standing. The babies clutched each other on the floor, wide-eyed and for once, not crying. Bella thought wryly that Stefan was right. In the end, her uncle would be the one taking the children to safety. Her aunt was slow to anger, but when her back was up, there was no one more fierce and unyielding.

"If you have a better plan, let's all hear it then, you stubborn old mule!" she retorted.

Bella used the distraction to escape to the street and headed swiftly towards the river where she'd last seen Malik. It was a relief to be free of her tense and frightened family and moving again. Yet troubling new thoughts from the revelation of the curse could not be left behind. The new image of her mother as the true leader of their clan made her feel odd, and slightly ashamed. She'd always just thought of her as a person who had to be obeyed, an annoyance most of the time.

Had the curse affected her all along? Had she never loved her mother? Was the stifled feeling she had anytime her mother came near because of the air binding of the curse? That couldn't be true. They had their differences, of course, and she was much closer to her father. To be fair, he was more fun, and hardly ever fussed at her. Was the curse why her mother was always so strict with her? Bella gave herself a little shake to stop the mental cascade of questions about her parents. Time for that later, when she could actually confront her mother about her ridiculous secrecy—why hadn't she been informed she'd been cursed, and a binding blood curse at that? After all, she was the focus of the curse. That would be a good starting place. It was so irritating!

Moving past revelers lighting early bonfires in the twilight, she heard raucous laughter and felt a stab of envy. Had it really only been an hour ago that she'd been happy?

CHAPTER EIGHT

As usual, it was Malik who found her. Bella had just finished giving the clothes a quick dunk in the river to make it look as if they had been washed and was wringing them out when he appeared next to her. The last vestiges of the day brushed across his cheekbones, giving him a beautiful gold dusting of color, as if he were a precious object. All thought of her mother and danger flew out of her head for a moment.

"You're so beautiful." The words were out of her mouth before she could stop them.

She was rewarded by his gorgeous smile, the one that made the dimple on his left cheek appear. His eyes shone as he looked at her. "I think I'm supposed to say that to you," Malik replied, in a light, teasing tone. "Need help with your wash?"

Malik looked surprised when Bella shook her head and dropped the wet clothes unceremoniously to the ground. Bella stepped closer, and his dimple deepened until she spoke. "Did you hear, they've arrested my mother for murder."

Malik's teasing manner vanished, along with his smile. He nodded solemnly. "Not the sentence, but I saw the soldiers bring her by the alley where I was tucked away. Good move throwing those fish, by the way, so I could get away."

Bella felt herself flush with pleasure at his compliment. She wanted to reach for him, loop her arms around him, but stopped herself. Now was not the time, especially now that she knew about the curse. She wondered if she should tell Malik about it but brushed it off. There were more important things to discuss. "Malik, we need to get her out by tomorrow at the latest. The hangman is due the day after that."

"You want to break your mother out of jail." Malik looked at her like she was crazy. She felt a prickle of irritation building. Bella looked him straight in the face, all romantic feelings evaporating.

"Of course I do, Malik."

"It's not possible, Bella. This is a big town, not some village where it'd be easy to do with some sleight of hand or a good shovel to dig with. They build with stone here. And have plenty of men on duty in there."

Bella felt the edges of her temper fray. "She doesn't deserve to be in there. Ma didn't murder anyone, but you know as well as I do that no one believes gypsies." She bit down on the last word, giving it the taint that all the townsfolk used when referring to her family and those like them.

"You're right, but it doesn't mean you can just break her out. Be reasonable." Malik's tone was the one he used when he was trying to make their ponies lift their hooves to be picked.

She hated that tone. Hated being told to be reasonable. Bella bit down on the curse words she wanted to use and forced her voice to sound calm. "I realize I'm not versed in breaking and entering like you are. I was hoping you might know a clever way in. Or that maybe you have friends clever enough if you are not."

Malik pretended to be shot by an arrow. "Ouch!" When she didn't smile, he scowled. "Like you, this is a new town for me," he protested.

"So that's it, you're not going to even try?"

"You're being unreasonable—"

"I'm trying to save Vadoma, Malik! A woman who is just as much a mother to you as your own. Doesn't that matter to you?"

They stood glaring at each other. The rushing of the river next to them filled the long silence. Bella refused to be the first one to look away or even blink, even if her eyes were burning. Malik broke first. He tossed his arms up in the air and strode away several steps. Bella stayed where she was. She knew his tricks. He returned and glared at her some more. Bella crossed her arms and raised her chin.

Malik rubbed his face with his hands. Sighed. "I'd need to go look at it."

Bella nodded. "Yes, you do, but you're not doing it by yourself. I'm coming with you."

"I won't let you put yourself in trouble."

"You can't stop me. You should know that well enough by now, Malik."

He shook his head, frustrated. "I suppose I should."

Bella inhaled and stopped herself from pressing for more. It passed for him agreeing with her. Time to move forward. "That's settled then. I'll meet you outside the jail after ten bells. I'm taking this laundry back first. Da's had enough worry for one day. I'll slip back out and meet you." She bent down and picked up the wet clothes. Now they had mud on them. No matter, she could give them a proper wash later.

Malik was looking at her when she stood. Bella ducked her head away, pretending to drop a shirt. He wasn't fooled. Catching her under the chin, he looked at her. "Don't be shy. I thought our first kiss went well, didn't you?"

"I can't be seen kissing you in public, Malik. There are… new considerations."

He stepped back. "New considerations? My, aren't we a fancy talker all of a sudden?"

"Don't try to pick a fight. I'll tell you more later," she promised. She stepped away before he could say more and hiked up the embankment. She wondered if she'd ever do the laundry again without thinking of this bizarre day that had changed her whole life.

Ugh. The area surrounding jail smelled even worse at night than it had in the daytime, if that was even possible. Bella moved carefully along the alley next to the low stone building. All manner of rotting, disgusting things slimed the cobblestones. She was grateful that the dark hid most of it and that she'd been smart enough to put on her shoes before coming here. The jail was just ahead of her on the left. She passed by a barred opening and risked peeping in, but could see nothing but darkness inside.

A breeze from downriver carried the pungent odors of the tanning yards. Her eyes watered. Stifling a coughing fit, she circled the block that held the jail and next to it, the charnel house. A high stone wall, more than twice her height, guarded the back of the jail from intrusion. Keeping her steps light, Bella moved around to the front side of the jailhouse. Passing its front door, she saw it stood open, the gleam of lantern light from within. Rough voices of men floated out into the warm evening. Not daring to look and have her face catch the eye of the men inside, she turned away and glided past.

The darkness felt even more oppressive after she passed the light. It had an almost physical presence, and she shuddered. *No need to fear shadows.* She calmed herself. *Just need to let my eyes grow used to the dark again.* Bella forced herself to stand still and be part of the dark rather than fight against it. Imagined it soft and inviting rather than fearsome. Several heartbeats later, her eyes adjusted, and she could see the edge of the charnel house clearly. It's wooden door was shut. A guard stood in front of it, his round helmet reflecting the dim starlight. The sharp edge of the sword tucked through his belt also gleamed, as did the long pike in his other hand. The man angled the pike across the door that led to the house of the dead. Their final watchman.

Bella pulled further back into the shadows to watch. Malik would come soon, and then they could cook up a distraction so she could get into the house of the dead. She waited long enough that her leg muscles locked, and her very bones were growing cold. The damnable watchman hadn't budged, except for one time when a cat had tried to twine its way around his boots. The guard had kicked the cat, sending it flying through the air with a yowl. Bella gritted her teeth to not protest the creature's treatment.

Where in the world was Malik? She'd been at least four quarters waiting here in the dark. Bella was impatient. She'd have to make her own distraction if the dratted boy couldn't find his way here to help. Bending slowly to the ground, she felt around in the disgusting muck of the street. *I'm probably glad I can't see what I'm touching.* Bella's hand finally felt on a square of loose brick.

She picked it up slowly and stood back up. Now how to make this work? She could just hurl it at the man, make him leave his post, and run after her. But he might just yell for the prison guards next door instead, and then her goose would be well and truly cooked. Maybe throw it down the alley so he'd investigate the sound? Bella discarded this idea as soon as she thought of it. The stubborn man hadn't moved from his post at all.

She frowned in the dark. If only Malik was here, it would be easy. Had he run into trouble? Or was he spurning both her idea and her? Bella felt anger rising in her. *How dare he! Worthless, stupid boy!* Maybe she should see if Stefan would help her instead. She could bully Stefan into it if he balked. Well, it was no good just standing here, with no clear plan.

Frustrated, Bella lowered herself down and dropped the brick. She'd started the slow process of creeping away when a burst of laughter from the jail caught her ear. She looked back and saw the guard at the charnel house door also look that way. Amazed, she watched him flex his knees and step away from his post. The man moved to the door of the jail.

"Wotcher laughin' about, ya lazy turds?" The guard spoke affably enough. Bella couldn't hear the response, but the guard laughed.

"Say, is that rum you lot are drinkin'? Selfish bastards, pass the pot here!" The guard stepped into the jailhouse fully, leaving his tall pike propped up outside.

This was her shot! Second thoughts would get her caught. *Run!* Bella darted to the door of the dead house. Praying that there was no need for a lock when a guard was posted out front, she pulled at the string latch and heard a gentle click. In a breath, she was inside the house of the dead. A series of openings high up on the righthand wall let faint light in and made her smile. They were small, just there to help ventilate the gasses from the dead, but they just might be her way out if the guard was back on duty when she was done here.

More relaxed now that she had an exit plan, Bella looked around. She'd seen dead bodies before. She wasn't bothered by the alternate stiffness and looseness of the limbs of the poor and destitute who ended up in places such as these. Living rough and travelling meant that a person saw all sorts of things, including death in its many forms. The difference here was that there were so many of them, stacked like wood along the sides of the room. Bella supposed death must be this way in any large city. A portion of people wouldn't live the night through, and the bigger the city, the more piles of dead in the charnel house. She said a quick prayer for the remission of their souls to whatever power they believed in, and that they'd found peace in the end. By the end of the day tomorrow, any unclaimed dead would have their belongs stripped from them and given to the rag mongers. Nuns from the nearby kirk would wash their bodies and wrap them properly before they were carried to a wide and deep common grave at the edge of town. A priest would say the words over them, lime scattered, and then they could rest until the next night's lot was dropped on top of them.

She was glad to see they kept the bodies as she had imagined earlier in the day when her idea had formed. In this keeping house, the bodies still had the clothes they died in for at least the first night, which was crucial to the success of her plan. Next, she moved to the wall nearest the jail, hoping that the two buildings might share a common entrance that couldn't be seen from the outside. There was no opening there, just more bodies, but moving towards the back, she saw a short door.

Tiptoeing so as not to disturb anyone's almost-final rest, Bella pushed the door. It was unlocked. She entered a small yard with the tall stone wall she'd seen from her reconnoiter. It delighted Bella to see that the jail had steps that also led down into the yard. She wrinkled her nose at the stench of piss. *No doubts about how they used this yard.* The dead smelled sweeter than the yard.

She moved to the jail door, hoping she would find this unlocked as well. Gingerly, she pulled at the dark iron latch, but it didn't budge. Looking closer, she could see that it needed a latch key. Or a person who could pick such a lock. She smiled. Malik's skill sets would come in handy here.

Deciding she'd seen enough, she moved to the back door of the charnel house and pulled at the door handle. The wooden door didn't budge.

"Drat, drat and damn," she muttered. Of course, the door wouldn't open from this yard if the jail shared it. It would be too easy for a lively prisoner to make a run for it. Shaking her head at her folly for not blocking open the door, Bella considered the high stone walls. She was an excellent climber, but they were easily twice her height, and had jagged stones placed along the top of the wall. Perhaps if she found something to leap upwards from, she could catch the top and ease herself over.

Looking around the small space, she spied a three-legged stool in the corner. It wasn't much, but it was all she had. If she placed it about a foot from the wall, and took a running leap off of it, she just might make it. The edges of the stone were going to hurt, no doubt, but she refused to be trapped here.

Bella picked up the stool to place it by the wall. Just then, the door from the jail opened, and a burly jailor blinked in surprise at seeing her. His hands paused where they had been fumbling with the last laces of his breeches.

"Wotcher doing here, then?" He growled.

"Just visiting!" Bella said brightly. Then she swung the little stool at his exposed man parts as hard as she could.

The guard turned away, so the stool merely glanced the tender area and then bounced away off his hip, but it gave Bella the opportunity she needed. Blessing the years of dancing that kept her limber, she arched her body past the roundness of the guards behind and slipped by him, into the jail. Turning around, she gave the man a good kick to the rear so that he stumbled into the yard. She pulled the door shut behind her. She heard keys jangle and grabbed them from the lock. Bella grasped the heavy iron ring and peered into the darkness.

The dank reek of unwashed bodies, mold, and misery hit her as she assessed the layout of the jail. *Saints, she hated being shut in like this.* Nothing for it but to grit it out. Just ahead was the long hall of the jail. A second murky hallway slanted unevenly down to her right, with a spiral stair at the end of it, which was no doubt the path to the lower dungeon. That was where the hangman would ply his trade, getting confessions from the poor souls that found themselves there. She heard moans come from that deeper darkness and shuddered. Up ahead, the light from where the warden kept watch showed the way out through the front door. Four tiny cells lined the hall where she stood. Moving past, Bella saw that the first two cells were empty. In the second two, she saw crumpled bodies lying on the floor, their faces turned to the stone wall.

She dared a whisper. "Ma, are you here?" One of the decrepit bundles stirred to sit up and look at her. A wizened face that sported full mustaches. Not her mother.

"Is there a woman in here?" she asked, keeping her voice low. "A woman who walks with a limp?"

The man looked puzzled but nodded, pointing back towards the dungeon. *Saints!*

Clasping the keys to the jail tightly, Bella turned to go back that way. Loud banging on the back door made her grimace. There was no time to make her way down into the dungeons. She'd be trapped there. Too risky. She'd have to trust the other guards would be light-blind when they moved into this passage.

The banging grew to include kicking. Bella heard the grunts of the guards in the front room, the scrape of their chairs pushing back. Crossing her fingers for luck, Bella moved as close to the doorway and its light as she could. She tucked herself into the corner.

Just in time. Two guardsmen moved past her hiding place. They walked in a reluctant stroll towards the back door, hitching up their breeches. Bella turned her face to the wall so they wouldn't feel her eyes upon them. *This is just like stalking game in the forest.* It was just a matter of timing and luck. Keeping still, she held her breath, tensed her legs, ready to move.

"Blast your bleed'n eyes, Belcher, you know t'use the stool to keep the bleed'n door open!" The first man called out. She could smell the cheap ale he'd been drinking.

She heard the second man banging his wooden club against the bars of the cells, forcing the incarcerated to wake up. Stealing the only relief from the monotony and wretchedness of this place they had. It made Bella angry, and she mentally kicked the guard as she willed them to just take a few more steps past her so she could slip out of the front door.

She snuck a peek through her eyelashes. It was almost time for her to make her move. But then the mustached man in the cell grinned and winked at her. He laughed, a high, manic laugh, and clapped his chained hands together.

The second guard noticed. "Hey what're you so happy about, ye daft drunk?" He stopped and stared at the grinning fool.

To her horror, Bella saw the prisoner raise his manacled hand and point at her. The guard was in the middle of turning around when she whipped out of her corner. She kicked him hard in the shin as she did so, making him howl in pain. The prisoner cackled with glee.

At least I got that kick in. Bella sucked in her gut and just avoided the man's outreached hands. She ran through the intake room. Thank the gods. The door to the street was still standing open. She grinned. Nearly free.

Suddenly she was jerked backwards and nearly fell on her face. The guard she'd kicked had hold of her skirts. He yanked back again, and she tumbled to the floor, hitting hard on the dirty stone. Panic seized her, and she reached around, tugged back as hard as she could. If only she could pull her dress from his fists, then she'd be away. No matter if cloth ripped. Bella knew she had only moments before the other two guards swarmed into the room.

The damnable skirts held. In moments, he'd have her in his grasp. She kicked backward and was gratified to hear his breath whoosh out from his body. He grimaced, and Bella saw he was about to grab her again. She twisted her body, then flung her arm around as fast as she could, the iron keys lending her momentum and weight. The keys smashed into the guard's face. His nose erupted in a fountain of blood, the keys scoring funnels through his cheeks. He screamed high and long and covered his ruined face with his hands.

Horrified at what she'd just done, Bella dropped the keys and scrambled backward on all fours for the open door. The man behind her bellowed as the other guard dashed into the space, his face contorted as he yelled at her to stop. Bella got her feet under her and fled into the blessed darkness of the street.

Pelting along the street, she let her feet take her where they would in her blind rush to escape. The stench of the tannery got stronger. She must be near the river. Behind her, she could hear the sounds of pursuit. A thud and then cursing, as if someone fallen. No time to look back and see. Gasping for air, uncertain of which street might allow her to lose the guards, she decided to run the easy way. Bella sprinted downhill. She heard the rushing of the river, felt the cool breeze of it on her face as the streets ended and the riverbank began. There were bonfires scattered along the grassy edge of the Neckar river. Bodies danced merrily around them. Panting, she stopped for a moment on top of the embankment, hands on knees. She had to get her breath, get her bearings.

"There's the mangy bitch!" The guttural shout was close. Bella forced herself to get moving again. *Not fast enough.* Her heart felt like it would beat out of her chest. There was nowhere to turn or hide, only open space and the dark gleam of the river flowing in front of her. The men behind her had longer legs. It was only a matter of moments before she was caught and condemned to the same prison she'd just escaped if she turned left or right. No doubt, assault on a guard of the city by a Traveller like her would mean a death sentence.

The rushing of the river was loud. It was moving fast. With a cry of despair, she bounded down the embankment to the quick flow and threw herself in. Thinking quickly, she grabbed her skirts at the hem and billowed them up into the air and over, making a makeshift float for herself. The river snatched her away from the bank and took her quickly into the middle of its greedy rush. The deep cold of it had her lungs constricting.

The men pursuing her wheeled their arms to stop from tumbling in after her. She grinned with relief and laughed at their furious faces that disappeared quickly as the river flowed on. Now to escape the river. She shivered, all the heat from the run dissipating.

Gulping in air, she kicked her legs and tried to stay up with the powerful flow. Thank the gods her father had taught her how to swim. She knew she had only a minute or so before her shoes and skirts dragged her down. The balloon of air that she'd captured in her skirts was disappearing through the rough weave of her overdress. The dress was now too heavy to try the same trick again. So heavy it was pulling her down. She flipped to her back so she could use both hands to undo the laces of the skirt.

She fumbled with the back ties, her fingers growing more numb by the moment. They were in impossible knots. Finally she got the top layer of skirts off and floated out of them. It didn't really help, for the underdress itself was just as heavy. Only her face was above water now. Her shoes! She pushed them off her feet. It did no good. Her woolen underdress would be the death of her if she couldn't get it off.

The river was getting wilder, the rushing of it gleeful, as if it delighted in having her in its grasp. The ties in the back of her underdress were impossible to unlace when they were wet. Screaming in frustration, Bella wondered if this was that wretched curse trying to manifest. The thought made her angry. *No.*

There was more than one way to get out of a dress! Bella yanked the front bodice up and got her teeth into it, biting and chewing like a mad dog. She got it to tear even as her head fell beneath the water. Kicking madly, she got up to the surface one last time and gasped in a final breath of air. The rest of this fight would be underwater.

Bella sank. She yanked at her dress, working at the rip she'd started. Just a little more, and she could wiggle free. Up and out was her focus. Her nails broke as she used the last of her strength and breath, straining against the stubborn homespun cloth. The river pulled harder, the darkness around her complete.

Her lungs burned. She fought. She felt fabric give way and then rip. She kicked and squirmed, finally feeling the weight of the dress fall away. She had to get air! Which way was up? A memory came to her, sitting with Malik on the bottom of a pond, watching their breath bubble to the top. Her mind was drifting into the eternal black. *Bubbles.* Bella forced herself to let the last of the air in her lungs go and watched for a bubble to show her the way.

There! The last bit of air in her lungs formed a round, glistening sphere that hovered and then moved. Kicking haphazardly, willing her legs to move, she followed it. The river pressed down and around her, wanting to claim her for its own. *No.* She would not give in, she would not. She forced her arms to reach up, pull down. Again and again. The bubble disappeared. She felt searing despair. Her guide was gone!

One final push and she broke the surface. Air. With deep gasps, she pulled it into her lungs. It hurt. Bella coughed. Spat up water. Breathed through the ache in her lungs as she floated. She was dimly aware of how cold she was. She had to get to land, get warm. Orienting herself using the light from the now-distant bonfires, she pulled and kicked her way to the bank. Finally reaching a muddy shore, she pulled herself up by the long grasses at the edge, and collapsed on the blessed earth. Looking upwards, she thought the sight of the glimmering stars had never been sweeter.

Bella got her breath back and then wiggled out of her wet smallclothes. She wrung out her hair and the linens. She giggled at the thought of wearing nothing at all into the town, but the giggles quickly dissolved into her teeth chattering. Movement was the only way to get warm. Shivering hard, she pulled back on her linens. She couldn't go into town in just her underthings. Even if she stuck to the shadows, it was too much of a risk. If caught by a night guard or even an upright citizen, they'd first be scandalized, then they'd take her straight to the jail. A place she only wanted to go one more time. When she broke her mother out.

CHAPTER NINE

V adoma flexed her hands, trying to keep the blood in them. They stretched agonizingly above her head, clamped in iron cuffs that were attached to the wall. She stood on her toes, trying to alleviate the pain in her shoulders. The straw scattered on the floor tickled her bare feet, but she was glad of something between her and the flagstones. Not that the straw was there for her comfort. It was there to make cleanup easier for the guards, absorbing various body fluids. The stink of urine and fear permeated the dank area.

She knew there were others down here in the dark. Vadoma could hear their sighs and moans. She'd tried talking to them when she had first arrived—was that hours or days ago? There was no way of telling down here. No one had replied. Perhaps their tongues had been removed. It was a popular option that jailers frequently used.

Vadoma eased her neck side to side, but nothing helped the strain. It surprised her that other than chaining her to the wall, nothing else had happened to her. She shivered at the thought. Vadoma had seen the metal torture devices on the table next to the doorway when they dragged her down here. She felt cold and was glad they had left her clothes on her except for taking away her shoes. It was something to be grateful for.

I'm catching at bits of hope. It might be better if she just gave up and let her fate come to her. It'd been long in the making. Yet she couldn't shake the idea that perhaps the curse could be lifted. If not for her, at least for Bella. She thought back to the moment when she knew Burgermeister Strom had recognized her. That grin of his had been so knowing, as if he'd been eagerly awaiting an old friend. He'd gestured to his Roundhats, and they had surrounded her before she could even think about running.

Luckily for her, there had been Travellers on their route, and she'd flashed some hand signals to them so that Ebbe would know where she was. Vadoma also thought she'd seen Malik peeking out from a filthy alley as she passed. She sighed, adding to the dim chorus of moans in the underground. Vadoma hoped Ebbe wouldn't try anything foolish. Not long ago she'd heard a scuffle in the jail above, and wild hope had flared in her. It shamed her to have it, and dread immediately replaced hope. She didn't want rescuing. She wanted her family to flee, leave this terrible town and its evil Burgermeister. Strom must be some sort of cunning demon. She was sure of it. How else had he not aged a day in fourteen years, save for the white streak in his hair? He surely had some sort of evil magic that kept him vibrant and in power.

It had been supremely stupid of her to think she could talk him out of the curse. She wondered now if the curse had an element that lashed her to him, something that became more powerful the closer she got to Strom. How else to explain her dashing to his home, unprotected and alone? It just wasn't something she would do. Or how she'd allowed Ebbe and the clan to come to this town in the first place, especially now when the curse was at the point of making its worst part known, Bella's death. It had been madness.

Realizing that her thoughts were doing nothing but whirling and circling like a flock of crows, Vadoma sighed again. She could only hope that her freely given confession to the murder of his wife and newborn babe would placate Strom. That he'd then lift the rest of his curse and let her child live.

CHAPTER TEN

B ella made her way north of the city, where space was allotted for the Travellers to make camp. The river had done most of the work for her, and the walking was easy on the road that ran beside it. Only once did she have to lie hidden in the undergrowth while a wagon passed by.

She found the encampment, and their carved and brightly painted wagon in swirls of red, violet, and yellow was easy to spot. Kezia and Timbo's larger, plain wagon was set up next to it, brown with a few splashes of green dye shaped like vines. Uncle Timbo was never one for decorations. She paused for a moment to make sure that none of her family was nearby. Stefan usually watched their camp, but he was nowhere in sight. Bella tiptoed past a few late campfires, staying well in the shadows. She didn't want to give anyone cause to tell stories of her creeping into camp in only her smallclothes. She'd never live it down.

Their sturdy ponies, Aethon and Pyrois, snuffled gently in greeting when she approached the wagon. She gave them a good scratch on their foreheads where each had a sun-shaped splotch of white on their coarse brown coats. She smiled to herself at the thought of these little ponies pulling the great sun-god Apollo's cart across the sky like the mythical horses they'd been named after. They might not have the stature for it, but they surely had the hearts. They nibbled at her hands in search of treats.

"Ah, nothing today boys, but I'll bring you something tasty soon," Bella promised. Moving to their wagon, she crawled inside. The first thing she did was open the metal box that carried their hard tack and eagerly bit into a biscuit. She let the rock-like bite dissolve in her mouth as she opened up the winter trunk. She sat back on her heels with a sigh when she saw that only her mother's yellow winter underdress was inside.

Bella then remembered that she'd thrown her own extra dress into the fire only last month in a pique of anger over a task her mother had set her to do. Bella frowned as she tried to think what had made her so angry at Vadoma. Reflecting, it seemed like she and her mother never saw eye to eye. Maybe there was something to that curse after all. Bella shook her head to get rid of the thought. She couldn't very well afford to believe in curses that ended with her own binding and destruction for those she loved.

She pulled on the dress, glad of its warmth, even though it would be too heavy later in the day. And it was yellow, not her best color. She took pleasure in the fact that it was too tight across her chest, but loose at the waist. Perhaps in the rush of what needed to happen on the morrow, her mother wouldn't notice. Bella frowned as she realized that was a false hope. Oh well. Vadoma was always angry with her over something. Wearing her dress would hardly add fuel to that particular fire. Bella found her father's knife belt and used it to cinch the waist. She added one of her own scarves and tied it to cover the knife, as Travellers weren't allowed to carry weapons in the town. She was exhausted. Maybe she could just lie down for a short while. Just until dawn. Finishing the biscuit, she moved to the long bench that lay on one side of the wagon, stretched out, and was asleep in moments.

CHAPTER ELEVEN

S tupid Bella! Rose dug through the disgusting heap of clothes her idiot cousin had dumped backstage sometime the night before. They were still wet and smelled like dirty river water and old sweat. She'd bet all her meals for the next two days that Bella had simply dunked them in the water and hadn't beaten or scrubbed them with sand or lye at all. Bella would have to do them all over again, but even so, nothing would be dry in time for today's show. If there was a show. For a moment, Rose stumbled over her inner rant. They had to do something about Vadoma, but she couldn't for the life of her figure out what that might be. They couldn't fight through the entire town guard to free her, after all.

Shaking her head and grumbling, Rose sifted through the wet pile. There had to be something here that would work for today. The last thing she needed was to trudge all the way over to the river and redo the wash herself, then do the calling of the crowd and the dancing again. That would make three days in a row she performed the show instead of being able to enjoy the market. It just wasn't fair. Bella just took up too much space in this family, she thought viciously. She made everyone's life harder.

Rose wished her cousin would just disappear. Not forever, just for a good long while. A year would be good. Or two.

Hands on hips, Rose blew her red ringlets out of her face. It was going to be a hot day, she could tell. She didn't want to wear her winter skirts again. Just then she spied a bit of red sticking out from behind the fake swords and shields that Ebbe and Stefan sometimes used when they were telling a tale with battles in it. She cocked her head and sidled over to the bit of red, as if it might suddenly dart away on its own accord.

Rose bent down and tugged. She grinned as her favorite red skirts came into view. *Oho! That Bella had been hiding them!* Grinning, Rose tied them on, and then spun. She always thought it looked like roses blooming when she twirled in this dress. Just like her name. And that Bella was dead wrong. This red didn't clash with her hair at all. They complimented each other. As they should. After all, it wasn't bragging if what you were saying was true!

Rose flounced out from behind the stage area feeling triumphant. She'd go find her mother at the booth, see if there was any news of Vadoma. For a moment, Rose wondered where her father, Stefan, and Ebbe had disappeared to. She also vaguely thought it might be wise for her to stay here to watch over their things, for this stage and costumes and props in the wings were how they all made their livelihood. But then she shrugged off the thought. She'd only be gone for a few minutes. What could possibly happen?

Pausing to make sure the back curtains were drawn tightly, Rose stepped out into the main square, feeling wonderful in the red skirts. The pocket on her left side felt heavy. Touching it, she realized it contained several coins. Rose frowned as she thought back to yesterday. *That Bella! She must have kept this coin back from the family. Again*! Rose shook her head. It was scandalous how selfish Bella could be.

Tucking the coins back into the deep pocket, Rose considered her options. She could secretly add the money into the family cache. Or she could tell on Bella and let her get what she deserved. On one hand, it was always good to have Bella owe her one. On the other hand, though... Bella had been secretive and mean for weeks, and Rose was sick of it. Bella would get punished if she told on her. Bella had been told multiple times that none of the family kept back profits from sales, no matter how well they bargained. It was the right thing to do to let the family know what Bella had done. Rose sniffed as she decided. It served her right. *I should take a finder's fee from the coins. Just a little one. Who would know?* Besides, Bella would never argue about how many coins had actually been tucked away.

Smiling, Rose agreed with her own calculations. *No one would miss a black pfennig.* They'd just thank her for turning over the rest of the coins to the family purse. She'd buy a sugared apple right now as her very own reward. The kind with cinnamon sprinkled on them. She could taste it already. Excited, Rose turned to cross the square on a diagonal towards the confectioner's cart. It wouldn't hurt to let as many townsfolk see her as possible in her pretty skirts. Might drum up some business for the show later. Rose smiled and bobbed her head to people as she passed.

It didn't bother her that while children smiled back at her, all the women pretended not to see her. Most pointedly altered their trajectory when they saw their path was about to cross that of a "dirty gypsy." That was just the way things were in the bigger towns. She knew to avoid groups of boys or men with hands that might be quick to grab. Ducking around a larger group, Rose heard a commotion at the far end of the square where she was headed.

Slowing her pace, for it was never wise to get caught up in trouble of any kind, Rose peered around the back of a particularly wide man to see what was happening. A group of Roundhats in full armor were shoving people aside as they moved forward. In their wake was a tall man dressed in deep red and black robes. The tall man had a white streak in his hair and was rather handsome. He seemed to meet her eyes and smiled in a most unpleasant way. The tall man pointed in her direction and the Roundhats trotted across the square.

Rose turned around to see who they might be after, but couldn't see anyone running away that might have made the man point like that. Shrugging, she moved out from behind the wide man. She could smell the crisping sugar and cinnamon wafting from the apple stall just a few feet away.

"You there, in the red dress, I order you to stop." She heard a man's voice call out.

Well, she had on red skirts, which were totally different from a red dress. Besides, she was quite sure she had done nothing wrong. Rose ignored the voice and skipped to the apple seller. The elderly woman had an odd look on her face. As if she were afraid of something.

"A sugared apple, please. With cinnamon." Rose held out the pfennig. But the wrinkly old woman backed away from her, cringing down behind her table. What was the matter with her?

Then a gauntleted hand knocked her arm down. The pfennig spun through the air and landed on the pavement as someone roughly turned her around. It was one of the Roundhats. He grabbed her and pulled both of her arms behind her. The rest of the brigade surrounded them.

"I told you to stop!" the guard said. "You're under arrest."

Baffled, Rose looked up at her accuser. "I haven't done anything," Rose gasped. Her shoulders felt like they were being twisted out of their sockets.

"We have sworn statements from both a local merchant and the Burgermeister himself that you purposefully disrupted an arrest last night." The men began marching her out of the square. Rose stumbled as they shoved her along with them. The man who had her arms yanked her up painfully.

"But I was performing all last night in the Traveller show!" Rose protested. "I wasn't even wearing these skirts. You have the wrong person!"

"I was there. I saw you and your dirty trick with the fish. You were there in these same red skirts. Now keep moving." With that, the man shoved her in the small of her back.

Confused and afraid, Rose moved with the soldiers. She hung her head down so that she wouldn't trip again. As she watched her red curls swing back and forth and beyond them, her bare feet trudging alongside the booted men, Rose was sure of one thing. This was all Bella's fault.

CHAPTER TWELVE

"What?" Ebbe surged to his feet, knocking the stool over in his haste. His face sagged even lower than it had been moments before. His red-rimmed eyes burned like molten coals. Malik swallowed, suddenly losing his words. His mother pushed him forward firmly.

"Speak up, son. Old Mistress Forge won't watch our stall for more than a few minutes and the clan needs to know."

Malik swallowed and gathered himself. He'd known Ebbe for many years and always had thought him to be a gentle man. Right now, the look coming from the man's golden eyes—so much like his daughter's—was feral. *He looks like a hungry wolf*, Malik thought.

Kezia and Timbo stood and moved to hear what he had to say. Each carried one of their young sons close to them. While Kezia simply looked worried and withdrawn, Timbo held himself tense and at the ready, as if he would join in any kill Ebbe intended to make.

"Malik, tell him what you saw in the streets last night and today, *sibi*." His mother's voice was firm but gentle.

Malik straightened to his full height. He knew these people. They couldn't intimidate him, even though he was sure they wouldn't like his news. "I planned to meet Bella at the jail last night. She thought we could break Vadoma out. I guess she got there before me. I saw Bella running out of the front door of the jail, then three guards rushing after her. I tackled one and kicked him down, but the other two went after her. I followed, but I didn't see where she went." Malik gaged the mood of the room and hastened to add, "They didn't catch her though, as they came back later empty-handed."

The reaction was quick. "Why on earth would you think you could break my sister out of the jail?" Kezia's voice was exasperated and scornful. "You're but ignorant children." Malik opened his mouth to retort, but snapped it shut again at her glare. The woman was fierce when angered. Kezia turned from him. "Has anyone seen Bella?" Kezia hoisted her son more securely onto her hip and looked around hopefully at the men in the room. She narrowed her eyes when Stefan shuffled his feet, but then the boy shook his head as well.

"You said there was more to tell," Ebbe said hollowly. His eyes glittered, telling of potent emotions held in check.

Malik nodded. He paused. Somehow, this was worse than telling them about Bella. With Bella, you always sort of knew she'd figure something out. Rose was just... soft. She wasn't at all resourceful or clever. He took a deep breath and told them about Rose being arrested.

"They thought it was her because she was wearing the red skirt that Bella wore when she threw the fish and made them take a tumble," he concluded. "You know we all look alike to them." He paused and then made himself say the truth. "But in the end, it's my fault she was arrested—."

With a roar of anger, Timbo thrust Pattin at his wife and then surged towards Malik, his mouth bared in a half-grimace. Malik stumbled back in shock, unable to continue speaking. He'd not seen the man move so quickly before. In a flash, Aisha was next to Malik. In her hand was one of the knives she wore strapped to her at all times. She held it up and spoke forcefully. "Have a care, Timbo. My son has simply told you the facts."

Timbo growled low in his throat and bunched his muscles. Malik felt his skin prickle, deep primal fear, triggered by Timbo's behavior. Malik had both an urge to run and one to fight. He'd pick fighting if had to. He didn't want his mother to fight for him. In less than a heartbeat, Ebbe pulled Timbo back roughly and bullied in front of him.

"You'll not be pulling knives on my family, Aisha." His voice was low and firm.

"Your family won't be threatening my son, Ebbe," she responded in kind.

The tension crackling in the room subsided after Ebbe nodded once. Aisha sheathed her knife. Malik let himself release the breath he'd been holding. Ebbe paced a few steps, shook his head impatiently. "We've no time nor space to be angry with each other. The executioner is due this afternoon. He'll use his instruments of torture on her, then early on the morrow they will behead my wife for murder. We must find a way to stop him." Ebbe's voice was firm as he clenched his fist defiantly.

Kezia moved next to Timbo. "Our daughter needs us to speak for her. They must be told Rose did nothing wrong, she's just not…"

"Capable of it?" Aisha finished Kezia's sentence for her. Kezia nodded mutely, holding tears in check, gripping her sons tightly to her.

"All right," Ebbe said after a moment. "Yes, someone must go speak for Rose, and quickly too, for we all know what can happen to any young girl in custody, no matter if the charge is false." Kezia moved towards the tent flap, but Timbo stopped her.

"Ye well know they'll naught listen to a woman," he said, anger still seething in his voice.

"I'll go," said Ebbe. "There'll be plenty who will have seen both of us up on the stage, and I can be persuasive." He looked at Malik. "But there is more that needs to happen. You said our Bella had concocted some sort of plan to get our Vadoma out. What was it?"

The dismissive tone aggravated Malik. He wanted to invent some fantastic plot that would make them realize how smart Bella was. Nothing came to mind. "She didn't tell me what she was thinking. We were just going to look at the place," he said defensively.

"Yet, she was running from the jail, you said. So she must have been inside."

Malik nodded. "And did something to make the guards chase her. They were mad, too. One of them had a broken nose and fresh welts on his face. I may have re-broken it when I tackled him." Malik risked a glance at his mother. Her mouth twitched ever so slightly, and he felt a rush of relief. It was never good to have his mother angry at him, even if he was a man in his own right now.

"Malik and I will search for her," Aisha said. Malik was dismayed. He could find Bella on his own, probably would've found her by now if his mother hadn't dragged him in here to confess first. Besides, if he found Bella, the clan would surely forgive him for creating the mess that got Rose arrested. He looked up at his mother, saw the look on her face, and realized that the hope of searching on his own was a lost one. He sighed, deeply frustrated.

Ebbe nodded gratefully, but still looked worried. "Perhaps I can speak to the wardens about Vadoma as well, change their minds before the hangman comes…" He trailed off and looked toward Timbo. It was as if they were silently communicating, Malik realized. There was a hum in the air. He had seen them do this in brief bursts during hunts in the forest, but this seemed to be more intense. Timbo nodded as if agreeing reluctantly to something, and then swung his gaze to Stefan, who had stayed out of the way of everything in the corner. Stefan nodded as well.

"No!" Kezia said weakly. "He's just a boy!" She moved as if she wanted to go to him, but was hampered by young Timbo's arms, which were clutched around her legs.

Stefan raised his chin and pointed at the babies. "Those are boys, Ma. I am near a man, and will go with my father. I can make the change; you well know I can."

Malik was baffled. Something had clearly been decided, but with no words spoken. He and his mother had travelled for many years on and off with this clan, but he'd never experienced something this odd. Since when was that annoying whelp Stefan 'near a man'? And what was the change? He was about to ask the questions aloud, but then felt his mother's hand on his shoulder squeeze tight, and then tighter still. Her message was clear. He forced himself to keep quiet for now. He'd shake it all out of Stefan later.

Timbo turned to Ebbe. "The boy and I will make sure the executioner is delayed. We'll find out the route he's most likely to take and waylay his wagon. Mayhap you can get everyone away with more time." He beckoned to Stefan with his good arm, and together they shambled out of the door. Malik noticed he avoided looking at Kezia, whose face was white with anger. Stefan imitated his father and gave her a wide berth.

As Stefan passed Malik, he gave him a condescending look. The boy leaned over and whispered mockingly in Malik's ear. "Have fun looking for Bella with your *mom*." Malik bared his teeth in the pretense of a smile. *Djinn's* flight, he wanted to pound that freckled sanctimonious face to a pudding. But not now. He'd settle up with Stefan later. Oh yes, he would.

Ebbe sighed and rubbed his face. "It's settled then. Kezia, can you manage to pack up the family stalls so we can leave quickly?"

Kezia's mouth worked, and her face turned bright red. "Oh, now you're asking if I can do something? I don't know, Ebbe, I'm such a lowly woman with no say in anything that concerns my daughter, my sister, or my own son. Maybe you can help poor little me out and tell me if I could *possibly* accomplish such a very great task, like packing up all the effing stalls by myself with two young ones in tow!" Without waiting for a response, she snatched young Timbo off the floor and marched out of the tent.

Malik wanted to laugh at the look on Ebbe's face but didn't dare. Instead, he turned to his mother. "Best we be off, too." Aisha gave him a strange look, like she wanted to strangle him, but kept her peace. She turned to Ebbe. "We will find Bella. Malik will get word to you if she has a reasonable plan." Her tone changed. "Now, as my son has so eloquently stated, we'd best be off." With that, she turned and stalked away.

Ebbe and Malik were left looking at each other in profound confusion. Malik had the vague feeling that both Kezia and his mother had won unexplained arguments. Ebbe shook his head. No answers there. Malik hurried out into the bright midday sunshine to catch up to his mother.

CHAPTER THIRTEEN

H er irksome son caught up with her when she was half-way across the square. Aisha heard the particular sound of his footsteps behind her. Taking a deep breath to calm herself, turned to him. "Son, you and I will have a long, long conversation about manners and a goodly reminder of how I expect you to speak to me later. Right now, I want you to go to the stall and pack everything. Bring it to our tent. We are leaving."

She saw the flush of outrage cross his face and watched him puff up his chest. Aisha sighed. *Djinns* preserve her from moody teenagers. She held up a finger, hoping clear direction would stave off whatever foolishness her son was about to spout.

"You will obey me. You're not a man yet, no matter what your balls tell you."

"But—"

"No buts, Malik. You won't remember what it was like to flee Alexandria by the skin of our knuckles. You were but a babe. When the law of the land is against such as we, the only answer is to run as fast and far as we can. We will leave Bella and her whole family behind if we must. You must trust me about this."

Seeing his face growing mutinous, she grabbed his hand. Pointed to his and her dark skin. "You cannot escape this, *sibi*.

This is how we are clad. You are 'other' to them, to be feared and blamed if things go awry. Always. No matter if one of them tells you she loves you or not."

The hurt in her son's eyes stabbed Aisha to her marrow. But this was no time to be gentle. The boy would misunderstand any softening. His face flushed with anger. "You understand nothing! I love Bella, we can't just abandon her! I need to be the one who finds her. I won't just leave with you!"

Aisha slapped him. And immediately regretted it.

His eyes rounded in shock as his hand flew to his cheek. She saw the ripple of dismay turn hard and her son looked at her in a way she hoped she would never see. Betrayed, filled with rage. She'd purposefully avoided ever beating or striking her child, determined to rear Malik differently from her own experience. That was ripped away now. The demon *ifrits* were surely dancing in glee that they'd created such a rift between her and her beloved son. No taking it back. She had to keep moving forward. She leaned into him and spoke in her softest voice, the one that she held in reserve for extreme anger.

"I understand more than you know. Now do as I say. Go."

With a final hate-filled glance, Malik strode away toward their stall. Aisha fought her instinct to run after him. Instead, she steeled herself to do the next right thing. Look for Bella.

Aisha wished she could blame the girl for romancing on her only child, but she could not. Bella was wayward as the day was long, but she had a good heart under her selfish, impulsive nature. They'd travelled with her and her family to many of the same towns and overwintered together. She should have foreseen that her Malik and Bella would eventually come together, fire meeting fire. Belladonna, she mused. An ill-omened name, one that she'd often wondered about since Vadoma named her. Why had Vadoma done such a thing? Ah well, such musings wouldn't help find the girl.

Now where would Belladonna go if she were being pursued? The girl was not the fastest runner, she'd need to choose the easiest path from the jail. That would be where to start. Aisha took off in long strides.

She noticed people stare and then avoid her and smiled to herself. It didn't bother her that many also crossed their fingers at her to ward off evil spirits, or viciously called her a spawn of the night demons. Far from feeling shame, she felt empowered by their ignorant prejudice and petty fears. In her own country, she'd just been one more swathed, unremarkable girl to be used and discarded. Disregarded. Here she was special.

Reaching the jail, she looked around at the streets radiating outward and spotted the downward path flowing with the muck and offal of a busy town. She followed it with purpose, looking into doorways. Mayhap the girl had squeezed herself into a hiding place or alley. The girl had some good sense to her. Aisha poked her nose into wretched corners filled with rats and crawling things. Stray dogs growled menacingly at her, guarding their territory. There weren't many places to hide. The city planners had done a good job of gridding off the streets so that dark alleys were few, even here in the poor section of town.

The sparkle of the river caught her eye. Perhaps the girl had hidden a mile or so further down the shore on the docks. It was a long way, but Bella was hale, and could have made it. Aisha moved in that direction as her mind caught in a web of possible outcomes. If Bella had hidden aboard a skiff, it might have moved on before she could get back off. Aisha followed the brisk movement of the river, noted the direction it flowed. She paused, thinking hard. Yes, the girl would certainly have the smarts and the guts to hide out on a boat, but perhaps—

"Hey-a darkskin, want some good white meat for a change?" Her thoughts jangled to a halt. Ice prickled up Aisha's spine as she inwardly cursed herself. She hadn't been paying attention to the here and now. She turned slowly to confront the scabby duo behind her. River rats in for the festival, from their clothing. Northerners from the accent. Not townsfolk, which was good if there was going to be trouble. One was larger and stouter than the other. The skinnier, scabbier one owned the mouth.

The mouth spoke again, scratching his head. She could almost see the lice raining out of his greasy hair. "We'a do two for one, no extra charge." He leered at her, revealing his brown teeth. "I'da say that be generous for a *skita*-ass tarskin, wouldn't you, Gunnar?"

"Ya, Yanick." The big one agreed, his voice rumbling up from his belly, chewing his words like gristle. "Woman wouldn'ta walk by herself down'a here less they're ready for takers." He flexed his hands convulsively, making his arm muscles pop. A man who would use his strength carelessly. One who was used to winning because of his size.

Aisha cocked her head to one side, looked the two men up and down. Yawned. "I don't see anything I fancy. Go somewhere else for your paid shag."

The two men looked at each other in surprise. The skinny one made an exaggerated face at her. "Oh, ya think ya better than we, do ya? Ya black whore's *skita*!"

"I'm sure of it." Aisha shrugged and let the knives strapped to her arms fall into her hands. "But you should absolutely come closer and give me a try." She spun the blades, so they flashed in the sun. She widened her stance slightly, and poised on her toes.

"What ya to do with those *liten* pigstickers? Tickle Gunnar here? Give poor Yanick a cut?" The mouthy one edged slightly behind his bigger companion and gave him a nudge. "Gunnar's been-a yearn'n for to fight for more than *das morgen*. Too many happy people during festival, makes him irritable."

"You really don't want to do this," Aisha warned.

"Oh, ya. A pounding is exactly what a stanky old cuss like ya needs. A bit a' softening afore we have our fun." Yanick had worked his way further behind Gunnar.

"Looks like your friend wants you to do all the work, Gunnar."

"It's vat I be good at, *ja*?" Gunnar lunged at her. Aisha did a neat sidestep, dodging his outstretched arms. Spinning, she dug a sharp elbow into his upper ribs and followed it up with a kick to his knee. It bent in an awkward way that had him howling and staggering to the side of the street. He slid down the wall of the building behind him, clutching his leg.

Scuffling behind her alerted her to Yanick's leap. Ducking, she used his own momentum to flip him over her back. He landed hard on the stone street; his head luckily cushioned by a particularly pungent pile of horse crap.

"Uggggh," was all Yanick could manage as he tried to roll back up. Aisha put a none-too-gentle foot on his chest and mashed him back to the street and held him down. Sheathing her knives, she bent low and spoke carefully. "I did warn you. Bless any saint you Northern scum prefer that I decided not to use my knives. If you follow me or make any trouble for me, I will think better of that decision. Nod if you understand, *ja*?"

With hate in his eyes, Yanick managed to raise his head a few inches out of the horse poop and nod. "Good," said Aisha. "That goes double for your friend. I'll hold you to it." She turned to continue down to the river.

It was pure instinct that had her ducking as Gunnar's meaty fist swung at her head. The savage punch clipped the side of her cheek as she dodged, his huge knuckles barreling into her eye. Pain throbbing from the side of her face, Aisha used the momentum of the blow to spin around. Using all her strength, she shoved him forward and down onto the pavement. She heard a crack as his nose landed first. Before the giant man could stand back up, she stomped hard on his right forearm and had the satisfaction of hearing the bone snap.

"It isn't nice to try and take people's heads off, Gunnar." Glad of the split skirts that hid her shaking legs, Aisha walked fast.

She needed to burn off the fierce grip of fear lodged in her chest. It happened every time she was forced to fight. She knew the cold sweat and nausea would come next, and she didn't want to let either the men she had just put down or any bystanders see that she'd been affected by fighting. Weakness was a liability that she knew only too well. Showing weakness could get you killed.

Aisha pushed against the flashes of memory that wanted to rear up. It had been years, but as always, the downside of a fight brought them back, hideous messengers from a time when she had no power to change her fate. A time when her name was not Aisha, but Mariam. Aisha struggled, but the memories flooded in. How it felt to be bound and chained, hand, foot, and neck. The heat and oppressive press of too many bodies in too small of a space. Despair everywhere. The wafting scent of cinnamon the only thing that could transport her out of the misery for a few brief moments. The sight of a bird in flight through the tiny window in a cell bringing a crippling mix of sorrow and joy.

Aisha reached the river's edge, and stumbled to her knees. She plunged her hands into it, throwing the cold water over her face repeatedly. Lathed her arms with the coolness. Took a kerchief from her pocket and dipped it in the water to hold on her rapidly swelling cheekbone. Breathed as she looked to the sky, the open sky. No walls or chains blocking her way. She was free, her son was free. And she'd be damned if she let Vadoma stay trapped. She owed a debt there, one that she had sworn she would repay.

Her head clear, Aisha stood. Bella had a wild, free heart too, and if she'd been trapped on this riverbank by the jail guards, she would've done anything to get free. If the girl was not drowned, Aisha knew where she must be.

CHAPTER FOURTEEN

The slam of the wagon door made Bella sit straight up. The figure in the door was in shadow, rays of sun seeping past them to spear into her eyes. She grabbed for the iron cook pan with her right hand as she got her feet firmly on the floor. In moments she was half-standing, knees bent, and swung the pan as hard as she could.

"All *Djinns*!" The figure reared back just in time to let the cookware whiz past. "Bella, it's me, Aisha."

Bella let her arm drop and collapsed back on the narrow bed. The cook pan dropped with a thump next to her. "Sorry. You startled me." She stretched her arms high, arching her back. She felt sore all over.

Her face still in shadows, Aisha crossed her arms. "Good, you need a scare. You've put your family through all seven hells, disappearing like that."

Bella didn't like the accusatory tone. "It wasn't on purpose! If you knew what I went through last night, you'd—"

Aisha waved Bella's words away as she interrupted. "We have more—"

Anxiety surged through Bella as it sunk in that the light seeping past Aisha's indignant form was dazzling. Much brighter than an early spring morning should be. "Oh, no! What time of day is it? I've slept too long!" She leapt to her feet and tried to push Aisha back from the doorway.

Aisha resisted her pushing and then, with a huff of exasperation, stepped down from the wagon's doorway. Bella bustled out and groaned at the sight of the high sun in the sky. Near noon! How could she get what she needed and be back before night fell? She was distracted from her harried thoughts by Aisha's violent movement away from her. It seemed as if the woman were arguing with herself. Aisha took three gigantic steps away from Bella before whirling back towards her. Aisha's face was a mask of anger, her teeth bared, eyes glinting. Bella saw the swelling on her cheek, the darkening around Aisha's eye.

"You will listen to me. Stop thinking whatever it is you're thinking, look at me." Bella raised her chin defiantly. Malik's mother would not scare her. She would not, no matter how tall Aisha was or how fierce she looked. Then Aisha's next words shook her to her core.

"Bella, they arrested your cousin for your crime of interfering with an arrest. The hangman is on the way to punish her and your mother. He's due later today."

"Rose arrested? But I just—"

"Threw fish. Aye, I know. And Malik said it was to help him escape Roundhats. But it was enough of an insult to warrant an arrest. She was wearing the red skirt, Bella. They think Rose is you."

Saints. How often had she wished Rose would be taken away over the years? Hundreds, most like. But she didn't really want that, of course not. Bella paced as she thought. Should she turn herself in? But then she couldn't execute the plan she'd concocted to get her mother out of jail. Bella looked up at Aisha, considering her options. The woman still looked angry enough to chew wood. Maybe her anger could be assuaged with good news.

"Aisha, last night I found a way to get Vadoma out. But I need your help. And Malik's too."

"You think I'm going to help you? After all the trouble you've caused?" Aisha started to shake her head, but then stopped, clearly in pain from the movement. "You're a hothead with no thought for others, just what you want when you want it."

"That's not fair!" Bella was stung by the accusation. After all, she'd gotten into trouble because she was helping people. Helping Malik escape, helping her mother escape. She bit down hard on the stream of reasons Aisha was so very wrong. She had to focus on what was important right now. She took a breath to tell Aisha her idea, but the woman walked over to her and had the nerve to clamp her hand over her mouth, grabbing her neck from behind so she couldn't move.

"You will listen to me," Aisha started. Bella squirmed to get out of the woman's grasp, but it proved impossible. "I can break your neck with a twist of my hands, so you'll want to stay very still."

Being pulled so close by Aisha's grip, Bella could see the bloodshot left eye and purpling bruising in detail. Bella had never feared Aisha before, but there was something new in her tone. Bella locked down her instinct to struggle against the pressure of Aisha's muscular hands.

"That's better. Your family is already working on a solid plan. Your father has gone to speak for Rose at the jail. There are plenty who saw her dancing while you were off tossing fish. Your uncle and cousin are off to waylay the hangman on the road. Meanwhile, your aunt has the unpleasant duty to pack up both the stage and your stall so we can flee this plagued town and never return. Malik is doing the same with ours. You will march yourself back with me to help your aunt. Am I clear? You need to understand your mother cannot be saved, Bella. She confessed. It's folly to think you can magically get her released or break her out with some wild scheme. This isn't one of your father's stage stories, child. This is real. Your mother is lost."

Fighting back fear at the thought Aisha might be right, Bella nodded her head, but in her heart, she refused to let the dark thoughts take root. She could rescue her mother. She wouldn't give up. She only needed to make Aisha understand what she needed from her, and a bit of luck in the doing of it.

She nodded her head again, as Aisha didn't seem to think the first time was vigorous enough. The woman released her, but still shook a finger. "I'll rope you to me if I have to, Bella. Don't make me drag you along."

"Aisha. I will do as you say. I promise on the heads of our ponies if you like. Or anything. Just hear me out for one moment."

"On the heads of your ponies? They aren't actually yours now, are they girl? To just give away if you don't keep your promise." Aisha seemed like she was dug in.

Bella wanted to scream but held herself in check. "Please. One moment." Aisha was unyielding. Bella gritted her teeth. Stubborn woman! "Give me the moment as thanks for saving your son from being the one arrested yesterday."

Aisha seemed even more angry, and Bella worried she had gone too far. Would Aisha actually just tie her up and drag her into town? *I could see her doing it.* Bella kept her mouth shut. She knew that Aisha only lost arguments one way, the same way her son lost them. She was confident that the next person who talked would lose this battle of wills. It wouldn't be her that broke.

The silence wore on. The cawing of crows echoed through the camp. Bella couldn't break her stare down with Aisha to count them to see if they boded for good or ill. *Please let it be two crows for luck,* she prayed inwardly. The silence stretched to an unbearable length. Aisha sighed and rolled her eyes.

"My son thinks he's in love with you." Aisha said bluntly. "I suppose you feel the same about him."

Bella's heart broke open and sang. "Yes, I think I really do." Bella smiled for the first time in what felt like ages.

Aisha scowled at her. "You're both idiots and know nothing, but for his sake, I will give you a moment. Now speak."

Bella was off balance from the admission that Malik loved her. Her! She wished she could wallow in the joy of it, but knew Aisha's forbearance had limits. Bella gathered her thoughts, then spoke quickly, her words tumbling out.

"Aisha, you make potions that can do anything. I need one that makes it appear as if I am dead. The watch will pick me up and put me into the dead house. Once I am in there, Malik can make the climb and sneak in through some windows I saw and wake me with another potion. Then he picks the lock on the back door to the jail I discovered last night. They connect! Then we go down to where I think, well, I'm sure Vadoma is, unchain her, and escape out the little windows! I'm sure I can fit, and Ma as well, it'd be easy to make the drop." Bella said the whole idea in one breath. She added, "The guards are at the far end of the building. They won't see us. Then we can all leave this town and never return."

Bella stopped, and beamed at Aisha, sure that the woman would clap her hands in delight at the brilliance of her plan. Instead, Aisha's frown deepened. "You think I know potions that will do that?"

Bella didn't hesitate. "I do. I've never asked you about them, but yes."

Aisha walked in a small circle. Bella waited, doing her best to appear confident.

"Knowing potions like that, it's a burning offense. Not even the quick death from the axe. You realize that, right?"

Bella had not known that, but nodded all the same, and tried to look profoundly serious as she did so. The smarter she behaved, the more likely Aisha was to go along with her plan.

Aisha paced. "I don't have everything I need. Oleander would be quickest, but that won't grow here. Wolfsbane would work if we could find some. There are the Belladonna black berries, but it's early for them, perhaps there would be some at the very edge of the forest. Lily of the Valley by a stream if the berries aren't yet ripe." Aisha was talking to herself now, low. Bella strained to hear her. The woman kept walking as she thought. "And honey, the bitterness is terrible. The baker has honey, and she's been wanting to trade for a sleeping draught—"

Aisha turned to her. "This is a terrible idea."

"Do you have another one?" Bella's patience with the older woman was at an end. If there were an easier way, she'd have thought of it. "I'm willing to do it. Isn't that enough?"

"I'm answerable if—which, by the way, is likely—you die in this foolish attempt, Bella. And you want to bring my son into it."

"Have you never done something that was dangerous?"

Aisha stopped short and barked out a laugh. "My whole life has hung on a thread, girl. Look at me. I'm a woman alone in the world, except for my only son. Would you take from me that which is most precious on a whim, on an ill-thought-out idea?"

Were those tears in Aisha's eyes? In all her years, she'd never once seen Aisha anything other than calm and collected. Bella's heart plummeted. No sharp remarks came to mind.

"Bella. I want to help Vadoma. She and Ebbe allowed my son and I to travel with them, protected us when no one else would. But I'm afraid, Bella. Afraid to lose the one thing in this world I love."

Aisha's face nearly undid Bella. It forced her to look deep inside of herself, and pull up words she'd never thought to utter. "Aisha, I know my mother loves me, just as fiercely as you love Malik. But she and I, we don't connect—I've never been able to show her I care about her. All my life I've fought against her. Now I need to fight for her."

Aisha nodded slowly. She reached out her hand to Bella. When Bella took it, the woman reeled her in to a close hug. "I understand."

It was strange, hugging a woman she'd barely touched in all the years she'd known her. Aisha was all hard angles and sinews and carried an attitude that discouraged displays of affection. But at the center of all that hardness was a heart that was beating strong and true. It gave her courage.

Aisha set her at arm's length. "All right, here's what you must do."

CHAPTER FIFTEEN

E bbe stumbled as he walked to the prison. He bumped his way through the streets, apologizing from rote habit to annoyed town folk. His normally quick wits had dried up. He was consumed by a despair he couldn't shake off. Ebbe tried his best to think of what he might say to convince the guards that they'd made a mistake when they arrested Rose. He couldn't say they were wrong outright, of course. That would get him clapped in irons alongside her. And his wife. His focus slipped from Rose to Vadoma.

The memories of Vadoma took over. He'd loved her from the moment she'd pushed him into the water during their first tryst. A ghost of a smile brushed Ebbe's lips as he remembered the moment. He'd rowed them out to the center of a small lake in a borrowed boat to better see the moon. That had been their excuse, at any rate. Anything to get them away from the busy camp and alone. He'd said something cheeky, and she'd shoved him into the water. Then helped him back into the boat, laughing. And one thing had led to another under the moonlit sky. They both nearly fell in the water again when he tried to get his wet clothes back on. Bella had been created that very night.

Both their families had thought them too young to handfast, but they'd been united in their desire to belong to one another.

And they'd been right. For fifteen years he and Vadoma had been as two halves of one person. He had trusted her implicitly. She was his constant in their ever-changing, moving life. Yet now he'd learned she'd kept a terrible secret from him for years. Years. It upended his entire world, and now he felt as if he couldn't trust anything anymore.

Ebbe found he had stopped in the middle of the street, and that his cheeks were wet with tears. People moved around him. He was an island, utterly alone. How much worse would it be when they killed Vadoma? Ebbe wished the ground would simply open up and swallow him whole, so he didn't have to take one more step through his crushing despair. He took a step forward anyway, and then another. He was the leader of their clan, and it was up to him to get them all out of this miserable, cursed town. One way or another.

The Roundhats didn't bother to acknowledge him when he stepped to the door of the jail. They were busy joking. One had his feet up on the table, smoking a long pipe. The stench of the tobacco permeated the room. Ebbe saw another man's nose was purple, the inner edges of his eyes blackened. Angry red gashes marched up the side of his face. Bella had done some damage escaping. He felt a pulse of pride that his girl had bested these burly oafs. Ebbe doffed his cap and cleared his throat. The men looked at him with beady eyes.

"What d'ye want, then, gypsy?" The fattest of the guards tilted himself off the wall he'd been leaning against. Ebbe noticed he moved gingerly, as if his balls ached. Another mark from Bella, perhaps. He was glad he'd taught his daughter how to scrap, even if Vadoma had frowned on the roughhousing.

"Well? Are ye daft? Speak up!" Ebbe realized he had drifted into memory again. He focused his attention. *Just pretend you're on the stage.* The notion drifted into his consciousness, and he grasped onto the idea. He straightened his spine and bowed deeply to the guards, wafting his hat through the air in a grand gesture. As he came up from the stage bow, it was as if a different person took over his body.

"I am but a humble servant of the stage, and of yourselves. Come to take an errant wench off your hands." Ebbe let his voice roll and fill the space, sure that it would reach the ears he wished it to reach.

"It's that gypsy feller what tells them stories in the square," remarked the fat guard with a partial smile on his face. "You told that one about the sleeping beauty and the ogre just yesterday."

"Stories? Wotcher listening to stories for, Belcher?" The one with the gouges on his face flicked Belcher's forehead irritably.

"My nephew wanted to go, didn't he? He's only four. Canna go to such a thing alone, and whatch'a have'ta flick me like that for anyway, Collins?" Belcher seemed indignant, glaring at his fellow guard. "It's uncalled for, that's what it is, plain uncalled for."

"Quit yer bellyachin'. Saint Adrian on a stick, yer right annoyin' today, Belcher." The pipe-smoking guard spoke up. He took his time removing his legs from the table to stand. He seemed to favor one leg. "Now, what do you want, gypsy? Hurry up and speak up or we'll show you the fast way out. Or in, makes no matter to me."

Ebbe smiled. "I am so glad you saw our little show, Master Belcher. Perhaps you remember the dancing girl who helped me call in the crowd, and then later demonstrated the ancient dance of our people? The one where she showed just a bit of leg from under her skirts?"

"Oh, yeh!" Belcher grinned. "Yeh, the red-haired one."

"Well, sir." Ebbe paused for dramatic effect, and then used his best all-knowing grin. "That is the very girl you have locked up here. She wore the red skirt one of our other dancers uses to do her marketing in, and—"

"Don't matter to us what skirts she be wear'n to buy her food," growled Collins. "If we has her locked up, she did sumthin' to be locked up for."

"No doubt, no doubt you are right, sir!" Ebbe continued brightly, even though his heart was sinking. "However, being as obviously intelligent as you are, perhaps you'd care to answer a riddle for me?"

Belcher snickered, and even the pipe-smoking guard chuckled. "Intelligent, you hear that, Collins? Someone's got you figured wrong!"

Collins scowled. "Hush it, Burke. Let's have the riddle, then."

"Very well. Master Belcher, will you swear to your fellows that you saw a red-haired girl with brown eyes dancing upon my stage yesterday afternoon?"

"O'course. I saw her, didn't I?"

"Wonderful! Then from that assertion, Master Collins, can you tell me how a woman can be simultaneously dancing upon a stage and throwing fish under the feet of guards many blocks away at the exact same time?"

Collins looked blank. Ebbe squelched the urge to explain to him what simultaneously meant.

"That's a good 'un!" Belcher said in his sluggish way after a long silence. "Say ya think the Burgermeister's guards got the wrong little gypsy?" His mouth formed a perfect O as he pondered the thought.

"Don't matter none. A gypsy is a gypsy," said Collins.

"It does though. We's to blame for mix-ups at the end of it, not them that made said mix-up." Burke tapped out his pipe on the table, leaving the ashes where they landed and waited for the other guards to follow his meaning. His face looked as if he'd just taken a bite of rotted fish. He glowered at Ebbe, who made himself look as pleasant and unassuming as possible. Burke turned to the fat guard.

"Damn it all, Belcher, did you really see that girl dancing on the stage yesterday?"

"Sure as shit flows from a goose." Belcher said earnestly.

Burke sighed. He waved hand at Belcher. "Go bring 'er up, let's see if she's the same one."

Belcher nodded, then took the iron key ring off its nail and disappeared through the door at the back of the guardroom. The other two men settled themselves back in their wooden chairs. Ebbe knew better than to say more until he was spoken to and kept his focus on his feet. His heart thudded wildly as he thought of Vadoma in this place. These idiots probably forgot to feed the prisoners in their care.

Ebbe wanted to clench his fists and pound the men into submission. He imagined breaking the legs off the table and beating their heads until they squashed like overripe melons. He realized he'd stopped breathing and forced himself to inhale. The ruckus such a rage would cause would undoubtedly bring more men pouring into the place.

Movement brought his eyes up. Belcher had Rose in a tight grip by an upper arm as he moved her roughly through the doorway. Ebbe restrained himself from going to her. The girl looked miserable in a daze. Her lip was split and swollen, her face covered with either dirt or bruises, Ebbe couldn't tell which. Worse, they had shorn her hair carelessly, leaving her partially bald, with just a few clumps of red still hanging onto her pale white scalp. The red skirts that had caused so much trouble were dirty and torn, looking more like a puddle of old blood than the happy crimson they used to be.

"Well, Belcher, is she the same one you saw dancin'?" Burke sounded as if he hardly cared.

"I dunno." Belcher stood away from Rose without breaking his grip. "Hard to tell without the hair or her movin' around some." Belcher stuck out his lower lip, dubious.

"Of course it's her, isn't it, Rose?" Ebbe started for her. Faster than he expected the man could move, Collins jerked up from the table and shoved Ebbe backwards. "Hands to yerself, dirty scum!"

"We need to know, Belcher. Kristoff the hangman comes later today to do his questioning of the prisoners afore the killin' of them tomorrow. If'n we's wrong about this girl, it'll be your thumbs in his screws." Burke kept his voice mild, but Belcher broke out into a cold sweat.

"Mebbe… if she were'ta dance… then I'd know?" Belcher seemed highly uncertain of his idea, but Burke clapped his hands together and stood with a grin. "Splendid!"

Rose swayed in his grasp. Ebbe stepped forward. "Surely you can see this is the same girl, fine sir?" Ebbe could tell he'd lost his grip on the men when Belcher pushed him back with a mean gleam in his eyes.

"I'm in the mood for a dance," Burke said.

"What if someone sees?" Collins asked in a worried tone.

"We're just doing the job, ain't we? Makin' sure as we have the right prisoner?" Burke smiled and then gestured broadly to Rose. "Go on, you little piece of trash, dance for yer freedom."

Rose looked up at Ebbe. He could see the confusion on her face. He nodded to her and spoke softly. "Go on, Rosy, do the final dance for these fine fellows. Here, I'll give you the beat." Ebbe kneeled on the ground and started the rhythm on his knees with his hands. Rose frowned at him. "Dance, Rose." He smiled encouragingly at her.

Rose moved a bit, her feet barely lifting, her body stiff as a board. Ebbe saw the men losing their interest rapidly. He lifted his voice into the familiar verses of the Traveller's song, still beating his hands to the rhythm. "Romale, Romale…" Rose seemed to understand, and moved a bit more. But it wasn't satisfying the guards.

"Put 'er up on the table, so we can see her dance better!" Burke said. Belcher grinned, grabbed Rose, and lifted her up onto the wooden table. Ebbe stopped singing in horror. Collins gave him another shove. "Keep going iff'n you know what's good fer ya." Ebbe reluctantly started up again.

Rose gaped at him, clutching her hands to her sides. She stared down at the guards looking up at her with nasty grins on their faces.

"Now that's more like it. Belcher, is this the girl?"

"Mebbe if I see more of her legs I could tell." Belcher licked his lips, leaving them glistening with spit. He squatted down and peered under Rose's skirts.

The men laughed. Ebbe wanted to kill them all. But all he could do was to start to sing and will Rose to find it in herself to prove herself innocent.

"Hike up that skirt, girl! Let's see if that red hair was natural!" Collins found his own comment to be uproariously funny and reached over to shove up the tatters of the red skirt. Rose seemed frozen at first as he kept pushing up, exposing more and more skin. Rose pulled back and put her hands out as if to dance. She got her balance, stood on one foot, and kicked him full in the face.

His nose re-broke in an impressive shower of red. Shrieking, he fell back, clutching his face as the other two men shouted and grabbed for Rose. Rose added her own screams as well, utterly terrified. Ebbe stood to go help her but was stopped by a gauntleted arm clamping down on his own.

The room darkened as several Roundhats and a man dressed in rich robes of green and gold stepped into the room. He was enormously tall, his shoulders wide. His entrance froze everyone in their places. The little room became utterly still, as if the man had sucked the chaos into his own body, and gained strength from it. The only sound was the patter of blood from Collin's nose.

"What is going on here?" The man's voice was quiet but penetrating. Ebbe's intuition was screaming at him to run, that before him stood a deep evil, but he held firm. He wasn't leaving this place without Rose.

"Sir, Burgermeister Strom sir. We was tryin' to determine if this girl here was the right one." Burke stammered the words out as he stood rigidly at attention.

"The right one for what?" Again, the tone was quiet, even gentle. It was the most evil voice Ebbe had ever heard.

"For what as done throw'd them fishes, sir."

"Ah." Strom said, allowing a small smile to wisp across his lips. His eyes glittered black as he tilted them up to Rose, who stood frozen on the table. He stepped closer, the tips of his beautiful gold shoes seeming to glide over the floor. Rose shrank back from him but also seemed fascinated, as a bird is when the snake is about to devour it.

Strom offered his hand to Rose, the generous folds of his sleeve falling back to reveal the smooth pale skin of his forearm. It looked like stone, as if he were an ancient a statue come to life. He gestured slightly with his fingers for her to take his. Everyone's attention was glued to the moment as she lifted her small hand into his huge one.

Ebbe thought he was handing her down from the table. Instead, Strom lifted Rose's hand to his nose, and smelled it. His eyes rolled back in his head, leaving only white to glare out in the dimness of the room.

Ebbe had never witnessed such a simple gesture convey such deep horror. Coldness seeped through the room. It was as if Strom was inhaling her essence, her soul.

Rose seemed frozen in place. Her eyes were glued to the place where her skin contacted Strom's. Her eyes went completely black as her pupils dilated fully. Ebbe saw the girl vibrating as if she were trying to flee her own skin.

Strom dropped her hand. His eyes clicked back into place. They looked disappointed. "This is not the girl I was seeking." He waved to his soldiers. "Put her outside."

The soldiers bustled to his bidding. They gathered Rose from where she'd collapsed in a heap onto the table and tossed her out the door. She landed heavily on hands and knees. Ebbe kept his eyes on her, and was relieved when he saw her stir, and then move to stand. Making himself as invisible as he could, he moved to tiptoe out of the door now that Rose was free. He knew how to make himself small and unnoticeable, and used that skill to ease behind the standing guards towards the open door. His heart gladdened as he watched Rose pull herself to stand and tilt her face to the sun like a flower opening at the dawn. Kezia and Timbo would be overjoyed that they had released their daughter.

"Not you." Strom's voice fell on his shoulders like a lead weight. Ebbe turned to face him, looking up at the man's pale face. Strom smiled as Ebbe's eyes met his. "You are Ebbe, handfast to Vadoma." He stretched out her name into three syllables that were loathed and despised. His nose twitched. "I can smell her on you."

Ebbe stood his tallest. "Vadoma did nothing to you or yours purposefully. She tried to help you."

Strom's face hardened. "She worked witchcraft. She stole my wife's life and my child's life to bring her own whelp into the world safe. Your whelp. Your Belladonna." Again he stretched out the syllables of the name as if it were a curse unto itself.

"She did nothing of the kind. If anyone be an evil spellcaster, it's you, Strom!" Ebbe didn't care what they did to him. He would tell the truth.

Strom smiled happily. "You have no power here, little man. And, ah, such a poor choice, you just verbally assaulted the mayor of this town." He looked over at Burke who had moved to help Collins staunch the blood still pouring from his nose. "You there, take this man down to the dungeons. I believe he has a confession to make in the coming hours."

"Yes, sir." Burke waved at Belcher to come help him. The two men took Ebbe by his arms. Ebbe didn't fight at all. He was glad he'd be seeing Vadoma again, no matter what the circumstances.

Belcher muttered, "Kristoff the hangman's going to be busy tomorrow."

Strom smiled again. "Oh, I don't think we need to wait for Kristoff, do we? We have all the tools we need downstairs. I think I'll take my turn at getting a confession from this man myself. Right in front of his wife." He gestured to Belcher and Burke to drag Ebbe down into the dungeons.

Ebbe fought then, but the two men were stronger. As they dragged him towards the prison area, Ebbe twisted around and shouted, "Run to your mother, Rose!" He got a cuff across the mouth but was gratified to see the girl pick up her tattered skirts and run.

As the darkness of the passageway to the dungeon closed around him, Ebbe felt all hope drain away, and his belly fill with ice at what was to come next at the hands of Strom.

CHAPTER SIXTEEN

B ella slowed the huge dark horse to a walk as she entered
the verge of the trees. He was blowing hard after the long,
steady trot punctuated by runs from the city. Bella patted him on
the neck and murmured, "Atta way, Destry. Good boy." Her legs
ached from the wide girth of the horse. It'd been ages since
she'd ridden anything but their ponies. This was Aisha's fine
horse that was the envy of all the Travellers. Aisha claimed she
won the charger from a knight on a bet years ago, but she'd
never told the full story. Aisha never let anyone but herself or
Malik ride him.

But they had needed the strength and speed of the stallion to
do what they needed to do in just a few scant hours.

The canopy of the trees was still in early bud, vivid spring
green tipping out of bare branches. The outliers of Darkwood
were beautiful. Miles further away in the heart of the forest, the
deep green needles of the firs stayed constant, but here the trees
created a mass of soft color as winter passed. Bella let her eyes
roam for a moment. There were times she wished the forest
spoke to her as it did her father, but she felt nothing from the
trees.

She'd have to find what she was looking for using her
ordinary senses. First here at the edge of the forest for the

poison, and then on further into the deeps of it for the cure. Sliding down the horse's side, bending her knees to absorb the landing, Bella flicked the reins over Destry's head and led the horse towards the babbling of the stream she heard up ahead. The horse plodded along with her with its ears pricked up and forward.

"You hear it too, don't you, boy? You must be thirsty." The bushy undergrowth grew thicker. Soon Bella was pushing her way through dense willow clumps. Destry snorted in annoyance as branches flicked against his sides, pulling up on the reins as if to tell her they should turn around. Bella's feet were sinking into the loamy ground, which was getting more and more damp with each step. Tiny gnats spun around her head with their irritating whine. This was what she was looking for, boggy ground.

The merry trickle of water was barely an arm span wide as it whisked past, eager to join the larger river some fifteen miles distant. Even riding the excellent horse, it had taken nearly two hours to get here. Bella felt impatience rise in her chest and forced it down. She just needed a few black berries—not green or red—from a Belladonna plant. Or if she spotted the pretty white flowers of glovewart, she could gather their stems, but she'd need a lot of those to get the sap. Or foxgloves would work as well. Bella reached into the satchel she carried slung diagonally across her shoulders and withdrew some gloves. She kept the knife Aisha had loaned her tucked into the satchel.

Destry nudged her aside and plunged his nose into the little streamlet. Bella let his reins drop, sure that he'd be content long enough for her to find one of the plants she sought. How hard could it be to find any of the three plants?

After nearly an hour, the confidence ebbed out of her. Panic seeped in. She'd found only a small patch of the glovewart, which she'd gathered, but was sure that it wouldn't be enough. She continued scouring the boggy area, brushing away the biting flies and mosquitoes, tugging an irritated Destry behind her.

Widening her search in ever-increasing circles, Bella finally spotted a bush that had the long leaves and bell-like purple flowers tinged with green of her namesake plant. She hurried over to it, but was disappointed to see that all the berries were still green. Those would not be strong enough to do the job of slowing her heart enough to fool the takers of the dead. Not strong enough to make her plan work.

"Gah!" Bella let out a shout of pure frustration. And shouted an extremely long line of choice curses at the top of her lungs.

Destry flicked his ears back as she stomped around the little clearing. He shifted on his feet, skin quivering. Destry didn't like loud noises. He whickered loudly and nudged her with his nose when she came close to him. Bella wasn't a crier, but she was close to letting go as she hugged the horse's neck. If she didn't find the proper plant, her mother would die.

Bella's thoughts filled with guilt. All the times she'd told her mother she hated her, or they'd argued. She felt a cold surety that it had been a long time—years perhaps—since she spoke in a kind way towards Vadoma, let alone a loving one. And now, there wouldn't be a chance to change that. She buried her face in the horse's neck, breathing in the earthy scent of him, willing herself to keep steady despite the ball of burning guilt that centered in her chest.

"What were you cursing about?" A blunt voice had Bella spinning around, pawing at her satchel, which carried her knife.

A girl who was perhaps her own age stepped back at the suddenness of Bella's movement. She wore a plain brown homespun dress and held a gathering basket looped in one arm. She had light brown hair kept back by a plain kerchief. Her nose was pushed oddly sideways, as if from a blow. The girl's eyes were striking, a clear beautiful blue like a rain-washed early morning. Those eyes watched Bella warily.

Bella scrubbed her nose with her sleeve. "I canna find a plant I be looking for," she said, using her best local accent.

"You talk funny," said the girl. "What're you looking for?"

Bella wanted to snap back at the girl but thought better of it. She pointed to the belladonna plant and dropped the fake accent. "These, but with black berries."

"The black won't come in for another few months, yet."

"Or foxglove or more glovewart, I only found a small patch."

The girl cocked her head sideways and regarded Bella with those penetrating eyes. "Heartstoppers. You mad at someone?"

Bella laughed. "You could say that." She found she couldn't stop laughing. In the next moment, she horrified herself by bursting into long-held tears. She stood and sobbed.

"Hey-a, now." The girl had ventured near to her and was extending her kerchief. Bella took it and blew her nose. The girl offered her hand for it, and Bella thought to fold it over the wet spot before handing it back.

"Sorry about that," Bella said, indicating the handkerchief.

"The kerchief will wash, and we all carry tears," the girl said, sounding wiser than her years seemed to be. "Now, if you be needing a heartstopper, yon plant can still give you what you need, but it be much more dangerous."

The girl moved by her and dug at the bottom of the plant, exposing the light brown root. Carefully, using her kerchief to guard her hands, she cut a long tuber. Bella moved next to her and offered up a serge gathering bag to put the root in. The girl patted the earth back around the plant.

"You must boil the root in five times the water until it disintegrates. Then no more than a half a spoon, unless it be a big man, then you can use more."

Bella stared at her. "You seem young to know so much."

The girl shrugged. "My ma's a witch." She laughed ruefully at Bella's look. "She's a healer really, but the folk of our village call her a witch behind her back. She's training me up to be a healer too," the girl added with some pride.

"They call my people worse than that, and to our faces too," Bella said.

The girl just nodded. "Aye, they do the same for the Travellers that pass through Hamsdorf. We are the first village you come to. It's a way after this outlier forest, but before the Darkwood proper along the eastern road."

Bella looked at the sky. Even with the trees in the way, she could tell the light was on the wane. "Saints, I need to hurry. Do you know where I can find the antidote for this?" she asked hopefully.

"Boxwood. Yes, this way." The girl walked confidently, and Bella followed. Destry seemed happy to get away from the midge flies. Part of her felt a fool for trusting a stranger. Every second that leaked away grated on Bella. To break the fear that was building in her once more that she'd be too late returning, Bella tried for some conversation.

"What's your name, anyway? I'm Bella."

"It's dumb. My name, not yours," she added quickly.

"All the same, I've given you mine."

"And I've given you a solution to your problem. Both of them." The girl pointed to a boxwood just ahead.

"Thank you, *girl*." Bella hurried forward to gather the leaves Aisha had told her they would need. "See how silly that sounds? Don't be bashful. What's your name?"

"Henna," the blue eyes darted away. "Everybody calls me Hen or Birdbrain." Her voice was dull, and Bella could hear the hurt in it.

Bella finished the stripping of the leaves and turned. She smiled easily. "I know a woman who does henna tattoos, and hair tonics for women who aren't ready to be gray yet. It's a beautiful plant."

Henna brightened. "You're the first other than my mother who's known that!" The girl's smile lit up her entire face.

Bella smiled back. For a moment, her troubles had been lifted. She led Destry to a log and clambered up on his back. He snorted and stamped his feet as if ready to leave as well. Bella untied one of the blue ribbons in her hair, leaned over and handed it down. "Thank you Henna, truly you have helped so much. I hope we meet again."

The girl nodded and stepped away as Bella kicked Destry into a quick trot.

CHAPTER SEVENTEEN

K ristoff the hangman clucked to his horses and wished for a dram of something to ease his throat. It was parched from the dust on the road. It had been days since he'd returned home. He was ready for his own fire and his own wife to tend to him.

"How much further?" His youngest son, Nicclos, sat next to him on the wagon. He'd brought the lad on this latest journey to dispense justice. It had been a mistake. Either the boy was too young, or just like his older brother, had no taste for the trade. Nicclos was spindly and his face wan like he might sick up again. Kristoff sighed. He'd have to take on an apprentice. Another mouth to feed and a bed to find in their inadequate home. Mayhap his two sons had the right of it in not wanting to take on their father's trade. There was no glory and little money being the hangman. Just the exquisite art of it.

"Papa, how much longer?" His son interrupted his thoughts with an even longer drawn-out whine to his repeated question.

Kristoff ruffled the boy's golden-brown hair. It'd been a long journey after all, covering his territory and dispensing the justice deemed necessary by the townships he served. "We be only four or so more hours on the road. We'll be home by mid-day. You'll have time tomorrow after the hanging to enjoy the festival."

"Do I have to help?" The boy got that anxious look on his face. His brown eyes pleaded for his father to say no. But until an apprentice was found, there was no help for it.

"We'll have a backlog of thieves to punish, son. Someone has to hold their arms out and steady on the block, so I cut their hands clean. It's not proper to not to do it clean, is it now?"

The boy shook his head slowly. He looked down at his hands and twisted them. "Do I have to help with the hanging as well?" His little face looked pinched at the idea. The hangman felt his heart contract for the love of the boy. It wasn't his fault he wasn't called to the profession. "No lad, I can have one of the guards help in that."

Nicclos sighed with clear relief. Kristoff focused his eyes back on the road. It was increasingly rutted the closer they came to the city and one wheel had been creaking more than usual. It wouldn't do to have a breakdown on the road that made them late for the duties of justice. Burgermeister Strom wasn't one for excuses. As usual, the thought of Strom caused the hangman to frown, and not just because he disliked the man. It was a puzzle. He'd been the mayor for nearly thirty years, yet had not aged in the slightest. He was a hard man who wanted to bring back burning prisoners alive instead of the more humane methods of dispensing justice. Kristoff was sure they'd have more disagreements about it in the future. The Burgermeister surely enjoyed getting his way in all things. The severing of the head was best and quickest. But if done correctly, hanging was almost the same.

Torture had its place, of course, in gathering confessions. But once the wrong-doers had confessed their sins, it was only right and proper their punishment be conducted smoothly and without malice. Else how to differentiate a murderer from a hangman? No, it was in the art of it that justice was best served. Not in making people suffer.

"Papa, what's that?" The boy's note of alarm brought him back from his reverie. He pointed up at a rocky outcrop which the road was obliged to go around in a slow, wide arc. The hangman squinted. The outcrop seemed perfectly normal to Kristoff, dusted as it was with some scrubby bushes.

"What do you think you see, son?" The hangman knew his eyesight wasn't the best, and wished for the thousandth time that he could afford spectacles.

"Two wolves, I think. Or big dogs, maybe? Or people in skins. Watching us from up there by the rocks."

Kristoff narrowed his eyes to help him focus but couldn't make anything out. "I don't think the wolves come down this low, son," he said reassuringly. "They keep to the mountains or deeper into the forest." Nevertheless, he swiveled his head to scan the woody section that edged close to the road. He'd prefer it be wolves, as they could be scared off. If it were rabid peasants, eager to rob a cart manned by only a man and a boy, that was cause for concern. Pain and hunger could make folks do just about anything. He'd been well versed in that over the years.

"Pull out the crossbow, lad. Just to be on the safe side." Nicclos nodded and crawled over the seat, back into the open cart they pulled. The boy knew which chest to open to retrieve the weapon, as it was his job to see all the execution gear stowed tidily. He grabbed the stout weapon and several quarrels as well as the windlass. Even he could load the crossbow using the crank.

"Good lad, get it loaded." The hangman clucked encouragingly to his horses, who were stepping a bit more briskly, as if they also had caught the whiff of danger in the air. Or had smelled wolves. Kristoff thought about the road ahead. It was much the same as this was, except straighter. Perhaps they could risk a bit more speed, once they were around this blasted outcropping. They were coming up to a point he knew was a blind corner, and anything could be waiting for them up ahead.

Kristoff leaned forward, taking a firm grasp on the reins. His boy was nearly done cranking the arrow in. They were as ready as they could be. Hoping all their preparations would be for nothing, he focused on his breathing as he did before a beheading. Focus was what mattered, not haste. They rounded the outcropping.

Clear road lay ahead of them. Even squinting he could see no movement, no shaggy wolves ready to rip out the throats of his horses. He smiled. Nothing to worry about except getting home.

His son screamed.

Out of the corner of his eye, the hangman saw two shaggy forms hurtling down the hillside. In a moment, they struck. Not at the horses but at the side of the cart, as if to push it over. His thoughts reeled as the cart rocked onto its bad wheel, nearly tipped, then thudded back to the road again. He slapped the reins and gave the horses their heads. They'd run straight and true on this section. He pulled the crossbow from his son as the horses moved from a steady trot to a dead gallop.

"There, Papa!" The boy pointed and Kristoff saw two shaggy bodies running after the wagon. One form ran faster than the other, which seemed to favor its left side. They were moving much faster than humans could. It must be wolves. But he'd never heard of wolves pursuing a wagon before, and to his dim eyesight, they seemed to run more upright than on all fours.

"Take the reins!" The hangman passed the leather to Nicclos, who handed him the crossbow in return. His vision might be blurry, but he just needed to hit in the center of the mass of movement. He could see well enough for that. He aimed. Shot. The slower of the two seemed to kick high into the air and then tumble down in a spray of dust. Got one! But the faster one was leaping now, gaining ground. In a moment, it would leap up into the wagon itself. Heavens above, why was the wild creature acting like this? Kristoff grabbed another quarrel and cranked it into the crossbow, blessing the strength of his arm as he did so.

He knelt on the bench facing backwards. Kristoff leveled the crossbow, braced it at the ready for the thing if it emerged up from the road and into the back of the open wagon. He'd by-god put an arrow right down its throat.

There was a massive bump. The back of the wagon heaved up in front of him. His son screamed again as the wagon pushed up and over, throwing them sideways as the wagon tilted violently and then crashed to the ground. Kristoff and Nicclos were tossed into the air, tumbling like puppets with their strings cut. Snippets of images tumbled together. The reins flapping free. Nicclos flying in the air above him. Reaching up to pull his child close so that he could cushion him from the blow of the ground. Frantic neighing from the horses. A crushed and broken wagon wheel whirling above them in slow motion.

He landed with a thud on the blessedly soft green grass at the side of the road, his arms wrapped tight around his boy. The crossbow clattered down next to him, empty of his arrow. Had he managed to get off another shot? The horses continued to snort and whinny in panic, rearing against the suddenly still and broken husk of the wagon. They weren't screaming. That was good.

Kristoff crawled to feet. The wagon was smashed to bits all around them. The boxes carrying the tools of his trade scattered. He felt whole, nothing broken. He realized he was still clutching Nicclos, who had wrapped his arms around his neck and legs around his torso.

"You hurt, son?" He whispered into his ear.

"No, Papa." The boy hugged him tighter.

That was good. That was all that really mattered. "I'm going to put you down now," he said. The boy nodded and let his feet unclasp. They stood looking at each other for a moment. The boy's eyes were steady in his scraped face. No tears.

"Where'd they go? The wolf men?"

What an odd way to put it, thought Kristoff. Maybe the boy needed glasses as well.

The hangman looked around but saw nothing. Perhaps they had run off. And then he heard it. An inhuman howl that turned into words coming from the road behind them.

"Papa!" The voice was filled with anguish. Not wolves then, but peasants bent on robbery. The hangman scowled. Served them right if one of the bloody bastards died then. Must have been dressed in furs for, to his eyes, they had certainly looked like wolves. No matter. They had to think of themselves now. And quickly, in case any more peasants came to try to rob them.

"Should we help them?" His son's voice piped up. Looking down at him, Kristoff was prepared to snap out a firm no, but then he saw the kindness shining from the boy's eyes. It was the same kindness that he had been drawn to and treasured in his wife. It was what kept him centered as he did his work, indeed what kept him humane in his work.

Instead of speaking sharply, he shook his head. "I think the one is beyond help now. We'll see to our horses, then gather what we can onto them."

He saw the boy still looked hesitant. Kristoff bent down, groaning a bit. He was going to be sore on the morrow. "Son, God has judged those people, and he chose to protect us. They failed in their task. It is not for us to decide what their fate. Do you see? We will not punish them further nor seek revenge, but neither shall we lend them aid. They chose their path."

Nicclos nodded slowly. He then brushed his hands together. "We've had an adventure!"

Kristoff chuckled and hugged his son to him closely. "We have indeed. And now comes the drudgery of walking on our own feet for home. That is our path, as tedious as it will be. Are you up for it?"

"I am, Papa. I'm sure we can be there by nightfall." Nicclos looked resolute and moved to untangle the reins and settle the horses. The hangman felt a flush of pride watching his lad. Behind him, he could hear the sobs of the other son calling out for his father. That pair had ended their adventure on a different note.

Glancing one more time behind them, he saw no movement. He spared a final thought as to why wolves or men would want to attack them in such an odd manner. Finding no ready answer, Kristoff turned and began to collect his things he would need for the punishments and execution on the morrow.

CHAPTER EIGHTEEN

H er behind would never be the same again. Bella groaned as she slid off Destry at the Traveller camp. Make that her behind and her inner thighs. She wobbled on her feet and mentally added in her lower back as well. She turned to the huge animal who twitched his ears at her and whickered.

"Are you laughing at me, you gigantic beast?"

Destry pawed at the ground with his hoof and bobbed his head so that his black mane bounced.

"Cheeky bastard!" Bella laughed despite her inner tension. She gave him an affectionate rub on the neck. "You are a most excellent horse, even if you do cause me pain and suffering."

Destry snorted in agreement and bowed down to crop some of the green grass at their feet. Bella let him have his bite and then picked up the reins to walk him to Aisha's tent. The horse plodded behind her amiably. Bella decided that someday she'd have a gorgeous stallion just like this for her very own.

Reaching the tent, she scratched on the front panel. Aisha swooped it open immediately and extended her hand. Noting the stress on the woman's face, Bella didn't say a word, but simply handed over the satchel.

"What did you find?" Aisha asked, digging into the bag.

"The belladonna berries weren't ripe, but I met a girl in the forest who said the root would work just as well."

Aisha froze, then carefully removed her hand from the satchel and closed it. She shut her eyes for a long moment before looking at Bella again. "You met a girl in the forest." Aisha's voice and face were flat. That was a bad sign. "You met a girl in the forest, and she said the root would work just as well. And you believed her."

"Well, yes." Bella felt her anger rising. Better anger than fear. "She was quite knowledgeable. You'll find the boxwood leaves in there for the cure. She took me right to the boxwood. She saved me a lot of time."

"How nice of her. Did she also mention that using the root will kill you if you have but an iota too much?"

"I... I don't... maybe." Bella stuttered uncomfortably in the face of Aisha's growing and seemingly infinite wrath. This was not going well. Panic welled up inside of her. She hurried on, as it seemed Aisha might just throw the satchel back in her face and refuse the task entirely. "She did. She did mention that. Henna said—"

Bella closed her eyes and willed herself to remember exactly.

Picturing Henna's face, Bella repeated the words. "You must boil the root in five times the water until it disintegrates. Then no more than a half a spoon, unless it be a big man, then you can use more." The words tumbled out in a rush. Aisha glared at her, unmoving. Bella buttoned up her lips, stared back, and waited for the woman to speak first.

The silence seemed endless. The wind blew between them, causing the chimes Aisha hung on the front of her tent to sound a few musical notes. Behind them, Destry blew and stamped his foot. Stray curls of her hair blew in front of Bella's face, but she didn't dare to lift her hand to move it away, even though it tickled for fear of breaking the impasse. Finally Aisha spoke.

"Her name was Henna? This mysterious girl in the woods? Odd name."

"She hates it. Her mother gave it to her. She's a witch." Off of Aisha's insulted look, Bella amended herself. "I mean, her mother is a healer. The village calls her a witch." Bella flipped her curls back out of her face.

Aisha sniffed. Sighed. Shifted her feet. Bella waited again and let the silence grow, but she was no longer anxious. She was confident this would go her way, and that they would move ahead with her very smart plan. She just needed to be patient a few moments more.

"Fine. But it's on you if I kill you." The words were reluctant, and Aisha seemed like she might take them back in her next breath. Forgetting herself, she took Aisha's free hand in her own and looked up at her earnestly.

"I trust you, Aisha. Completely."

For the smallest of moments, it seemed as if Aisha was going to cry. Aisha's eyes squinted shut, and her lips trembled. The emotion alarmed Bella. The woman never cried, not when she was hurt, not when people said horrific things about her or to her. Not even when her own son broke his arm falling out of the tree he and Bella had been climbing. Never.

Aisha's warm brown hand gripped her own tightly. "Swear you won't haunt me with your annoying spirit self if this goes the wrong way. Swear it to any saints you believe in." Aisha seemed serious.

"By Saints above, I promise I will not haunt you."

"Or curse me with your dying breath."

"Or curse you with my dying breath."

Aisha took her thumb and forefinger, held them together, and then flicked Bella in the middle of her forehead.

"Ow!"

"The promise is sealed." Aisha's face relaxed. She grabbed a wooden pail and held it out to Bella. "Go fill this and take Destry with you to get a drink. Mind you, put that bucket in the cleanest part of the river you can find. Hurry now, we don't have long."

Bella rubbed her forehead and gave Aisha a look. She took the bucket and Destry's reins and ran down to the river. Her legs and back throbbed, and she was glad of the movement to work out the aches. As she let the horse drink, she waded out into the cold flow of the river to fill the bucket. The waters tugged at her legs as if encouraging her to go deeper. She thought back to the previous night, when this very river was both her savior and also nearly the death of her. She thought about how her father always took a moment and thanked the trees that gave them shelter and fruit, and the animals that gave their lives so they could eat, and their skins so that they could be warm. Perhaps a river should be thanked as well for saving a life. Bending down, she cupped some of the sparkling stream into her hand. It felt awkward, but she pushed through the feeling.

"Thank you. Even though you tried to take me for your own. In the end, you saved me." Bella breathed the words into the captured water, then let the water flow back into the river. Watching the droplets trickle from her hand, she felt an odd peace in her heart. Maybe it'd been a silly thing to do, but she was glad she'd done it all the same.

"Well, 'tis done," Aisha grumbled. With a steady hand, she poured the small amount of liquid from the pot into the flask that Bella held ready for her. Aisha stoppered it with a bit of cloth and pushed the flask into Bella's hands.

Aisha rocked back on her heels, away from the fire. She looked up at the sky. At first it seemed ironic that the sunset was so beautiful tonight, a purpling sky above reds and golds that lit the camp area with a clear light. It was as if she could see everything more clearly. As she considered it, her thoughts changed. Perhaps it was fitting that such beauty and clarity came as death neared.

"The golden hour," she whispered to herself. In another life, she would be bending in prayer. But she was no longer of that tribe, both by circumstance and by choice. Instead, she took the moment to breathe in deeply of the cooling air that spoke of the night soon to come.

She stretched and then stood. Faced the young woman who was trusting her with her very life. "Bella, I have to ask once again. Are you sure you want to go through with this?"

"I have to." The simplicity of the answer surprised Aisha. She was used to the girl spouting outrageous nonsense, or babbling on using twice as many words as were needed. Half the time it seemed she'd rather lie than tell the truth about something. This was different. Aisha nodded.

"Tell me one more time about how your plan is supposed to work."

"I go back to the stage. Drink this. The dead watch takes me up on their cart. Malik is waiting for me at the charnel house. He gives me the cure. We rescue Vadoma." Bella rattled it off.

"What if something goes wrong? What if the night watch is late? What if you are not revived? What if you and my son get caught?" Aisha folded her arms and prepared for Bella to stumble. Again, she was surprised.

"I can only answer the last one—you know as well as I do, Malik is as wily as they come. He won't let them catch him. And he won't let them catch me either."

"Your mother will be weak and ill. How are you going to manage her?"

Bella smiled. "I thought of that. I'll make Rose or Stefan meet us with a wheelbarrow. They'll do it," she added firmly as Aisha quirked an eyebrow. "I can make them do it. Or you could meet us with Destry. He's a great horse."

"He is a great horse, and no, thank you, I won't be taking him into town. Destry will be hitched to our cart and ready to leave. You should do the same with your ponies as well, so your clan can disappear into the night."

The girl nodded, and a wry smile crept onto her serious face. "I'll have Aunt Kezia do all that. I'll be too busy being dead."

The joke fell flat. The surrounding air seemed to go still and heavy. Bella looked at the stoppered flask and swallowed. Aisha put a hand on her shoulder. "It's good that you are taking this seriously, Bella. Now. You must not eat or drink anything before you take this. If you sick up when no one is around, your own vomit will choke you."

"Ewww." Bella made a face.

Aisha ignored the face and the comment. "After Malik revives you with the second draught, you need to drink as much clean water as you can. I'll be sure he brings you some. You should try to be sick."

Bella looked horrified. Aisha shook her head at the girl. "I can read your thoughts. If he truly loves you, he will not mind the sick. If he truly loves you, he'll hold your hair away while it happens."

Bella looked up at her, considering. Then her beautiful smile broke through. "You're right."

Aisha smiled back. "When all of this is over, we can have a long talk about menfolk if you'd like."

"I would." Bella's face changed from happy to perplexed in the course of a moment. A swath of sadness passed over her features, and her shoulders slumped. "I don't think Vadoma would have that talk with me. Ever. We've never been close, and I've told her so many times and in so many ways how I despise her." Her voice trailed off.

Aisha busied herself with putting away the herbs and oils she had used to make the two potions. She knew all too well how Bella felt. The bruise inside that never healed when you could not bring yourself to love your own mother. Maybe it would end differently for Bella and Vadoma than it had for her, so long ago. She took Bella's face in her hands, tilted it so that their eyes met. "It takes two people to build a wall, Bella. It only takes one to start to take it down."

Bella looked miserable and pulled away. "I just wonder if it's the blood curse that's made it so we—so that I—don't know how to be with my own mother in comfort. It feels like I can never take a full breath around her. Even if I try."

Aisha was taken aback. What could the girl be talking about? "Bella, what is this curse—" Bella interrupted Aisha, giving a loud whoop and holding her arms out wide.

"Malik!"

Aisha saw her son moving towards them. His slender form seemed dwarfed by the wooden cart he pulled via two long handles. Each step he took dug into the soft earth, heel slipping slightly before it got purchase. The two large wheels on the cart turned slowly. He looked exhausted, with sweat beaded on his face, his mouth grim with strain.

Bella ran forward and grabbed one of the handles. Malik barely glanced at her, but together they finished pulling the cart to the tent. Malik bent forward to carefully place the wooden handles on the ground. Then he put his hands on his knees and let his head hang down, breathing hard. Bella ran to get him a dipper of water from the pail. He took it and drank, then stood slowly and puffed his cheeks out in relief.

"I could've used the horse," he said shortly. "I see Bella has been found."

"I'm about to be lost again, too." Bella's voice was bright as she spoke. *Too bright*, thought Aisha. The girl was scared. As she should be.

"Tell Malik your plan while I make him something to eat. He'll need the energy for what you have in mind." Aisha turned to go inside the tent to give the two some privacy as she saw

Bella move forward to hug Malik, and Malik pushing her roughly away.

She heard shouting as she moved to make her son a quick meal of the last scrapings of this week's pottage flavored with cardamom and ginger spice. She noted that their personal spices were running low. Perhaps they should go back on the spice road early this year. She served the stew up in a hollow round of black bread and brought it back outside.

Malik looked pale and had walked several strides away from Bella, who had her hands on her hips and a scowl on her face.

"I don't care if you don't like the idea, Malik! You have to participate. No one else can do the parts you have to do!" Seeing Aisha, Bella pointed at her. "Your mother thinks it's a good idea, or she wouldn't have made the potions for me!"

Malik turned to his mother, anger suffusing his face, red spots rising in the middle of the pale. "You made this death potion for her?"

Aisha reminded herself that keeping calm was the best approach. "Aye. And I made the one that will revive her." She pushed the food into his hands, along with a wooden spoon. "You must eat now; we all have a long night ahead of us if we're to escape this cursed town."

Malik took the food and dug in. He spoke around mouthfuls. "Cursed is right. Ebbe's in jail now, as well as Vadoma. I never would have kissed you if I'd known."

"I didn't know about the curse either! And you didn't tell me Da's in jail too!" Bella's voice was shrill and rising in volume.

"Didn't give me a chance, did you? Came at me yammering about this crazy idea of yours."

"I didn't come *at* you. We're short of time, and it's the only plan we have! Now we have to get both of them out. We'll need a cart. Or two wheelbarrows. What on earth was he arrested for?" Bella paced as she talked.

"Ebbe went to get Rose out of jail. They let her go, but locked him up in her place." Malik tore at the bread bowl as he finished the pottage inside of it.

"Oh." Bella looked stricken. Aisha moved to ask more questions, but Malik continued. "There's more. Your aunt had a terrible time getting Rose to stop crying, but eventually she got it out of her, and then told me. Rose says the mayor of the town has a special interest in Ebbe and Vadoma. And in you, Bella."

Aisha felt the chill of a warning shiver up her spine. "Why would the mayor have any interest in Travellers, and by name, too? It's not like we live in his city."

Malik gestured with the last of the bread he held. "Go on and tell my *ommah*. Kezia told me."

Bella clenched her fists at her sides and looked up at the sky as if for answers. Or perhaps she was just stalling. The girl swallowed, and then spoke. "Burgermeister Strom put a blood curse on my mother and me when I was born. Accused her of killing his own wife and child to give their strength to me. I'm supposed to unleash all manner of hell and suffering on those I love after love's first kiss. Be bound, and a lot more generally awful things." Bella folded her arms defiantly and pasted a smirk on her face, acting as if she thought it was all bollocks, but Aisha could tell the girl was deeply frightened.

"Good thing I don't love you, then." Malik said nonchalantly. Bella's eyes went round. She flew at him, using both hands and feet to land as many blows as possible. Malik fought back, deflecting instead of attacking. Aisha waded in to separate them, getting a solid kick in her own shin for her troubles.

"That's enough. We don't have time for this now." Aisha fought to keep her own alarm from making the critical situation worse as she pushed them further apart.

"Why'd you say that! You don't mean it!" Bella flushed with rage. Tears glinted in her eyes. Aisha gave her son a little shake when he clamped his mouth shut and turned his head away.

"I don't know! I guess because if it's not true, then you don't have to die." Malik practically spat out the words and flung his arms out into the air. He glared at Bella as he shook off his mother's grasp, his chin jutting out as if he was begging Bella to slug him again.

Bella narrowed her eyes, head cocked to the side as she studied him, then her whole demeanor changed. She pointed at him. "You said it because you care. Because you love." She flung her arms around Malik, who, after a moment, hugged her back just as fiercely. Aisha looked away when Bella planted a kiss full on Malik's lips. "I knew you loved me," the girl whispered. Malik's eyes gleamed.

"If you're quite done." Aisha said dryly. "The light is on the wane."

Bella looked as if she might impulsively give Aisha a kiss too, so she prudently took a step backward and spoke briskly. "All this will keep for later. Bella, go talk your cousins into doing what they need to do tonight. Have one of them bring the little ones to me. I'll start along the road with the babies so the two of them can finish packing your family more quickly. We'll head east towards the Darkwood and meet everyone there at the forest camp by sunrise the day after tomorrow."

Striding into the tent, she picked up the flask with the antidote. Bella and Malik stood in the last waning light of day, their hands clasped together. She handed the antidote to Malik, ignoring how cold she suddenly felt. There was no room for caution now.

"Bella, your heart will be so slowed that none but the most talented of healers could detect a beat. It will happen quickly, so lay down before you take it. You have one hour to take the antidote, or you will die in reality."

Bella nodded and looked up at Malik. "Malik will get it to me."

"The antidote will be bitter, and smell of rotting elderberries and bark, but you must drink all of it. I had no time to sweeten it with honey."

Aisha turned to her son. Saw both the boy she had raised and the man he was becoming. In her heart, she wept. Outwardly, she laid a gentle hand on his face. "Bring yourself home to me, *alhabib*."

He smiled, placed his hand in return on her cheek. "Always, *ommah*."

The pair turned from her, Malik's right hand clasping Bella's left, and they strode away into the deepening night. Aisha felt her heart fill with foreboding. So much could go wrong. She kept her eyes on them until they disappeared from sight, yearning with all her heart to call them back, keep them safe.

CHAPTER NINETEEN

K ristoff the hangman eased his weary feet out towards the low fire and sighed contentedly. Young Nicclos had been right. They'd entered the gates of the city just as the night was falling. Their weary horses were now stabled, and his youngest son was fed and tucked safely in his bed. He reached out to clasp the hand of his wife. Bringing it to his lips, he kissed it.

"Your youngest son did well today," he murmured. "He takes after his mother, courageous in the face of danger."

Johanna smiled indulgently. "Yes, Nicclos told me all about your 'wolfen adventure,' as he called it, several times over. At supper, in his bath. He was still embroidering the tale as he fell asleep."

Kristoff nodded. That was Nicclos, all right. Perhaps his son would become a bard and travel from town to town. entertaining the nobles. "And how have you been busying yourself while we were getting waylaid by shaggy peasants?"

Johanna gave him a keen look and moved to the small cupboard they kept locked. Opening it with one of the set of keys she wore at her waist, she pulled out a leather-bound book and brought it to the table. She pulled the candlesticks closer. The hangman looked at her askance and stood to pull the curtains over the window.

"You know women aren't supposed to read," he scolded.

"Then you should not have taught me, husband," she replied. She continued over his sigh. "Look at this." She pointed to an illustration of a leg being cut off. Next to the bleeding limb was a bucket filled with a black substance.

"They dip the remaining limb in hot coal tar directly after the cut. They say here that most survive without putrification of the wound after." She moved her fingers to stroke his arm. "You could do the same."

He looked at the drawing for long time. Tried to imagine how it would work. The condemned lined up on the outdoor platform so the crowd could see the punishment. The hard anvil and his sharp axe. The chop, the screams, the cheers of the crowd. Then bustled to the side of the stage to be thus tended to by Johanna. He shook his head vehemently and shut the book. "For those going to a barber for surgery, 'tis a fine idea. Not for those who've committed crimes."

"You always say that the moment the punishment has been delivered, the condemned have paid their price." Johanna folded her arms and nodded her head firmly the way she always did when she felt she'd won an argument.

Kristoff stood, frustrated. Paced the stone floor. He hated that she was using his own words against him. He shook his head again, but slowly this time. He was reluctant to admit that he wasn't ready to embrace such an idea, but it was the truth. "'Tis too radical. They'd have me in chains for it."

"Who'd have you in chains? The mob? You know better than that. You're a respected man in this town."

A chill came over the hangman. He moved to poke the hearth fire higher, held his hands to it. Bitterly, he formed his next words. "Aye, I am respected by many. Yet there is only one who lays down the law and you well know it. I'll not cross that man, if man he truly be."

He glanced over at his wife. Saw a shadow cross her face. Her lips turned down. She was about to take a breath to speak. He moved to her, took her by the arms, pulled her to his chest, dipped his head down to her soft crown of braids. He whispered to her. "Johanna, you may think me a coward for not standing up to him. I think it myself often enough. But do not ask me to risk my position or our lives. The Burgermeister cannot be fought by such as we."

She stiffened in his arms but didn't pull away. Slowly, Johanna nodded her head. "You said I was courageous, but you are in the right of it, I would not have you jeopardize our son's future. We are the lesser for our cowardice."

Kristoff kissed her. "The line between prudent wisdom and cowardice seems blurred to me in this case, wife. Who's to say which is true and right? We are but mortals doing our best on each day, are we not?"

His wife sighed, shook her head. "That Strom has too much power. He's had too much for nigh on our entire lifetime. It's not right." Johanna's forehead creased, and she seemed about to criticize further.

Something banged against the wooden shutters outside. A chilly wind blew down the chimney, causing sparks to fly through the room. They jumped and clutched at each other. The hangman wondered for the hundredth time if the Burgermeister somehow had magical ears that heard all. Or perhaps it was just his own fear doing him in, filling his head with nonsense.

Johanna relaxed after the wind died down. She pulled away and regarded him, then held up a finger and waved it in his face. "I'll bring strong port wine tomorrow and let the prisoners drink deep of it, then. I'll not be denied giving them that small comfort. We are Christian folk, after all."

Relieved that she would not fight him on the matter, Kristoff smiled, took her hand, and kissed it. "You are right, my dear. You shall not be denied that."

Outside the house, Stefan stood rigid. It would be so easy to kill them all. Just crawl into the sleeping boy's window. Make them pay for what they did to his father. Waves of grief flooded him as he remembered his father's lifeless body crumpled in the dust of the road. The rising cold wind blew like a howl from his soul, but he remained silent, watching the shadowy figures of the hangman and his wife embrace in the flimsy false safety of their home.

CHAPTER TWENTY

The flickering torchlight cast the world into simple colors of red, black, and grey. Strom looked up from his task briefly, and cocked his head, listening. Satisfied, he smiled and returned his attention to the last of Ebbe's fingers. The last one that remained straight and whole.

Strom picked up his mallet and struck. How he loved the muted sounds of agony coming from Ebbe's crushed face. They paired so sweetly with those coming from Vadoma, chained to the wall nearby.

He looked up at the woman who had caused him so much pain for so many years. Ruined his plans. Made him wait. He wanted to simply rend her in half, rip her like his wife, his one love, had been torn. But that wouldn't get him what he wanted. What he needed. What he would have. He forced his teeth to show in a grin.

"Well, sadly, we are all out of fingers to break. Shall I start on his arms or his legs next?" He looked at her expectantly. "Not so many small bone breaks there. Just the fibula and the tibia." He moved the wood and metal hammer up Ebbe's leg. Was disappointed that the man's flesh didn't shiver. Well, it soon would. He moved his hands and picked up a sharp bone blade.

"Or perhaps slicing up here along these brawny arms would be better?"

"Please." Vadoma's word was a breath of air. Strom chuckled.

"Polite until the end. Vadoma," he said in a chiding tone. "All you need to do to stop his pain is tell me where your Belladonna is. She's been a slippery one." He laughed, but there was no mirth in it. "She's eluded my soldiers for over a day now. That black boy too."

"She's done nothing to you. Nothing. It was my mistakes that —"

He raised the knife and slashed down Ebbe's chest. Blood bloomed black from the wound. Strange how what should be red only seemed black in the dim light of the dungeons.

"Oh dear. I made that cut rather deep. I'd say that wound will kill him if allowed to continue to bleed," he said conversationally. "Or I can have someone fetch some hot wine to splash on it, then bandage it so that it doesn't." He hissed as Vadoma shook her head mutely. Ebbe raised his head, his eyes astonishingly fierce in the flickering light.

"You'll never have our daughter," Ebbe said.

How he hated being talked to like this! Strom slapped the man violently so that the chains holding him to the stone block rattled. Strom realized he was breathing hard. How uncouth that mere gypsies had brought him to such a state. He was getting too agitated by this work. He needed fresh air. Strom stood. Collected himself. Bent low over the man and squeezed Ebbe's face between his hands until the gypsy's eyes opened again.

"I shall have her. Listen to me well. Ebbe, your daughter will replace the girl that your wife murdered. It must be, for I have willed it so. I shall have Belladonna in my bed over and over again until she bears me the son I lost. Then I'll kill her and hire a wet nurse. You can take comfort in knowing your grandchild will be a great man in this world. Your race is strong, and mine is powerful. Together, we will make something quite unique.

Something… unstoppable. It's time for those insipid Luxembourgs to conclude their reign and a new bloodline rule Germany. You see, there is a renaissance at hand."

Strom smiled happily at the panic he observed on both Ebbe and Vadoma's faces. "Think on where Belladonna might be while I take the airs above. It's so dank down here." He moved to the staircase and carefully placed his rich outer robe on his shoulders. Smiled as he thought of a charming pun.

"I'd say you have at most an hour before your blood has ebbed, Ebbe. I'll return before then to see if you've remembered anything."

CHAPTER TWENTY-ONE

M alik led her through the dark alleys he seemed to know so well. Halting in hidden doorways to let guards and ordinary folk pass, moving softly and silently, they made their way across the city. Bella was glad to let him take the lead. It was a new feeling, this trust of someone else, but Bella was glad of it. Maybe it meant the curse was breaking, or at least losing power. She was sure that when they freed her parents and escaped this place, that the curse would become fragile and easily broken.

She thought back to the incessant nagging and cajoling she'd used to get first her father, then her aunt and uncle to join her campaign to come here to this festival. Not because she truly wanted to come to this town, but because her mother so vehemently did not. Bella shook her head, angry at herself for such pettiness. Moving forward, she would do better by Vadoma.

At last, they came to the square where their stage was. Full night had fallen and there was only the tiniest sliver of a moon to give them light. The only sound was the trickle of the fountain in the middle of the square. Keeping to the edges of the courtyard, Malik and Bella made it to the curtained off area of their stage. Holding a finger to his lips and motioning her to stay back,

Malik ventured forward and dipped behind the fabric. Bella shifted impatiently outside.

Malik pulled her in. Bella sighed with relief to be amongst all the familiar things. The costumes half-packed into crates, the prop table. It was like she was seeing them for the first time, all lit by the warm soft glow of the lanterns on the table. Even seeing her cousin Rose crying like she did at least once a day gave her a sense that all was right in the world. Bella saw they'd cut her pretty red hair off and felt compassion spring up for her cousin, crumpled in a heap on the ground, sobbing into the fur of the little orange kitten she'd found yesterday. She stepped forward with a smile on her lips, intending to comfort her cousin and rescue the kitten from getting any wetter. Then she saw the pale, drawn face and red-lined eyes of her aunt Kezia, who slowly rocked Pattin in a sling at her breast. Young Timbo was strapped onto her back, head lolling in sleep. She seemed laden with the weight of not only her children, but with the worry of the world. *They must be concerned about Vadoma and Ebbe,* she thought. She gasped when Stefan grabbed her arms roughly. She hadn't seen him in the shadows.

"Where in all the hells have you been?" He snarled the words at her.

"Hey, let go of her." Malik stepped in and pushed him away. Stefan stepped right back up until he was nose to nose with Malik, and growled deep in his throat.

"Stop it, both of you," Bella said. Putting herself between them, as she had only the day before, she glared at both. "We've no time for posturing." The two boys showed no signs of breaking their tension, so Bella went on. "I have a plan to rescue Ebbe and Vadoma, and I need—"

"My father is dead." Stefan's voice was grating and harsh. "Killed by the very man that is to kill your mother and father on the morrow. That's who we must stop tonight!" He whirled and confronted his mother, who shook her head at him sadly. "We need to go kill him! Kill the hangman and his whole family! I followed them. I know where they live."

"Stefan." Stunned, Bella blinked back tears. Rose sobbed even harder. Kezia rubbed her pale face with her hands.

"I'm taking the boys and Rose to collect his body from the western road tonight. We are not. Not," she repeated as Stefan surged forward again. "Not going to allow him to lie out there. We are collecting him and giving him his due rights and respects. We will bury him according to our custom."

Kezia had never looked more beautiful, Bella thought. Her face had an ethereal quality to it, as if her grief had transformed her into another type of being. She moved to her aunt, took both her hands, and touched her forehead to her aunt's. Continuing to clasp her hands, Bella spoke softly. "I grieve with you, Kezia. We will honor him. But I will not allow my parents to die as well. Please, just hear me out," she begged as she saw her aunt turn her face away.

"We don't need any more of your stupid plans!" Stefan erupted. He picked up the three-legged stool and smashed it to the ground. His eyes glowed golden with rage. Rose screamed and sobbed harder. Young Timbo woke and added his cries to the mix.

"You'll bring the night watch down on us!" Malik spoke in intense, hushed tones, but they carried.

Bella hurried to her aunt's side and plucked Young Timbo from his carrier. She turned and plopped him in Rose's lap. "Both of you stop your crying!" The pair looked up at her, startled into quiet. Bella turned on Stefan. "You do not honor your father by acting this way."

She faced Kezia. "Aunt. Of course I'll not stop you from what you must do. But I need Stefan to help me tonight. Aisha can take the boys for you; she is waiting at the camp to do just that. That will leave you and Rose free to do what you need to do for

Uncle Timbo. Then we can all go into the heart of the Darkwood and honor him. All of us. Together."

Kezia's lips trembled, and Bella felt fear clutch her gut. If she refused, then Stefan would, too. Without his muscle, it would be impossible to maneuver both of her parents to safety, especially if they had been hurt. Bella refused to let her mind drift to what may have happened to them in the dungeon. She had to make Kezia agree.

"I know you want your sister to be safe again, Kezia. You won't abandon Vadoma." Bella whispered.

The woman cast her gaze downward, at where, impossibly, Pattin had slept through everything. Kezia brushed his brown curls away from his flushed cheeks. Then she lifted the sling over her head and moved over to Rose. She draped the carrier and the child over her daughter.

"Dry your eyes, child, and take your little brothers to Aisha. Then take our cart and go with Stefan to find your father. You have strength in you, Rose, I know it. Time to call on that now." Kezia kissed her daughter on the forehead. Then turned to her oldest son, pulled him towards her so they were eye to eye. It surprised Bella to see that Stefan was of a height with Kezia. When had he grown so tall? "I know you would face anything, Stefan. You are ferocious and wild, just like your father. I would keep his fire alive tonight, in you. Go with your sister. Show her the way." Stefan jutted his jaw, as if to disagree, but she stilled him with a look. He moved to pick up Little Timbo from Rose's lap, then helped his sister to stand.

Kezia turned back to Bella. "Tell me what you need from me. I'll not abandon my sister, but neither will I risk my children. We have lost enough for one night."

Bella looked at her aunt, and wished for a moment that this was her own mother, standing there, strong and resolute. Someone she could love and be proud of. Well, she'd just have to find those same qualities in her own mother. Bella nodded her head and told them her plan.

CHAPTER TWENTY-TWO

B ella had to admit that Kezia's change to her plan was a good one. Instead of waiting for the dead cart, she'd make it come to them. That would give them more hours of night to escape the town once Ebbe and Vadoma had been rescued. Now she and Malik waited together in the dark of the backstage area. He'd shadow her to the house of the dead.

Stefan and Rose had left hours ago, carrying the babies and large packs of clothing and items that couldn't be left behind. There'd be no returning for their stage or most of the props and costumes. Bella had asked Rose to take the little kitten too, snuggled up in the sling with Pattin. Bella had sentimentally tucked a pair of the metal finger cymbals into her own bodice. She wrapped two shawls around her body and wore an extra dress. She'd also tucked several baby nappies into the top of her skirt.

"So I can clean up after I sick up," she explained to Malik.

He looked at her critically, then spun her around. "I might like you a little round," he commented wryly.

Bella had whapped him gently but smiled. Now the frivolity was gone and only the waiting remained. There were only a few hours left before dawn. Malik's hand took hers. She clasped it and squeezed it tightly. In her other hand, she had the poison that would slow her heart and breath and feign death. They both listened intently for Kezia.

"Malik, if you find something going wrong with the plan—"

"What could go wrong?" Malik said in his driest tone. "It only involves you dying and the rest of us risking death."

Bella nodded. The plan could go wrong a thousand ways. "Well, if you find things going wrong Malik, just think to yourself 'what would Bella do'? Then you'll be all right."

Malik smiled at her, and Bella wished that she'd kissed him more, for what if this were her last chance to do so? She was just turning to him when she heard creaking wheels and above it the wails of Kezia's voice.

"My niece, she collapsed when she heard of her parents being taken. I couldn't revive her!" Male grumbling sounded underneath Kezia's exaggerated cries and moans. "Come this way, she is just here. Dead, deader than dead."

Bella's breathing quickened. Malik squeezed her hand and then let go. It was time. Bella felt as if she was wandering within a dream. Disassociated, she watched her hand unstop the flask and move it to her mouth. She opened her mouth, poured, and swallowed. Remembered to lie down. She waited, aware that Malik was staring at her with wide eyes.

Pure panic set in. Nothing was happening. She surged to her feet, tried to run, but then her legs felt as if someone had chopped them off. She stumbled, felt Malik's arms around her, lowering her back to the ground. The last thing she saw was his beautiful face, fading away to a pinpoint of color in utter black. And then the void.

Malik didn't want to let her go. It'd been surreal watching her pass from being a living, breathing person into a sheath of clothes wrapped around a form that had no animation, no spark, *no Bella* to it. While he'd privately always doubted his mother's tales about everyone having an animating spirit that was the essential, everlasting part of that person, he had no doubts at all now.

Lost in his thoughts, staring at Bella's still form, he forgot where he was for a moment. Kezia's crying voice saved him.

"She's inside, my niece, oh, my niece!"

Malik scurried behind the trunks and ducked down just as the curtains parted. Two scrawny men with arms roped with muscle bent down and picked up Bella as if she weighed nothing at all. He heard the thump of her body land in the cart. His own heart seemed to skip a beat at the sound.

Kezia kept up her caterwauling. "This be all Master Strom's fault that our Belladonna is dead!"

"Hush!" Malik heard one man say. "Ye no be wanting to bring his guards down to take ye away too, do ye now?"

"I want Strom to see! I want Strom to see what he has done to my family!" Kezia got even louder. Her voice carried from years of calling wares.

"Fer Saint Gertrude herself, pipe down woman!" The guard was yelling himself now. Malik had to smile. "I'm sure he's heard ye by now. Or ye can go over to the mayor's house after we finish our rounds."

"Don't pile more of the dead atop of my beautiful Belladonna!" Malik had to peep out to watch. The cart horses were waiting patiently, their heads hanging low as the men hauled Kezia back. She fought them, but not so very hard, Malik saw. Just enough to irritate them. One of the men grabbed her from behind while the other got up into her face.

"Lookit," the man said, exasperated. "I'm done with ye. Now, we're taking this—your—Belladonna, you say; yes? Belladonna is going to be tucked nice and safe-like into the house of the dead, just for tonight. Then in the morning ye can claim it—her —iff'n you want to. Them's the rules. Understand?" He gestured and the second man put Kezia down. She shrugged her shawl more tightly to her and glared at him.

Kezia turned back to the man who had been talking, sniffed, then waved a hand. "Take her, then. Follow your rules. I'm following *you* and if we see that Burgermeister of yours, I'm giving him a piece of my mind!" The men rolled their eyes at each other but got the cart rolling. Malik could see Bella's limp form on top of several more, her hand dangling. How strange he'd just been holding it minutes before.

Now to get himself in position at the charnel house. Best be inside before they got there, so he'd waste no time reviving Bella. Malik checked he had the earthenware flask with the potion that would save her safely stowed, grabbed the water she'd need after they revived her. He eased out of the backstage area. He quickly moved at an angle away from the horse-drawn cart and Kezia's continuing sobs and protestations.

Kezia had no problem letting her sorrow flow. In a way, it was good to have this outlet for it, as it stopped her from feeling the true grief she knew would come. It felt good to be annoying to the men with the dead cart, to misbehave in public. For ages now, she'd been a good wife, a good mother, doing the jobs those entailed every day without complaint. There were too many in their clan who needed center stage to feel whole. That was not her norm, but now she relished the role. Besides, it was important that Strom think Bella dead, that he saw her as dead. Then perhaps whatever the horrible curse he'd put on Vadoma, and Bella would lift. One could hope so, at any rate.

She'd caught movement out of the corner of her eye up ahead at the dead house. It must be Malik, swinging up into the small windows Bella had spotted. He'd play dead when the doors opened. The cart slowed. They were in front of the jail.

Kezia took a deep breath. By all the gods, she'd let Vadoma and Ebbe know she was here. Hopefully, they'd understand her words and prepare themselves. "Ebbe! Vadoma! Your child is here!" Kezia used her best calling voice, the one that could be heard for long distances. "Your Sleeping Beauty has taken her draught, and is no longer in the land of light!"

The two men with the cart looked at each other and shrugged. They'd given up trying to quiet her blocks ago. Kezia took a deep breath from her belly and continued, hoping her sister and her husband would understand her message. "Where, oh where, is the dark prince who can wake her with a kiss now? Will he come within the hour? Oh our beloved Belladonna, our Sleeping Beauty!" The stone walls echoed her words, amplifying them and repeating them into the canyons of the city. Lanterns flared to life in windows, people's sleep disturbed. That was fine with her. She'd had enough of being subservient and quiet for a lifetime.

The dark doorway to the jail darkened further as Strom erupted from it in a fury. Heavily cloaked in rich fabric, his ruby ring glinting in the faint moonlight, the angles of his face caught in the torchlight at the door of the jail. He looked like a demon from hell, his face thunderous, and his black eyes focused on her. Kezia gasped and clutched at her throat. It was as if someone had sucked all the air from her lungs. The cart creaked to a halt, and the two men snatched their caps from their heads and bowed low.

Strom took his time moving to the cart, as if he didn't want to see what lay there. Obscenely his nose twitched as if he were a predatory creature of the forest, not a man. Kezia had to lock her knees to stop from falling as he approached. She struggled to pull air into her lungs. He brushed past her as if she were nothing and reached into the cart.

Strom moaned, and pulled first Bella's limp hand to his nose, then he reached in, and pulled her body up and to him like a lover. He caressed her hair, kissed her lips, smelled her throat. He bent down and listened to where her heart should beat. Kezia shrank back as he breathed in and out, latching onto her lips, trying to breathe air into her from his own lungs.

It was horrifying to watch him paw at her in desperation, pushing her chest, willing it to move with the power of his hands. Kezia felt tears come to her eyes unbidden, and she didn't know if she wept for herself or for Bella. Or for Strom. He seemed to age a decade in moments.

The guards from the prison had come to the door to watch. They were speechless as Strom inhaled Bella's scent a final time, then eased her back on the cart. He clutched the side of the wagon as if he couldn't support his own weight. Noticing all the eyes upon him, he looked around. Pointed at Kezia.

"You. Speak. How did she die?"

Kezia moistened her lips and pulled up all the sorrow she'd held in check over her husband. It rolled up, threatened to take away her voice. She swallowed, then spoke. She spoke in vibrating, low tones, ones that sounded like bells tolling in mourning for the dead. "Of grief," she said. "Grief you created by imprisoning first her mother, then her father. This girl's death is on your head!" Kezia felt cold, but sure. She spoke truth and every ear that heard it would know.

"And what is she to you?"

"My niece, the daughter of my heart." As she said the words, Kezia felt a ruffle in her mind, as if someone were thumbing through a deck of cards. Strom held her gaze intensely. Kezia's memories of Bella flooded up, despite her trying to hold them back. Precious memories were pulled from her. Bella as a baby, nursing at her own breast, Bella toddling towards Ebbe, arms outstretched, Bella playing in the pond with Malik, Bella dancing on the stage, her scarlet ribbons and curly black hair swinging to the beating of Ebbe's bohdran drum.

Kezia's heart thudded in tempo with the memory of Bella's dancing feet. Kezia's anxiety rose, replacing the cold surety she'd clung to only moments before. Strom was pulling memories out of her skull! What if he saw the deathly deception they were in the midst of next? Kezia fought the pull of Strom's mind, but he was strong, so strong. His face swam into her vision, coming closer, pulling harder.

She heard his voice inside of her head. "If I cannot take and make my own the daughter of the witch who murdered my wife and child, her sister will do. Yes, you will do to create a new child for me. Four live children you have borne, you are a fertile wench, a breeder."

Kezia screamed, tried to break free of his hold on her. The pain started then, immense, bone cracking pain that moved up her spine, across her shoulders, into her head. She saw Strom smile. His nose twitched as he inhaled. The pressure inside of her brain increased. His eyes bored into her.

She heard his voice again, pounding, insistent. "There's more. You've conceived a deception…"

Kezia struggled, but found herself immobile. Trapped, she was trapped. In a moment, he'd discover that Bella wasn't really dead. Strom's hands cupped like a mendicant, reaching for the sides of her face, his mind intent on forcing all her memories from her, insistent on learning the secret she was trying so hard to keep hidden from him.

Kezia did the only thing she could think to do.

She spit in his face.

He startled back, shocked. The feeling of fingers shuffling through her mind stopped. The rictus of pain up her spine lessened. Kezia knew in some distant part of her she should try to run, disappear into the dark, but she was utterly drained.

Strom turned away from her and wiped the moisture from his face. He turned back again, disgust and anger wracking his face so that he resembled a gargoyle on a church roof. His eyes flipped back in his head, blind whites gleaming. Kezia felt a tremor move through her body. A cold breeze blew up the back of her neck. He raised his left hand, the sleeve fell back from it, his pale skin throbbing. The ruby on his ring caught the light from the flames of the torches. Strom opened his mouth to speak a binding curse Kezia could feel it roiling and building in the air between them. In a few seconds, he would possess her utterly.

A snarl broke from the darkness. A shaggy form leapt on her, knocking Kezia to the ground. Her head knocked against the stone of the street. She welcomed the solid pain of it, instead of the hideous pain of possession she'd been fighting. Kezia could feel the hot breath of the creature next to her, heard its panting. She tried to raise her head. Shouts of alarm and confusion from the men echoed down the street.

"Wolf!"

"Nay, 'tis a man!"

Above the cacophony, Strom's voice carried through clear. "Kill it."

Kezia felt a hand, or perhaps it was teeth, tugging at her sleeve, trying to get her to move. With all the strength left in her, Kezia pulled herself up and faced the creature that had knocked her to the ground and had broken the binding spell. She saw brown eyes with golden flecks that shone bright and clear. Saw the curling red hair of her son. The son that had just saved her from betraying Bella and had saved her from Strom's possession.

She heard men rushing towards them, saw the fear in her son's eyes. Knew the guards were closing in with their weapons. With a smile only for Stefan, infused with all the love a mother holds for their child, Kezia surged to her feet and stood tall. She flung her arms out wide, using her body as a shield to block the three sharp spears that were aimed at her son. Her breath huffed out of her body, and she saw the tips of the three blades that had pierced through her back emerge from her chest. Her eyes swam with tears as she looked one last time at her boy. Everything was darkening so quickly. Her last breath sighed out like a blessing.

"Run."

Kezia's final mortal vision was her unscathed son loping into the darkness. She sank to her knees, and as she collapsed to the ground, her smile remained. For there, standing next to her, was Timbo, whole and unmarked, his face full of love, his hand extended to lift her home.

CHAPTER TWENTY-THREE

Malik crouched low in the house of the dead. He'd carefully placed the waterskin Bella would need in the back corner of the room when he'd entered. Surely it would only be a few moments before the door opened, and they brought Bella inside. He'd heard the commotion when the cart arrived, had smiled when Kezia used the Sleeping Beauty trick to alert Ebbe and Vadoma. That was smart. But now, time was clicking away, and Bella's life with it. The cart had pulled up outside long ago. Why weren't they bringing Bella inside? He shifted his weight back and forth as the rumble of conversation continued. He couldn't just sit here and do nothing. Maybe he could at least get a head start on their rescue attempt. He moved to the back door of the charnel house and opened it. After examining the mechanism, he carefully tore a strip off a dead man's shirt. Malik carefully tied it around the metal hasp so that the latch couldn't fall and lock him out.

He paused, then went back and took another strip from the man's shirt. He tried not to touch the cold greasiness of the man's skin as he did so. Stealing from the dead was frowned upon by everyone, but he thought perhaps in this case, he would be forgiven. Muttering a thanks and a blessing in the man's direction, he hurried back outside again.

In the small courtyard, Malik saw the walls were indeed too high to climb, as Bella had said. There was a big pile of straw in one corner, no doubt there to use in tomorrow's executions and punishments. The sight of the straw filled him with resolve. He moved to the jailhouse door. Removing his lock picks from his pocket, he got to work pushing the iron pins back. He blinked back the burn of sweat in his eyes. The shouting outside was even louder now. Malik's anxiety caused him to rub his tense neck. He wondered if he should sneak back into the dead house, but he was close to conquering the lock.

It was the stern command to "Kill it." that shook him. Kill what? The shouting outside grew in volume. Something terrible was happening with their plan. He had to decide. Should he go back and wait for Bella? Any delay in giving her the reviving potion would result in her dying. Or should he use the distraction outside to get Vadoma and Ebbe out of the jail on his own? His stomach churned, and he nearly gave up on the jail lock.

Then the lock clicked back with a solid thump. The choice was made. He had to move forward now. Taking a deep breath, he pushed the door. The hinges on the door creaked. He froze, but could hear nothing from inside the jail. Binding the lock open with the second piece of cloth, he eased his way into the empty corridor. Bella had said the stairs to the dungeon were on the left. As his eyes adjusted to the musty dark, Malik could discern an orange glow below him.

Feeling his way forward, he found the curving stairs that led down towards that orange glow. He was committed now, no turning back. He descended into the stench of the dungeon. Blood, overtopped by vomit, piss, and excrement. Turning the final corner of the spiral, he saw they had left a single torch burning, along with a hot brazier used to heat some sharp metal implements. Their tips glowed red in the dark.

Malik saw the shapes of a half-dozen people languishing in the shadows of the terrible place. Some were chained by their ankles, others hung by their wrists. He felt his courage ebb as he caught glimpses of the wounds they bore in the dim light. Most of the prisoners didn't have the strength to look at him, but one pair of eyes did. They were in the pale face of an ancient old woman with flowing white hair, chained by her arms above her to the wall. She was shaking her head at him, as if she were telling him not to do something.

"Malik." The woman spoke in a horse croak.

He startled; his heart raced. How did this stranger know his name? Maybe these prisoners really were witches after all, imbued with secret knowing. He backed up a step, anxiety flaring. He heard chains clanking on the stone, saw that the old woman was straining to lean closer to him on hideously bloated legs that seemed to belong to another creature. She'd been crippled from hanging by her arms too long, his mind whispered to him.

The woman spoke again, more clearly this time. "Malik. Get out of here." The effort seemed to drain her utterly, as she fell back against the wall, the fall of white hair obscuring her face.

A man covered with blood chained to a stone block in the center of the pit shifted and moaned. He tried to speak. Despite his growing fear, Malik shuffled closer to the wreck of a human. The man's face was blackened by filth and bruises. One eye was swollen completely shut, the other barely slitted open. Blood and straw matted in his hair, and his shirt was in tatters, barely covering multiple bloody cuts across his chest.

"Help Vadoma," the man said. He raised his arm with great effort, pointing it towards the woman who had just spoken. His hand was swollen to twice its normal size, fully black. The fingers dangled as if they were attached solely by the putrefying skin. The man's single working eye glinted gold as he tried to convey his need.

Malik gasped. The ancient white-haired woman hanging on the wall was Vadoma, and this broken man before him was

Ebbe. Malik fell to his knees, aghast at what had happened to two of the strongest people he knew. How had her hair turned white overnight? How could Ebbe endure the pain?

He was in danger of being overcome by grief and fear. He must channel it into something else. Malik smashed his feelings into a hard anger and used it to brush aside Ebbe's plea to help Vadoma first. She wouldn't be able to walk. He'd have to carry her. Glancing down, he saw that Ebbe's feet were still intact. He'd put Ebbe up on his feet ahead of him. He could carry and push the pair at the same time if he had to. Malik knew he had to.

Teeth gritted, Malik went to work with his lock-picking tools, blessing the long lessons his mother had insisted on, working on picking multiple locks. She hated seeing anyone chained. If it were his mother down here, she'd insist on freeing all the prisoners, but Malik knew he only had minutes to get these two people up the stairs and hiding in the room of the dead. He gritted his will against feeling guilt and worked the locks.

Once Ebbe was free, Malik pointed to the stairs. "I'll be right behind you with Vadoma, but you have to start up those, Ebbe. Can you do that?"

Ebbe grunted. Malik put his arms under the man and, with an effort, pulled him to his feet, steadying him as he swayed. "Walk, Ebbe, *asrae!*" The man put a slow foot in front of the other in a shuffle. Malik turned his attention to Vadoma.

She seemed to have regained some of her strength, seeing Ebbe crossing the floor. She tried to help Malik, making the chains tight so he could more easily work the locks. He avoided looking at the way the cuffs had ripped the skin off her arms and wrists nearly down to the bone. Another problem he'd have to solve. Neither of these people could climb anything, let alone maneuver themselves through the narrow windows in the charnel house. Well, one dilemma at a time. He caught Vadoma when the chains released. As he expected, the woman could not stand.

Malik swept Vadoma up in his arms. "Put your arms around my neck and help me as much as you can," Malik said.

Ebbe was on his knees and elbows, crawling up the stairs, his ruined hands dangling painfully. They had to move faster. Malik edged around Ebbe and took Vadoma to the top of the stairs. He set her down in the corner, then rushed back down and grabbed Ebbe around his waist. He hauled the broken man to his feet. Malik groaned at the weight and nearly fell over. "You must try to walk, Ebbe. I cannot carry you." He could feel the man's chest wounds open up and gush blood over his hands, making them slick with gore, but he didn't let go, lifting Ebbe up with each too-slow step.

They reached the top of the stairs. Vadoma looked panicked, pointing down the hallway. Malik listened and heard the voices of men muttering as they filed back into the jail. They'd be back here in moments!

Keeping his grasp around Ebbe, he bent down and commanded Vadoma. "Put your arms around my neck. Use all your strength!" Malik's limbs shook with the effort, but he stood and propelled Ebbe out the door, dragging Vadoma behind him, her arms choking him as she hung on, her useless legs dragging behind. They both tried their best to help him, moving what they could. Now they were in the courtyard. Only a few more feet to go before they were in the house of the dead.

Later, Malik had no memory of how he managed those final yards, nor how he was able to open the dead house door and tumble into it with his burden. He eased Ebbe and Vadoma down to the floor, and then rushed to pull the cloth from the back door allowing it to shut, plunging them into darkness with the dead. He lay on his back, panting, his arms and legs burning.

The darkness lasted only a moment as the front door creaked open, not long enough for Malik to convey a plan. He just had to pray that they had the sense to stay still. The two men charged with collecting bodies started carrying them inside. Malik closed his eyes so that he was only peeping out from under his eyelashes. He tried to make his breathing slow and silent.

The two men were efficient in completing their task. They worked silently as they piled over a dozen bodies onto the shelving lining the room. Once done, they shut the door shut again. Malik placed a hand on Ebbe and Vadoma to make sure they were still breathing and to reassure them he was still with them. Only Vadoma seemed responsive. Malik wondered if Ebbe had mercifully passed out from the pain of his wounds.

He had to find Bella fast. Malik was sure more than an hour had passed since she'd taken the deadly poison. He might be too late. He moved silently forward. It'd seemed that the men had placed men's bodies on the right side of the room, and women on the left. He wished there were more light, but he couldn't risk opening the back door. Someone would discover that Ebbe and Vadoma were gone at any moment. He felt his breath quicken at the pressure of not having enough time. A small part of him simply wanted to crawl out of the window and flee.

He couldn't see, so he'd have to go by feel. He squashed the dread that continued to build inside of him and focused on finding Bella. She was counting on him. He reached out his hands to where the newest bodies had been tossed. The first body was wizened and cold, not Bella. The next was cold and stiff. The third body was warm to the touch. Maybe it was her! He raised the body up so that the weak light coming through the windows shone upon the face.

Malik gasped in horror and nearly dropped the body. It was Kezia. Her face was peaceful, with a smile etched upon her lips. Malik bent back towards her, hoping that it wasn't true, that she wasn't dead. He put his ear to her lips but heard no breath. *Djinns,* their plan had gone terrifyingly wrong. Malik's heart thudded. He heard rustling in the back. Ebbe or Vadoma were perhaps trying to rise. He must not let them see Kezia! It would be their undoing. Quickly, he rolled her so that her face was to the wall. Fighting tears, he continued to search for warmth, for life.

At last, he touched another warm body. Tugging it from the pile, he looked. It was Bella! Praying he was not too late, Malik scrabbled for the flask containing the potion inside of his clothes. His heart clenched as he touched broken edges. *No!*

He pulled out the remains of the container. Only a small amount of liquid was in the flask's bottom, the rest lost and soaked into his shirt. He stared at the broken thing, wishing with every fiber of his being that it wasn't true.

He must have crushed it while he was trying to lift Ebbe up the stairs. Despair filled every part of him. He'd failed her. Failed all of them. Malik slumped to the floor, wishing he were one of the dead, too. He prayed for an answer, something he could do with all his might.

Bella's words came to him. "If you run into trouble, just think to yourself, what would Bella do?" He almost laughed. He didn't know what she would do. He couldn't think. She always had such crazy ideas. Even when they were little, it'd been Bella who thought up their adventures.

Then an idea came to him.

Malik pulled his shirt over his head, felt with his fingers, smelled for the potion. It smelled like rotted elderberries and tree bark, he remembered. He found a large damp patch that smelled like that. Taking a deep breath and holding onto hope this would work, he sucked at the damp spot. No matter that there was dirt, sweat, and blood mixed in as well. His *ummah* made potent mixes.

Malik nearly gagged at the bitter taste, but was heartened. He had perhaps half a spoon in his mouth now. He quickly put the rest of the potion that was still in the bottle into his mouth as well. Malik moved to Bella and lifted her limp form in his arms. Held her head up with gentle fingers.

He bent and kissed her. He teased open her lips and let the liquid antidote trickle in from his mouth. Malik stroked his thumbs along her neck to make her swallow the precious fluid. He stayed in the embrace, murmuring encouragement softly into her ear. "Live. Live."

Nothing happened. Bella stayed limp in his arms. Her body seemed cool. Had he been too late?

He held her closer to him, kissed her in earnest this time. He tasted the salt of tears and realized they were his own. "Bella," he whispered. "Come back."

Thump.

Malik held his breath, continued to hold Bella tightly to him. He hoped, oh, he hoped.

Thump, thump.

Her heart. Her heart was beating. He kissed her again. "Bella," he called softly.

With a giant gasp, Bella sat upright, gulping in air as if she had never breathed before. Inside the house of the dead, life bloomed once more.

CHAPTER TWENTY-FOUR

S he was going to be sick. Pushing the solid warm body she knew was Malik away, she leaned over and vomited. Saints, it was gross. Bella only had time to take another deep breath when the next wave took her. She felt gentle hands gather up her hair, holding it back for her as sicked up yet again.

Malik was holding her hair. Bella would've smiled if she could. It sounded more romantic than it was in actuality, but he was doing it all the same. She felt in her bodice for the nappies she had tucked there and wiped her face.

"You did it," she whispered. Her throat felt raw and painful. It was all she could do to roll back over and lie flat on her back. Every joint ached. "Is there water?"

"There is." Malik moved out of her sight and returned a moment later with it. He raised her up gently and helped her take a drink. The first swallow was painful, the second less so. She breathed in and out, getting used to the feeling of her lungs filling again. Every breath hurt.

Malik seemed agitated. He pulled the water away when she reached for the skin again. "There're others here who need it," he explained. Bella was confused. Did he mean himself? Malik moved to the back of the dead house. She heard him murmuring to someone. Cautiously, she maneuvered to sit up. She edged one foot down on the floor, and then the next. Using her hands to help, she stood up. It was touch and go for a moment, but then she found her balance. Her vision was still a bit grey around the edges, but she assumed that would clear up as she rid herself of the poison she'd ingested.

She shuffled to Malik, focusing on pushing one foot in front of the other. She had to concentrate on each tiny movement of her feet and legs, as if she were learning to walk all over again. Bella made a promise to herself. *I will never, never drink a potion made with Belladonna again.* She felt like apologizing to each of the bodies she used to keep her balance as she moved. Her sense of smell was coming back, and the putrefying bodies were triggering her gag reflex. The last thing she wanted was to be sick again, so she breathed through her mouth.

Malik was helping an old woman to her feet when she reached them. Had they put someone in here who wasn't dead? Her thoughts scrambled as she looked at the woman, who seemed nearly beyond help, broken and defeated. Her long white hair was matted and stained with blood and more. The woman's hands shook. Then she looked up. It was her mother.

Bella clapped her hand over her mouth to stop the scream that wanted to erupt as she recognized her. What had Vadoma endured to make her hair turn white overnight? It was horrifying. Tears sprang into Bella's eyes. Vadoma held her arms out, and Bella saw how savaged her wrists were from being bound. Carefully, for she felt like her mother might break if she held her too hard, Bella hugged her mother, and realized this might be the first time she had done so willingly in her life. She heard Vadoma whisper, "My Bella, my sweet girl."

Her mother was looking at her with love from a ravaged face. It was all too much. Bella had to step back and nearly fell over a dead body. She didn't know how to feel about her mother. She'd never practiced saying loving things to her. Bella saw her mother shiver. This she could help. Pulling off one of the extra shawls she'd worn for just this reason, she tied it around her mother's shoulders. "Here, I have an extra dress for you as well." She stepped out of it and helped Vadoma dress as if she were the child and Bella the adult. It was all so odd.

Malik's voice broke in, low and urgent. "We must go."

"I know!" she whispered back. Bella rounded on him, her voice filled with a mix of regret and wonderment.

"You rescued her without me!"

"Them. I rescued them. Now we need to get them out of here."

Bella cursed herself for being so slow to understand. She looked past her mother and saw the wreck that was her father. She pulled back a sob. "Da, what've they done to you?"

Vadoma spoke. "He stood up to him. To Strom." Pride seeped through her voice.

Malik pulled Ebbe up to a sitting position. "Please drink the water," he begged. Bella knelt and joined him. "Come on, Da, we need to leave." Together, she and Malik helped him take a drink. Bella saw her father's hands. How could such broken things ever be fixed? *No time to think about it now.*

Malik pulled her aside. He looked worried. "Your parents cannot climb out the windows in their condition."

Bella nodded, thinking hard. "They'll have to go out the front. I'll distract the guard."

"Bella, are you sure?"

"Of course, what, are you going to borrow my dancing skills do it?" Bella covered her nerves by scoffing at Malik. "Let me check something," she said.

Clambering up the pile of bodies, she peeked out the narrow windows and down into the alley below. Good, the cart they used to haul the dead in was stored right next to the building, as she'd remembered from the previous day. So much had happened in less than a day.

She scrambled down. Hurried to her parents and spoke with authority. "You must stand right by the entrance and be ready to get into the cart quickly. I know it will be difficult, but then we'll be away and to the Darkwood and safety." She waited until she got nods from both, then turned to Malik. "Malik, you pull that cart around from the side. We could wish for a horse, but we've got none. Once they're in the cart, I'll help you pull, and we'll run for the river." She paused, took a breath. "I know the way," she added wryly.

"The river's a dead end. Why would we do that?" Malik asked.

"We're going straight into it, use the cart as a float, and let the river carry us to the camp." Her mother's mouth dropped open, and she turned to Ebbe. Ebbe nodded slowly. "Aye," he said.

Malik opened his mouth as if to protest, then shut it again. "It doesn't matter if it's a crazy plan. You're just going to say it's the only plan we've got, aren't you?"

Bella nodded. "That's right. The cart is wood, so it'll float well enough. Let's hope so, anyway. Ready?"

She and Malik climbed up the heap of corpses a final time. Malik let Bella wiggle through first, holding her wrists so that her drop to the ground was shorter. She landed hard but remembered to roll. Everything in her body still ached from the poison she had taken, but she forced herself to keep moving.

Malik landed beside her, light as a cat. He looked at the large, sturdy cart and winced a bit. "I know you can do it," Bella said, more stoutly than she actually felt. She peeked around the corner. As she expected, just a single guard was posted. She couldn't tell if it was the same one from the night before. Pulling out the finger cymbals she'd sentimentally taken from backstage, and then yanking down the bodice of her dress so that she displayed as much of herself as she dared, Bella took a deep breath. She shook out her long, flowing hair. It was time for the performance of her life.

CHAPTER TWENTY-FIVE

T ing, ting. Ting, ting. The bright, metallic sound bounced off the cold stone walls and street. It was an odd sound for this part of the city. The guard peered into the darkness. He was already shaken from the events earlier in the evening and wanted no more surprises tonight. He tightened his grip on his spear, ready to use it at the slightest provocation. The guard listened intently, but after a bit, he relaxed again. Maybe it had been some tinker working late, the light breeze bearing the sound from far off.

Ting, ting. Tinga-tinga-tinga. Ting. There it was again. It was closer this time, or at least louder. He moved a few steps into the street to look up and down, cursing to himself when he stepped in a wet pile of filth. Probably someone's foul body part that had fallen off the dead wagon. He leaned on his spear and shook his foot to get rid of whatever it was he'd stepped in. This was the worst posting in the city, he thought to himself. Sure, all the youngest guards had to do it, but he'd been stuck in this post for nigh on two years now.

He sighed as he stepped back to the door of the charnel house. Looked over to the door of the prison. It was shut now; the night guard were probably all sleeping off a good drunk, the rat bastards. Here he was, having to stay awake. He shifted his feet.

Even though the summer was nearly upon them, at this early hour of the morning, it was chill and damp. A light fog swirled up from the river, bringing with it a musky stink that had him wishing for the crackle of a warm fire and a nice bowl of soup to warm both hands and belly.

Tinga-tinga-tinga. There was that sound again! This time, when the guard looked out into the street, he saw movement. Remembering protocols, he stood straighter and stared straight ahead, although he shifted his eyes to keep the movement in sight as it got closer. It was sinuous, flowing like skirts, perhaps. Yes, it was a girl with long dark hair, moving down the streets using finger cymbals. One of those gypsies in for the festival, no doubt. Although word was that most of them had fled during the night after the arrests had been made. Pity, he'd wanted to see one of their shows.

Maybe a show was coming to him. He perked up at the thought as the girl entered his full range of vision. She smiled at him, her long, slanted eyes taking him in. He wished there was enough light to see the color of them. He could see that her hair was dark and bountiful. Her dress certainly left little to the imagination. He felt a smile creeping over his face. At first he tried to stop it, after all, he was on duty. But then, why not? What harm was there at smiling at a pretty girl?

The gypsy girl swayed before him and raised her arms so that the dress slipped even further down her chest. She moved, her feet making little pivots, unmindful of the filth they trod in. She moved her hips in a suggestive way and the guard found he had to adjust himself. She moved closer, all of her attention upon him. He felt himself heating. Beads of sweat formed at the top of his head where the round metal helmet weighed so heavily. She saw the sweat, he could tell. She was only a foot away from him now, swaying so seductively.

With a smile on her face, she removed the finger cymbals slowly, tucking them into the low bodice of her dress. He followed the trail of her fingers as they seductively dipped low, and then lower still. He licked his lips. She inched closer, raised her arms, and removed his helmet. Using those long fingers that had just been in such an interesting place, she brushed his hair back.

She pressed herself close to him. Moved her hands to his shoulders. Slid down his arms. He was rock hard now, his mind focused fully on her. She was beautiful. She was so close that he could see the velvet of her skin, the golden gleam of her eyes, the powerful arch of her lips that were parted ever so slightly. It mesmerized the guard to see her tongue extend, run around her lips. He felt her take away his spear. He didn't care. His hands freed, he reached around her and pulled the gypsy to him, using her round buttocks as leverage. Kissed her deep and long.

She responded eagerly, her hands racing down, down to clutch him, untie his breeches. He moaned and pushed up against her. She kissed him even more passionately, moved her hands to clutch at his wrists, spinning with him to roll away from the door, so that her back was to the wall. Away from his post. Dimly, some part of his mind was sternly telling him to do his duty and let this strumpet go on her way. In the next moment, he was gleefully discarding that voice. He'd have this girl that was so intent on having him. After all, she was just a gypsy.

Roughly, he pushed her against the wall, reached inside her bodice and yanked the cymbals out, tossing them to the ground. She made a surprised sound and broke the kiss. He grinned. Oh ho! So she had just been in for a tease. Thought he was just a boy to toy with. Well, she was in for a surprise. A big surprise, if he did say so himself. He scrabbled at the strings holding on his breastplate and shoved it off. There, now he could pin her properly against the stone. She was peasant stock; gypsies could take the rough. She seemed to be trying to say something, but he covered her mouth with his own. No talking, just pleasure. His pleasure for the taking. He pulled up her dress, eager, so eager.

Blinding pain. Cold penetrating pain. It swept through his body like an ice bath. Grunting, he bent over, understanding at a primitive level that the little bitch had kneed him in the balls. He couldn't catch his breath, but when he did, she was going to pay for this. As he was bent over, he caught a flash of movement. He turned his head and saw too late that he was going to be knocked out by his own helmet. He felt it crack against his head and knew no more.

CHAPTER TWENTY-SIX

"Did you have to kiss him so thoroughly?" hissed Malik as he hauled the wagon around to the door. Bella looked up from where she was dragging the hapless soldier into the dead house. Malik's face was red, both from the effort and his pique.

"I was pretending it was you!" she said in a huff. "And anyway, it worked!" She thanked the stars above the man had discarded the heavy armored breast plate as she pulled his bulk inside. She put the breastplate and the helmet inside as well. Double-checked to make sure the guard was still breathing. Her parents hobbled forward, and Bella helped them get into the cart. It was an awkward business, with Vadoma barely able to walk and Ebbe unable to use his hands. Bella's alarm grew when she realized she could see them clearly as she helped boost them up and into the bed of the cart. Full dawn wasn't far away. They had to be long gone before then.

Malik had the oddest look on his face as she climbed down from the wagon. At first she thought he was still angry at her seduction of the guard, but then Bella realized it was something else. Her impatience to leave caused her voice to come out with a snap.

"What is it, Malik?"

He was silent for several moments, tried to speak. She was about to brush him off and move to pull the cart when he took her by the shoulders. "There's someone else in there, someone we have to bring with us."

Confused, Bella thought he meant the guard at first. But then she realized he was fighting some deep emotion. The muscle on the side of his cheek was popping, and his eyes pooled with tears. Cold gripped her heart. What else could possibly have gone wrong? Malik pulled her into a fierce hug and clung to her. She wrapped her arms around him.

"I want you to blindfold your parents, Bella. They can't see her right now, it would finish them, I'm sure of it," he said in a harsh whisper into her ear. "Please, just do it."

Surprised, Bella nodded, and climbed back up into the cart, her legs aching with the effort. Ripping pieces off her skirts, she moved to her parents. "This will make your journey easier. Just trust us, we'll get you safe." At any other time, she would have gotten protestation, but both Ebbe and Vadoma were utterly drained. They were like discarded rag dolls leaning back against the sides of the cart. She tied the cloth around their eyes, then turned around.

She clapped her hands to her mouth when she saw who Malik carried in his arms. The scream welled up inside her, wanting to rip free. It was only by the strongest effort of will that she stopped it from coming out. It couldn't be. It couldn't.

Choking down sobs, Bella reached down to help put the body of her aunt into the cart. She clamped her lips tight, trying to keep her devastation from seeping out. She could see everything so clearly as the sun rose. The blood covering Kezia's torso, the unearthly pallor of her cool skin. She swallowed hard, forced her mind back to the task at hand. Tradesmen and the change of the guard would walk the streets at any moment. They had to leave.

Malik shut the door to the charnel house. Bella hopped down and grabbed one of the wooden shaft poles that were used to hitch the horse to the cart. Malik grabbed the other one and together they pulled. At first, the laden cart refused to budge. They dug in, and it inched forward. A few more heaving steps and the cart rolled.

Bella was beyond grateful that the road to the river was nearly straight and travelled downhill. The cart moved faster and faster as they went. "Lay down and hold on!" Bella called out to her parents as she moved into a quick jog, then a run, she and Malik racing to keep the cart straight between them as it bounced down the uneven paving stones. The road got worse the closer to the river they got, and Ebbe cried out in pain as he was jostled and flung side to side.

Bella heard shouts from behind them, and glancing over, saw Malik heard them too. His face hardened, and his focus intensified. They reached the slope of the riverbank, and the fast-moving cart slowed to a crawl halfway up the steep-sided embankment that kept the water from pouring into the city during floods. Straining, they hauled at the wagon, the weight nearly more than Bella could move. Just a few more feet, then they were over the crest. The river fog was thicker here, the early morning still greyed. Her feet slid on the wet grass as they tilted down the other side. She tried to brake with her legs. The momentum of the cart was overpowering after only a few yards.

"We just have to run with it!" shouted Malik.

Bella gasped for air and nodded as they made the final sprint to the river, fighting to keep the wooden arms up and the cart from tipping over on the uneven grass. Bella stumbled and nearly fell, her upper body tilting dangerously far forward beyond her feet. Somehow, she stayed upright as they raced down the embankment.

The river glistened pink in the early dawn. A layer of fog floated above the water. Golden rays filtered horizontally, bestowing color onto what had been simply graduated greys. Moments later, the sun shot a brilliant pathway straight across the river, marking a golden path seemingly just for them. They arrowed down it. The sparkle off the water was blinding. Angling her head down to make sure she didn't trip again, Bella noticed she was covered in dirt and gore. The wagon twisted and rattled down the final few steps, wheel hubs groaning with the strain as they reached the river's edge.

"Don't stop!" Bella called out. She and Malik rushed into the river along with the cart. Gasping at the sudden cold of the water, Bella hoped she was right, that the heaviness of the cart wouldn't simply sink and take all of them with it. Hoped that her thanks to these waters earlier had somehow graced the way for them to survive this last bit of their flight.

The coldness of the water felt like it was sucking the life out of her. Bella breathed in tiny gasps as it moved over her legs and then her waist. It swept her feet from beneath her as the current caught them. She saw Malik clinging to the other shaft as he, too, was caught.

"Kick!" he shouted. Bella did so, just as the first arrow struck the water by her face. She felt the breath of it whiz by her cheek and ducked down lower into the water. She kicked harder, felt the cart swing out behind her, also taken by the current. Two more arrows splashed by her in quick succession, and she thought she heard another strike wood. Hoped the time it would take to reload quarrels into the crossbows would allow them to get out of range. Thank the heavens that the rising sun was in the archer's eyes.

Risking a glance backwards, she saw the cart was low in the water, and the river was slopping over the sides of the cart. There was nothing she could do for her parents right now except to try and keep the cart balanced and flat in the freezing cold water.

She shook with cold and exhaustion as she kicked. Her legs moved more and more slowly. Vicious cramps seized up first her toes and then her calves. That last run had pulled out her final bit of energy. Bella clung to the wooden shaft, utterly drained. She knew she had to hold on, but it was all so hard. Her aunt was dead, her uncle too. Her parents were broken, just like the curse had promised. *She had caused all of this.* She struggled to breathe, even though her head was still above water. Her head lowered closer to the water, and it greedily reached up, soaking her hair, lapping at her lips. It would be so easy to slip away. Maybe everything would stop hurting. Maybe no one else would suffer.

"Bella!" She realized Malik had been calling to her. She looked at him weakly. She could no longer feel her hands on the wood. All she had to do was to just let go. "Bella, keep trying!" he begged. Part of her wanted to. But it made more sense to let go, really it would be better for everyone, she was just so tired, so sad, so very…

She heard her father's voice. Singing. She tilted her head, the one that felt that it weighed ten thousand pounds, out of the water to listen to the tune. He lifted up the song as he had a thousand times before on their journeys. It was a melody she'd heard as a baby. A song her father's father and his before him had sung. She clung to the sound of her father's voice like a lifeline as the river continued to tug them along.

"Would you like to come for a ride? We'll go so high. And if you've got the faith, we'll climb up to the sky; Our wagon wheels keep rolling on, our caravan keeps movin' on. Through streams and over mountains, through valleys and over the hills, through meadows and across the plains, our wagon wheels keep rolling on."

Her father's voice quavered. The words slurred, but it was enough. Bella sucked in the cool morning air, let it fill her lungs and on the exhale, she released her bitterness and self-pity, gritted her teeth, and forced her cramping legs to kick. The town flowed past them on the left, giving way to fields. Each breath she took became easier. At last, in the distance, she saw the open space where the Travellers had made their camp. Thankfully, the current slowed as the river curved. Bella wearily pushed and kicked to move the cart out of the main current so they could come ashore.

Bella saw that the Traveller's camp was already empty. News must have spread quickly. With all the troubles, their caravan had decided to move on. Just two wagons remained at the site. One had the bright swirls of red, violet, and yellow that meant home. Next to it was a plain brown and green one. Both were hitched up and ready to leave.

Bella's heart twisted when she saw the girl who stood atop the brown and green wagon. The girl waved both arms, and clambered down from her perch, running to the river to help. Rose. She was about to discover that not only her father, but now her mother, too, was dead. Bella felt like she would split in two with sorrow. She focused on getting the cart to the shore. She had to take everything one moment at a time.

Bella's feet brushed the bottom. Grateful to feel solid footing again, she pushed her feet down into the mud. Tugged with Malik until the wheels of the cart wedged into the side of the river. She desperately wanted to collapse onto the shore and rest, but instead she staggered up the bank to clasp Rose in her arms. The girl was laughing and crying at the same time. Her cousin hugged her for a moment, then pushed away.

"You're soaking wet. Let go of me, Bella!" Rose said, wiping her eyes. "I just got into a dry dress, and—"

"Rose, look at me. Look at me." Bella held her at arm's length, saw that Rose's beautiful hair had been shorn, leaving her nearly bald. She swallowed. "Be strong, now. Stronger than you've ever been."

Rose looked at her with confusion, swiping her cheeks with her palms. "What do you mean, I see you rescued both of them, they're alive! Saints, your mother's hair has gone completely white!"

A broken cry of pain stopped Bella from responding. "Kezia! No! My sister!" Vadoma's voice cracked as she groaned in agony.

Rose's face blanked, all the color draining from it. Bella couldn't think of anything to say or do, except let her go. She buried her face in her hands, not wanting to see the agony on Rose's face as she rushed into the river and looked over the side of the cart.

"Mama!" Rose shrieked. She tried to climb into the cart, but fell, her skirts tangling, soaking in the shallow water. Bella rushed down and with Malik, they raised her up out of the water, held her back.

"You'll upset the cart if you try to climb it," Malik said quickly. "I'm sorry, Rose, I'm so sorry."

"What happened? What happened to her?" Rose turned to Bella and sobbed into her shoulder.

"I don't know." Bella hugged her as hard as she could. Over the girl's shoulder, she looked at Malik, who shook his head. In the wagon, she heard the low moans of her mother, saw Ebbe crawling to her side.

Bella realized she was shaking, and not just with cold. The whole rescue was in danger of being for nothing if they didn't pull themselves together and get to the safety of the forest. The guards would've alerted the authorities. They'd gained time by using the river, but they were losing it.

"Malik, help me get Ebbe and Vadoma to our wagon," she said with authority. "Then go ahead and start driving, don't wait for us." He nodded and moved to the back of the wagon. Bella heard him murmuring to her parents, urging her father to step out and onto the bank.

Her father gave her a wan smile. "My brave girl." Bella warmed at his praise, and without thinking, reached to take his hands. She stopped herself just in time. Instead, she held his dear face in her palms, and kissed him on the forehead.

Ebbe nodded and then slowly made his way up the hill, his hands dangling uselessly at his sides. They were hard to look at, the once strong and expressive fingers now black and limp, all the bones crushed. Inspiration struck, and she grabbed Malik's arm as he walked by. "Malik, the first village you come to on the eastern road, past the first outliers of the forest, you must take Ebbe there. There's a girl there, with sky-blue eyes. Her name is Henna. Her mother is a healer. Henna knows who I am."

Malik looked uncertain, looking back towards the city. He knew as well as she did that Strom would mount a hunt for them. He had a wildness about him that spoke of wanting to run and keep running. Bella grabbed his hand. "You must, do you hear? I'll be along as soon as I can."

He pulled his hand from her grasp. "Don't tell me I 'must' do something. You know asking for help from villagers is not our way, Bella. It only invites trouble." His voice was hard.

"Aye, I know well that we Travellers are distrusted and disliked, Malik. Ebbe needs a healer."

"Haven't I done enough for them? For you?"

Bella felt like he'd slapped her. A few hours ago, she thought they'd always be united by this rescue. She'd felt so full of love for him, had thought he felt the same for her. Her hurt boiled into sarcasm.

"You don't have to stay with them. You can move on if you're that afraid."

Malik clenched his jaw. "It's not safe, Bella. T'was sheer luck we're all not locked away waiting for the hangman this morning. I didn't take you for a fool before, but now you're showing nothing but foolishness."

Bella grabbed him and pulled him close so that Rose could not hear. "If you don't find him a healer, our rescue of him will be for nothing. He'll die of those wounds. The grief of it will carry away my mother too. Do you want that on your conscience?

That you could've finished the job, but didn't, out of cowardice?"

Malik fisted his hands. His nostrils flared as he fought to keep his temper in check. Bella didn't care if he was mad, she was just as furious with him. He took a careful step back from her, and his eyes raked her with their fury. "Have it your way, princess. Fine, I'll risk my life and theirs once again on something you say must happen. I'll find Henna and leave your parents if they'll tolerate it. But I'll not be staying with them. I'll be moving on without them. Without you."

His mouth twisted as he turned away from her. She wanted to yell at him. She wanted to run to him and tell him she was sorry. Instead, Bella found herself rooted in place. She watched as he carefully lifted her mother from the cart and strode past her without another word.

He'd given his promise to find Henna's mother. That had to be enough for now. He was angry, and sure enough, she'd given him reason to be. It'd been a terrible night, and they weren't out of danger yet.

She turned to her cousin, found her staring into the distance at nothing. Bella wanted to shake her into wakefulness, but instead spoke in soft tones as she would to a wounded animal. "Rose, we're going to put your mother into your wagon with your father. We're going to put them together and take them into the forest."

Rose's breathing hitched. She struggled to get her words out. "Mama is dead. Papa is dead. How can they both be dead?" She looked at Bella with bewilderment and pain etched on her face.

Bella wished she had answers, wished she could magically whisk Rose's anguish away. She settled for holding her hands. "It's awful. But we have to go, we have to get into the woods so that Strom's soldiers don't catch us. Can you do that?"

Rose took several fast breaths, and then nodded. Her tears continued to fall as she waded into the river alongside Bella.

Together they pulled Kezia's body out and carried it to the shore. Bella shoved the cart back into the river. She pushed it out deeply enough so that the current took it once more. Hopefully, the soldiers would find the empty cart and deem them all drowned by the river. Dipping her blistered, raw hands in the wet coolness, she breathed a silent thanks for what the waters had done for her family. She glanced back up the green banks, saw that Rose held her mother's body in her arms, her face buried in her mother's neck, crying bitterly. At least the water had washed away most of the blood. Bella felt compelled to look away, and let Rose have her moment to grieve.

Further up the hill, Bella watched Malik climb up onto their family wagon and take the reins of Aethon and Pyrois into his hands. The sun hit his lean, dark body, making it gleam. He didn't look toward her, simply shook the reins. The wagon moved forward as the sturdy ponies pulled, eager to be away.

Her heart snapped painfully, but there was no more time to waste in grief. Bella steeled herself to deal with Rose and waded back to shore. She reached down and squeezed Rose's shoulder. "Let's take her up to your Da in the wagon, all right Rose?"

Rose was unmoving. Bella saw only blankness on her face. The girl had retreated far inside her own mind. Saints, what to do now? Feeling pressed for time and wishing mightily that someone else was around to be in charge, Bella lifted Rose to her feet. She placed Rose's hands under her mother's legs. Bella picked up Kezia's shoulders and started moving. Sighed a breath of relief as Rose followed suit with her end. They stumbled slowly up the hill.

The girls worked together, but it took a long time to move Kezia's body to the family wagon. They laid her next to her husband on the floor inside the little cabin on the back of the wagon. Rose took a moment to straighten her mother's clothing, then Bella shut the cabin door. Rose seemed incapable of moving anywhere on her own, so Bella led her by the hand and helped her climb up onto the buckboard.

She followed her up. Bella sighed as old Cyclops swished his tail in discontent and tossed his head, trying to be rid of the annoying reins. She clucked to the big brown horse encouragingly, and with a bump they trundled forward, bouncing in the ruts of all the wagons that had gone before them. They were the last of the camp to leave. Bella peered ahead but saw no sign of Malik. She wondered how much time had passed since he'd left. She wished they had more than the one horse pulling them, for it would be slow and heavy going with the burden they carried.

Sometime later, Rose seemed to wake up with some inner thought. She turned around and looked behind them. Turned back to Bella, worry mixing with the sorrow on her face. "Stefan went back to help you last night after we brought the boys to Aisha. Why isn't he with you?"

Bella shook her head, feeling gut-punched. When Stefan hadn't been with Rose at the wagon, she'd assumed he'd gone ahead with Aisha and the little ones. This new uncertainty made her feel ill. She simply couldn't bear any more worry or fear at that moment. Certainly, Rose couldn't bear more either. Bella forced her face into a calm mask. "He's plucky, your brother is," she said, pushing surety into her voice. "I'm sure he's fine. He knows where we are headed."

Rose still looked uncertain. At least it was better than the blankness she'd been displaying before. Bella gave Rose the best smile she could muster, then snapped the leather for Cyclops to pick up the pace. She looked up the track toward the distant green blur that was the promise of safety in the Darkwood and hoped she'd told Rose the truth.

CHAPTER TWENTY-SEVEN

S trom stood over the woozy guard, who held his head in his hands. Blood dried on one side of his face where his own helmet had gashed his forehead. Strom plucked at his lips. He disliked being woken so exceedingly early in the day. Beside him, his manservant stifled a yawn. Strom used his toe to kick at the offending helmet. It had a large dent on one side. *The gypsy had a good arm on her.*

"This strumpet came out of the alley, you say?" He asked in a nonchalant tone.

"Aye. She was wearin' those finger clinky-things, weavin' her spell with 'em."

Strom spotted the finger cymbals on the ground, gleaming the torches his guard held high to fend off the grey fogginess of early morning. He pointed to them and snapped his fingers. His manservant splayed his legs wide to accommodate his belly as he bent down and plucked them from the ground with a grunt. Strom held out his hand. The cymbals clattered together into his palm; their music muted to a dull clank.

"Doesn't seem very seductive to me," he commented to the air.

"You didn't see she who was wearin' them," the injured guard said defensively. "All golden eyes and dark hair and fingers that..." He trailed off at Strom's look.

"You allowed her to seduce you. Knock you out. And help valuable prisoners escape to the river. Does that cover it?" Strom's clinical words dropped like stones.

"Yes." The guard sounded miserable. *As well he should.*

Strom nodded slowly, then signaled for two of his personal guard to come forward. The well-trained men stepped forth with alacrity. Strom turned to the injured charnel house guard, beckoned him to stand. The man did so slowly.

"Tell me, do you have any relatives?" Strom made his voice purr with kindness. The guard looked surprised. "Just me old mam, sir."

"Very good. We'll see she gets your death benefit. Such a shame you died in the gypsy attack. We'll be sure to punish the wench when we catch her."

Strom signaled to his men, who promptly stepped forward with their short swords and stabbed the guard through the heart. Blood bubbled from his lips, and he died with a puzzled look on his face. Strom stepped back so the geyser of heart blood wouldn't sully his shoes. He turned to his manservant.

"Have the prison guard clean this mess up. Send a crier and soldier squads along both the east and the western roads. I want the girl who did this, along with her entire clan, rounded up and brought to me by the end of day. I'm sure I've made myself clear."

His manservant's jowls quivered as he nodded. "Perfectly clear, Burgermeister."

CHAPTER TWENTY-EIGHT

B ella snapped her head up from where it had drooped to her chest. She couldn't remember the last good sleep she'd had. The monotony of hours on the road which rolled out over the meadows kept lulling her to sleep. She glanced over at Rose, thinking to hand the reins to her for a while, but the girl was back to staring at nothing again.

At least her clothes were dry, and she was warm again. Bella looked up at the sky. The sun had favored them most of the day, but now descended behind them. Bella had hoped they'd be at Henna's village by now, but the road had been so rutted by the recent traffic it had forced her to take horse and wagon onto the verge of the road, slowing them. Then there was the time they'd spent hidden in a dense stand of willows as a group of six roundhats had galloped past. Thank the Saints she'd spotted their dust behind them and had the time to hide the wagon.

Her stomach rumbled. Bella thought pulling over again and making camp might be wise. They could cook some travel rations, but the idea of rummaging around the dead bodies of Timbo and Kezia quelled the notion. Besides, her aunt and uncle deserved a proper Traveller send-off, and they couldn't get one until she reunited with the clans up inside the Darkwood. They had to keep moving.

Her thoughts tumbled in a circle, going over, and over the questions she had. How had Kezia come to be killed? Where was Stefan? Had Malik found Henna? Were the soldiers going to circle back after them? Would Malik stay angry with her? The thoughts harried around her mind like midge flies around a horse's eyes. Just as annoying, too. And where was this dratted village Henna had spoken of? Perhaps the girl had been jesting, or flat-out lying, Bella thought viciously.

"Smoke." It was the first word Rose had spoken in hours. She pointed and Bella followed the line of her hand. Sure enough, it looked like there was a town or perhaps a Traveller camp ahead. Ten miles perhaps, Bella thought, weighing the space. She sighed and clucked at the horse. Not that it would make it go faster. The cranky old thing seemed to have only one speed. Now that they'd sighted the smoke, Bella's anxiety grew again. What if it wasn't a town, or clans she knew? What if it was soldiers burning Traveller wagons? She shook that thought off. If she was smart enough to pull off the road when she sighted soldiers on the road, then so was her clan.

The shadows grew and changed to twilight before Bella rolled to the edge of the village she hoped was Henna's. It was a shabby place, fifteen or so houses with crabbed yards, some empty, others in disrepair, wisping the smoke they'd spotted. They huddled next to the road, along with the requisite chapel, what she guessed passed for an inn, and a cold smithy with a large barn on the far side of it.

Spotting a watering trough next to the barn, Bella clambered wearily down from the buckboard. She felt like she needed a butt replacement. She was so sore. Bella gave the tired horse a pat and led it over to the trough. Cyclops sucked water greedily. Bella splashed some of the water on her face. It was odd that no one had come out to see who'd driven into town. They must've heard the jostling of the wagon. Bella's thoughts were foggy. She simply couldn't figure out one more puzzle. She stayed standing, for she was sure if she sat down, she'd fall asleep in seconds. Maybe if she just guided the horse around behind the barn, they could sleep for a few hours out of sight of the road.

A pinprick of light in the gathering gloam emerged from the far end of the village. Low for a star, she thought. It grew bigger and bobbled a bit. A lantern, she realized. Perhaps a drunk looking for trouble, or—her thoughts failed her. It could be anything. She'd just have to wait until whoever carried the lantern got closer. No time to flee now. Bella wished she had knives strapped to her arms and legs, as Aisha did. *If I get through this cursed night, I'll find some and do just that.* She looked around for some weapon to use; even a loose board would do.

"Bella?" a voice called out of the dark. "Bella, is that you stumbling around in the dark?"

"Henna!" Relief flooded through Bella. She moved towards the girl, her thighs protesting with each step. "Did Malik find you, did—"

Henna interrupted. "We need to get your wagon and horse out of sight. There was a town crier through here earlier, shouting about your clan. Strom is paying a hefty price for your 'return to justice', as he called it. Here, I'll take care of your horse, I can feed him." Henna grabbed the reins from Bella's hands. "Take your cousin to the last cottage on the left. Your folk are there with my mother."

"But—"

"Make haste, you silly thing. There are those in this village who'd happily give ye up for the coin." Henna gave her a little push.

Bella lacked the energy to do anything but obey Henna. The girl certainly had a bossy way, to be sure. Taking Rose by the hand, she moved quietly down the main street. In a few homes, curtains twitched back, the light from within shafting onto the street. She averted her gaze and kept moving in the shadows. Her skin crawled as she thought of watchers in the windows.

Rose stumbled next to her, and she propped her up. "Only a little further," she said. Half to Rose and half to herself. Her feet were dragging. She was moving forward with sheer willpower.

Finally, the end of the village. Bella turned to the tumbledown cottage on her left and pushed open the wooden door a crack.

CHAPTER TWENTY-NINE

B ella peeked inside, hoping she had the right home. On one side, a fire burned low, a pot set on a tripod above it. The smell of stew permeated the air. A large table filled the center of the room. Ebbe lay upon it, one hand swathed in linens by his side, the other elevated above him in a sort of harness attached to a hook in the ceiling. He seemed to be unconscious, his breathing so slow as to be nearly undetectable. Vadoma sat in a chair pulled up to the table. She smiled when she saw Bella and Rose.

"You made it." Vadoma stood as they entered the house fully. Bella saw that her wrists, which had been so savaged by the metal cuffs, were bandaged in clean white linen. A glance downward showed her that her mother's legs were wrapped as well, still swollen to three times their size from hanging on the wall. A crisp voice sounded from the gloom in the back of the cottage. "Sure, and I told you as to stay off your feet as much as ye can."

Vadoma rolled her eyes and sat back down. Bella stifled a surprised smile. She'd never seen her mother obey anyone so immediately in her life.

"Shut yon door, if ye please." The voice sounded again. Bella pulled Rose in behind her and did so. The tiny room seemed very crowded.

"Now who is it we have here?" A tall, aging woman with a face wreathed in wrinkles like a dried apple and bright blue eyes the color of washed skies moved into the flickering light of the fire. She wore long homespun skirts and carried a soft goatskin flask by the neck, gently swirling the contents inside as she moved closer to Rose and Bella with a speed that belied her apparent age.

The intensity of her gaze was astonishing. Bella felt like the woman was looking through her and out again, into her past, or perhaps her future. Or maybe she was so tired she imagined it. For a moment later, the woman's eyes lost their brilliance and became hazed over with milky strands. The woman tut-tutted at whatever she had seen inside Bella and waved to them to move further inside.

"Ye be the lost girls. My Henna found you right enough. Ye must be famished. Sit and have a bowl of stew before you drop and litter my floor with your prone selves." Bella moved to the rich scent of the pot. The woman certainly had the knack for ordering people around. Now she understood where Henna got it from. Bella ladled up stew for both herself and Rose. Seating themselves on short stools near the fire, they gulped down the food. Bella didn't mind that the meat was a bit gamey, and the broth thin. There were mushrooms, carrots, and turnips that helped bolster the meal. Bella was glad to have it.

She watched the woman pour a thin stream of the potion from the flask into a cup, and give it to Vadoma, who dripped it into Ebbe's slack mouth, then worked his throat so that even in his unconscious state, he'd swallow. Ebbe seemed like a blown husk of his former self, tiny and wizened as if he'd aged fifty years in a day and could be blown into his grave by a gust of wind.

"Ye'd be smart to have a swallow of that poppy juice yerself," the old woman commented to Vadoma. She simply shook her head and stroked Ebbe's shoulder.

The woman grunted dismissively, then turned around. "Eaten enough for now, you two? Wash it down with plenty of that ale. The brown jug there. You need fortifying, for yer rest here is but short unless ye want to travel straight back to the city dungeons."

Her tone was so matter of fact it gave Bella a dose of courage. It was easier to know what one was facing instead of running ever forward into the dark. She drank as she was told to do. Rose mechanically did so as well. The girl was pale and needed rest. Bella eyed her critically and spoke up.

"Is there a pallet for Rose to lie down, Mistress—" Bella realized she wasn't sure of the woman's name. "Mistress Henna's Mother?" she winced as she completed the sentence.

The woman grinned, and Bella saw several of her teeth were missing. No wonder the village called her a witch behind her back, for she surely looked the part.

"I be that title sure enough, and proud of it. I'm also mother to Jon, Gunnar, and my poor mites Helgi and Einar in heaven, rest their souls. I be Mother Sigrun. Or That Witch." She snorted contemptuously. It was clear she wasn't bothered by anyone calling her names. Sigrun continued, "It be all the same to me. The answer to yer question lies behind ye."

Bella guided Rose to the back of the cottage where two neatly made pallets, complete with blankets, lay side by side. She helped her down and looked longingly at the other empty bed. If only she could rest for a few minutes.

"We could use your strength here, girl." The woman's voice interceded. With a gusty sigh, Bella moved back to the light.

"The sooner we set these bones back where they belong, the sooner ye'll be gone from here. I nay want ye in my house when the Roundhats return, and return they will." Mother Sigrun raised her wrinkled face from her mixing bowl to make sure they understood. Silence held sway, but Bella nodded agreement, as did her mother. Sigrun added a few more grains of some herb to the mixture in the bowl and a large dollop of honey, smelled it, and then began tending to Ebbe's hands.

Bella felt like she should feel resentful at the woman's brusque way, but instead she felt steadied and focused with the task at hand. Which was holding down her father's torso while her mother dripped milk of the poppy into his mouth to keep him sleeping.

Mother Sigrun pointed at Ebbe and the mass of new-wrapped bandages that still seeped blood on his chest. "Keep him still and listen close to his heart, girl. That's right, put your ear right across it, gentle now, you don't want to rip his stitches yer Ma put in so careful. If the heart slows too much, tell your Ma. If it speeds up, tell me."

The woman deftly manipulated Ebbe's elevated hand and finger bones, tsking and muttering to herself the whole time. Things like, "what people will do to each other," and "ought to be given a taste of his own medicine." As she set each of the finger bones straight, she slathered the digit with the poultice of honey and the pungent green herb that stung Bella's nostrils. Then she wrapped each set bone in linens.

It felt comforting laying on her father's chest, something she hadn't done in a long time. The thump of his heart and the sound of his slow breath gave her hope that everything will be all right.

"Everything will be all right." It was her mother, looking at her with her slanted green eyes. Bella gave her mother a small nod, as if agreeing. But in her heart, she didn't think it was true. Nothing would ever be all right ever again. Timbo and Kezia dead, Rose a walking corpse, Stefan missing. Malik no longer in love with her. Roundhats after them. It hurt to think about all the wrong that'd happened in such a short amount of time. Bella felt the tickle of tears in her nose, and sniffed to keep them bottled up. Snuggled closer to her father, listening to his steady heart and breath like a lifeline.

She must have fallen asleep laying across her father's chest, for when she opened her eyes the work on his hands was done, and Henna was in the room with them, eating a bowl of stew by the fire. The girl raised her wooden spoon in greeting but didn't stop eating.

"We'll bind his hands up on his shoulders, thus." Sigrun demonstrated by crossing her own arms. "He must keep them at heart level, so the blood doesn't pool in the hands. He must sleep sitting up. Every hour or so, he can let them lower for ten minutes. It'd be best if you'd come back in a week, and let me see how they are healing."

"We'll be far from here in a week." Vadoma had a determined look.

The woman grunted and shrugged. "The honey and herb will stave off infection. Time must do the rest. I'll send along supplies for the re-bandaging then, and more milk of the poppy. Seek out another healer when you can. Some of these will not mend; they were beyond my skill. They'll need to be re-broken and set if you want your man to have the use of his fingers return."

"Mama, can I go with them? Show them the way?" Henna stood up from her place at the fire and spoke urgently. Bella felt her heart tug. She liked this girl, she realized.

Her mother shook her head firmly. "Nay, daughter, you must stay behind with me. It would look amiss were ye to be gone at the same time as the Travellers. I'll not have you in danger, my *hjarta*."

Henna frowned. "Mama, she be my friend."

Bella's heart gave a huge thump, and she felt her eyes go strangely misty at the simple declaration. She'd always had her family, of course. But with their constant movement, she'd never made a genuine friend. She wished fiercely that Henna could come with them, but in the next minute knew she'd not want to put her in danger. It seemed that the curse she and her mother carried could bring ill luck to anyone who helped them. Maybe this was how true friends behaved. Putting other's needs before their own. She wiped her eyes with her sleeve. Saints, she'd had far too many emotions over the last few days. It was exhausting.

Mother Sigrun had gone still, her bright blue eyes sweeping over Ebbe and Vadoma, stopping at Bella, then moving on again. She nodded slowly. "Aye, she be your true friend, for she is willing to let you go to keep you safe."

It startled Bella to realize that the woman had somehow read her mind.

Mother Sigrun looked slightly haunted and uncomfortable as she nodded once more. "You've been bound to each other, I think. Mayhap in the future your paths will cross again."

Vadoma took the woman's hands in her own, kissed them. "We are beyond grateful, and will send payment as we can."

Mother Sigrun nodded. "Now, time to get ye gone and into to the Darkwood 'afore daybreak. Move past the woodcutter's house and the two sisters who be bakers, some five hours' journey from here. All of them ye should avoid, for the woodcutter takes after his father. That is to say he's a mean-to-the-bone, selfish young man, and those sisters are born gossips even if they make fine loaves. They'll turn ye in as sure as anything you'd like to swear upon just for the coin and the delight in others' misfortunes." Sigrun shut her mouth with a snap and began the task of cleaning the kitchen table.

Henna pulled Bella aside, held her hands. It was as if she had something important to say. The girl blew out her breath, and unshed tears made her eyes sparkle. "I scattered some sweet flowers upon your dead, so their smell won't attract the animals." Her blunt way of speaking made Bella smile, but she had the feeling the girl had wanted to say something entirely different.

"I'm glad we met Henna," Bella said. "You helped save us all."

The girl turned scarlet with embarrassment but had a pleased smile. She seemed about to say something happy, but her face changed, going sheet white in the space of a breath. Bella saw Henna's forehead crease with pain. "You're not safe. There's a watcher in the woods," Henna panted out before collapsing into a chair.

Mother Sigrun darted over. Her distress was clear in every flustered movement. "Henna's had one of her visions. I beg ye, keep what she said to yourself. Don't tell anyone. Henna has enough troubles being female and a so-called witch's brat without being named a witch herself."

Bella didn't know what to think, but nodded to placate the woman. She was used to her father using the long talk with the trees, so why would she doubt others had ways of seeing that she did not? All the same, it was irritating, having other people proclaim things about the future you. It was as bad as being cursed.

The moon was a faint sliver in the cold air. The ponies had been unhappy about being hitched to the wagon again. They'd stamped and tossed their heads, but in the end, Bella had managed to get them hooked back up again. They lay Ebbe in the back, and Vadoma was going to drive.

Bella wanted to climb in the back of their wagon and sleep, but she had to drive the other cart. Rose was still lost to them, staring at nothing, pliable as a rag doll as if she'd lost the ability to move herself. She felt annoyed with her cousin for being so weak, but knew it was unfair of her to have such thoughts. It made her doubly annoyed that she was wrong for having them.

Mother Sigrun walked outside. She beckoned to Vadoma and Bella. Her breath puffed out white in the cool air of the night. "A piece of advice. Just hear me out." Bella crossed her arms. When people started sentences out that way, it was sure to be something she didn't want to hear.

"I know the Traveller ways to honor the dead. There is a circle of rowan trees not far from here. It might be wise to… unburden yourself." Vadoma shook her head and got the stubborn set to her lips that Bella knew well.

Mother Sigrun persisted. "The Roundhats be right idiots, most of them. Finding a burnt 'gypsy' wagon with two bodies would fool them and let the rest of you escape without pursuit." Sigrun paused, then sighed as Vadoma gave her a steely look. "Think on it."

The woman handed Bella a cloth bundle. "Here's medicine and some food for your journey. And may all the *Sinti* blessings be upon you." Her keen eyes gave Bella a final sweep. She pushed her lips together like she was keeping a secret. Bella had an incisive pull to stay with this woman and Henna for a time. She could pretend to be part of a different sort of family. Would it be so bad to live in one house, in one village, for a span? Her skin began to itch. Bella sighed. No, being cooped up in one spot was not for her.

Her mother climbed up onto their wagon, where Rose was already perched, gazing at nothing. Bella gathered herself and shoved down her awkward feelings as she climbed aboard the second wagon bearing the dead. She raised a hand to say goodbye to Mother Sigrun, but they'd already shut the door. The cottage looked just like all the rest now. A small, insignificant refuge in a small, insignificant village.

Bella felt a little of the tightness in her chest ease as she clucked to Cyclops and felt the animal pull her forward into the unknown. Something settled bone deep in her. Acceptance that she was a Traveller by blood and birth, with a constant, deep need to see fresh places, even if they held danger. For just as like, they could hold adventure. Or even love.

CHAPTER THIRTY

Vadoma couldn't get the thought out of her head that
Mother Sigrun had planted. It made sense to fool the
soldiers following them, and with only one wagon, the travelling
would be easier for all. She'd seen how weary Bella was. A
surge of pride filled her as she remembered how her daughter
had climbed up to drive the other wagon without complaint.
Much had happened over the past two days, but not all of it had
been bad. Maybe surviving Strom had cracked the curse apart,
freeing her daughter to find a way to love her. It had been a
heroic and loving act to rescue her. Or had she been after
rescuing her father, whom she loved easily and well? And
releasing her mother an afterthought?

Vadoma felt her thoughts turning bitter. There'd been no time
to find out the why of anything in the chaos of escaping Strom.
Best to continue their long escape from that terrible city and
make the sacrifices of her family count for something. Her
thoughts drifted ahead to where she hoped she'd find more of
their clan, including Timbo and Kezia's babies.

Her heart clutched at the thought of Kezia. What had
happened to her sister that they'd stabbed her through with
spears? Thinking about her sister caused guilt to overwhelm her,
and she wanted to weep for a thousand years. Or die in her

sister's place. After all, it had been her own weakness that had gotten them into this disaster. If only she'd not succumbed to Bella's pleading to go to that city, knowing that Strom might still hold sway there. She'd been trying to please her daughter, had been trying to find a way to connect with her by making her happy.

Was that the curse at work? Or was she just not good at mothering? Her next thought had her wrinkling her nose and frowning. *My own mother was terrible at mothering.* Maybe the apple didn't fall from the tree. What did that bode for Bella's future? Would she continue the 'bad mother' trait? Or would it all somehow be different?

She certainly seemed to have formed a crush on Malik. Vadoma wasn't sure it was a good match. She was grateful to both Malik and his mother, to be sure. But was it genuine love? Or had Bella not had the opportunities to meet enough boys? Again, that was her personal failing. They should've journeyed this past winter down to the camps in Aragon, or Valencia by the sea. There were many Sinti clans there, many boys to fall in love with. She should've realized that her daughter needed such interactions, as did Rose, and Stefan for that matter. They would become her children now, and young Timbo and Pattin.

Vadoma resolved that once Ebbe had healed enough, they would trade what goods they had for furs from the Rutgar clan in the Darkwood. Then head south past the Bodensee, climb overmountain through the pass and on to Casale Monferrato and the winter resting grounds. It was more difficult than the Rhone river route, but would keep them far away from Strom and his power, the further the better. If they found no other clans willing to start the southern journey so early, they'd go alone. It was a relatively safe journey in the summer months and would give Ebbe a chance to heal. He would heal, she thought ferociously. He would.

Vadoma stirred from her thoughts to realize she could clearly see the road ahead. A faint tinge of pink filled the sky in front of her. The stars were pale; the moon dipped below the horizon. Vadoma strained her eyes. How much further did they have to go before reaching the sanctuary of the Darkwood?

It was still a green blur on the horizon. Hours away. Hours in which the Roundhats could easily recapture them. Vadoma weighed their options. She wanted to give Timbo and her sister the full clan Traveller sendoff they deserved. However, she knew them both well. Vadoma smiled at the thought of the grins they'd have that even in death, they managed to stymie Strom's pursuit. The vision of their delight convinced Vadoma.

As if she'd conjured it, the circle of rowan trees Sigrun had mentioned appeared to her right. A breeze beckoned her with the light sweet scent of the flowering trees. Here was protection from evil; here was a passageway; here was the gate from past to future, from death to life. Vadoma turned off the road and headed for the sacred rowan trees.

Looking behind, she saw Bella followed, although the girl had her signature forehead crease, which meant she had plenty to say once they stopped. Vadoma looked at Rose. The girl seemed as if she was in a trance, staring at her knees. If she'd been herself, Vadoma would have asked her permission to send her parents on, but that seemed beyond Rose.

She trundled to a stop just outside of the circle of mature trees. They reached up nearly sixty feet in the air, their light green leaves just darkening and a few clusters of the pretty creamy flowers showing. As she had hoped, a small stream trickled nearby. They could make a meal for themselves and let the horses drink and crop the young meadow grasses.

"What do you think you're doing, Ma?" Bella's strident voice broke her concentration. Bella stood with her hands fisted on her hips, glaring up at her. Vadoma felt the familiar prickle of irritation she always got when confronting her daughter. There'd be no time for a gentle conversation. This was a good idea, but it still had its dangers, for the smoke from the fire would draw eyes.

"You know well enough." Vadoma kept her words short and her tone authoritarian. She saw Bella take a breath, and she held up her hand and looked at her daughter sternly. "I'll brook no argument. Pull Kezia's wagon into the center of the trees and unhitch the horse. If there is anything not of Kezia and Timbo in their cart, take it out, along with the cooking oil." Vadoma turned away from her daughter to clamber down. Saints, it was hard to do with her wrists so painful!

Vadoma felt sturdy hands around her waist as Bella helped lift her down. The hands turned her around. Vadoma gathered herself for a fight, but what she saw was compassion. "Get yourself food, Ma. See how Da is doing. I'll care for the animals. Maybe you can get Rose to help you."

"We've not long." Vadoma couldn't help herself saying. It got the sideward glance and huff of impatience she expected.

"I know, Ma. I know." Bella moved to the ponies to unhitch them. Vadoma watched her move away. It was an improvement, to be sure. Perhaps she'd never find perfect harmony with her daughter after so many years of outright war, but less arguing was good. Vadoma nodded to herself. Better was better. She'd take it.

Ebbe sat on the back of the cart and sang the song of parting with a cracked voice. Bella's kitten sat next to him, watching the flames take the brown and green-vined wagon that contained the bodies of Timbo and Kezia. There'd been no time to properly wash and dress them, but Vadoma and Bella had strewn wildflowers in with them, and placed the personal items they'd held dear in life around them.

Vadoma cast the long locks of white hair she'd shorn from her head onto the blaze. Bella tossed the ribbons she'd made onto it as well. Rose sat and plucked at the grasses outside of the circle of trees, seeming to not comprehend what was happening.

The flames built in size, fed by the dry wood of the wagon and the cooking oil they'd cast upon it. Soon the whole thing would be engulfed. Ebbe's song came to an end, and all that could be heard was the crackle of flames and the faint breeze in the rowan trees that surrounded them. There was peace to be found in the scene, Vadoma thought, if you tried hard enough. Tears fell as she mourned the sister and brother-in-law that had moved from this plane to another.

A scream ripped through the air, startling Vadoma. She turned and saw a wild-eyed Rose running towards the wagon full out. Her arms were outstretched, her mouth stretched in agony as she ran for the flames. It was clear she meant to fling herself on top of the pyre.

"Bella, stop her!" Vadoma cried out.

Bella tackled Rose to the ground and rolled with her, coming so close to the burning wagon that Rose's dress caught fire. Vadoma ran over and stomped on the flames, and helped corral the grieving girl, who was fighting Bella's strong arms. Together, they moved the girl back from the flames.

"Saints!" Bella gasped.

"You have no right! No right!" Rose raged through her tears.

"I have every right as her sister." Vadoma said sternly. "We will do more for them with the clans when we're safe."

"Come on, Rose, they're gone now." Bella was soft in tone as she helped Rose rise. Vadoma noticed she kept a tight grip on the girl.

Rose seemed to comply for a moment, then tried to break free again, struggling against Bella. Vadoma stepped in front of Rose. She wished she could grip the crazed girl, but knew her wrists weren't up to the task. "Don't let your parent's sacrifice be for nothing! They want you to live, Rose. You must live for them. It's meaningless to die here."

"It hurts. It hurts so much." Rose's voice was barely a broken whisper.

"It does. I know it. But we have to move on. Life is for the living, Rose."

Rose wept even harder. Bella clutched her cousin close. "Come cousin. You must ride with your Uncle Ebbe and be sure he keeps his hands at heart level."

Vadoma watched as Bella bundled Rose up into the back of their wagon. She scooped the kitten up and handed it to her. "Keep Selena warm. I think she really likes you." The orange kitten purred in agreement and didn't seem to mind when Rose wiped her wet cheeks on its fur. The girl seemed to take comfort from the little creature.

Vadoma met her husband's eyes, and he nodded. He would watch over the girl. Seeing they were settled, Vadoma shut the door to the cart, and with an ache in her heart, looked one more time at the tall flames. The wagon was a crumbling silhouette inside the orange and red. It was everything she could do to crawl back up and take up the reins of the ponies.

Bella had Cyclops' reins in her hand. "I'll walk for a way," she said. Without looking back, Bella started walking ahead of the wagon, cutting across the meadow at an angle to regain the road. Vadoma knew her daughter grieved and felt guilty. Just as she did. It was wise of her to walk for a while and let the rhythm of it free her mind to wander as it needed to. It was certainly something, she thought. To see your own daughter leading the way, to realize that overnight your child had become a woman in her own right.

CHAPTER THIRTY-ONE

" I want the bones. I'll know to whom they belong." Strom said as he gazed down at his town from a high window. He struggled to catch his breath. Perhaps he'd caught a chill. He regarded his hand in the sunlight. It looked old to him, with new lines he'd never seen before, and dark splotches. Was that a tremor?

He turned away from the window into the comforting darkness of his bedchamber, glanced at the portrait of his long-dead wife. Her clear eyes the same color as the square-cut emerald she wore around her neck seemed to reproach him for his failure to revenge her. He stepped out of the unforgiving sunlight. His voice felt weak as well. He cleared his throat as he pinned the hapless young messenger with a look. "Did you hear me, boy?"

The messenger stood far back from Strom, his face red from the exertion of his run. *Smart lad.* Strom had half a mind to chuck him straight out the window for bringing him the unwelcome news that those gypsies had not yet been caught. He had felt his sense of the woman he wanted in his grasp fading.

The messenger twisted his cap in his young hands. *No lines on them. The boy was fresh.* "The bones, yes, sir. They were burnt inside the wagon, so I don't know how much you'll be able to make out, sir."

Strom nodded, smiled as he saw the boy gulp. He modulated his tone carefully. It wouldn't do to let anyone see his distress over losing his prey. Nor what he really wanted the bones for.

"Nevertheless. Have them brought to me." He brought his gaze up to lock with the messenger's. The boy gulped again and shuffled back another foot. "Of course, sir, right away."

The boy fled the chamber. Strom moved back to his high perch and looked out over his city. He didn't believe Vadoma, or even her daughter, were dead. He'd know it, connected as they were. Best to check all the same. The bones would speak to him. He had the knack, just as his grandfather had before him. What an inspiration that man had been.

She fooled you. You thought Bella was dead. A tiny whisper mocked him.

He shifted his gaze to the bed that his wife and son had died in all those years ago. It was distressing that a simple gypsy and her brat had so far thwarted him. Yet their success validated his desire to bed the daughter. He could use such wily strength in an heir. In a sacrifice.

Strom fingered his ruby ring that shone with its heart fire, thought about the bound leather book that, along with the ruby ring, had been passed down to him by his grandfather. The grimoire in which he'd found the air, earth, and blood curse. It was a strong conjuring, and had required much of him over the years, binding it as he had to his own life and breath.

He paused mid-stride, his difficulty in pulling in air suddenly worrying him. Had the wretched creatures found a way to loosen the first bond of air? He shook his head, chuckling at the thought. They weren't clever enough for that. No, the thrice-wrapped curse on Vadoma and Belladonna would hold. It might change form, take on a different aspect, but it doomed both the women to sorrow and pain—and their children, and any who might aid them—until he released them from it.

I'll win in the end.

Calmer now, Strom reached for the cooling potion only he knew how to make and drank deeply from the cup. The iron taste of the thick, red liquid was muted by the ground bones, rosemary, and rue he'd included. It fortified him. Renewed his vigor, as it was brewed to do. He planned to live for a long time. He'd take his revenge, sow his seed, and conquer a nation.

CHAPTER THIRTY-TWO

The horse and ponies stumbled from weariness as they entered the clearing that held the Traveller camp in the Darkwood. Bella had been so tired as she rode Cyclops through those last miles, she'd almost missed the sign on the road. Cyclops had stepped on the thick sticks that pointed the way off the main trail. It was the deep snapping that had alerted her. She felt a surge of relief that they'd found the way to the camp. Signaling back to Vadoma to turn, she followed the occasional fluttering ribbons that first detoured them to the right, then guided them along a narrow path. It was full dark, with only a sliver of moonlight filtering through the chestnut trees.

The glow of banked firepits and the sound of a single mouth harp guided them in the last distance. A dozen tents and wagons lay scattered in the open circle ringed by the giant trees. As she entered the final clearing, a few late-night watchers stood. They all loosely held weapons, but relaxed when they saw who it was. Soft calls of "Hey-ah" greeted the tired travelers as they rolled in. The smells of roasting rabbit and venison still left in pots made Bella's mouth water. Gratefully, she slid off Cyclops' back. She was sure the old brown horse was just as glad to be rid of her.

Bella spotted Destry hobbled by Aisha's tent. She felt nervy about seeing Malik again after their abrupt parting two nights ago. She tiptoed to the tent. Aisha's tent flaps were tied together. It would be rude to scratch at them so late at night. She'd have to wait until morning to satisfy her curiosity. Perhaps such a meeting was best done after a few hours' sleep, anyway. She had no proper plans for what she wanted to say to Malik. She only knew she longed to see him and have him hold her again.

After seeing to the horses, Bella unrolled her sleeping mat and blankets and spread them under the wagon. The watchman brought her a container of stew scraped from various pots in camp. She shared it among four of their own bowls and dug out the last of the bread and cheese Mother Sigrun had pressed upon them. Bella urged Rose to climb down and join her underneath, leaving the covered section of the wagon for Vadoma and Ebbe. She left Vadoma spooning stew into her husband's mouth. Her mother had looked at her with pride in her eyes.

"You've grown up these last few days," Vadoma said.

Bella felt vaguely insulted but kept the sharp comment she wanted to snap back with to herself. She'd been grown up for over a year. It wasn't her fault her mother only now was noticing. She took a deep breath.

"Be sure to eat some of that yourself," was all she said to Vadoma. She climbed down, proud of herself that she'd held her tongue. She found Rose already lying down. As if the girl hadn't been lying down the entire journey here!

She poked at her and pressed the hot food into Rose's hands when the girl sat up. At first, Rose pushed away at the bowl. Bella sighed. "Starving yourself won't change anything, Rose." She knew it wasn't the nicest thing to say, but Bella was all out of nice.

Rose ate a few bites mechanically, while Bella tore into her food. It had been a long time since the bowl of thin stew at Mistress Sigrun's home. It felt marvelous to chew the grained bread and soft cheese, and to eat something warm. Bella felt sleep coming over her almost before she could finish. Rose was already gently snoring, her arms cast over her head in surrender. Bella curled up close to her cousin's warmth and fell into a blissful sleep.

"Hey." Someone was shaking her shoulder. Bella grunted and rolled away. She'd just been having the most wonderful dream about a castle and tables of food just for her. She wanted to get back to it. The shaking grew more insistent. "Bella."

"I'm sleeping!" She felt like throwing things. The beautiful dream was fraying around the edges. She'd lose it entirely in a moment.

"I've got apple crumble for breakfast, *jameela*."

Apple crumble was her favorite.

She opened one eye. Bella could tell by the light that it was full day already. She shut it again, but it was too late. The dream and the hope of more sleep had fled. With a groan, she rolled out from underneath the wagon and sat up. She felt like every inch of her had been beaten with hazel rods. Even her fingernails hurt. She stretched her arms up, heard cracking all along each joint as she yawned. Her mouth felt like ducks had pooped in it. She really just wanted to go back to sleep.

The irritating voice spoke again. "You've got dead leaves in your hair."

This time, she cracked open both eyes and saw the critical face of Malik just inches away.

"Take them out then," she said in her grumpiest tone.

She felt his gentle fingers tugging at her hair, fingers combing through it, gently unsnarling her curls as he went. It felt wonderful.

"Much better," he said. Then he rocked back on his heels and stood up in the sinuous, lithe way he had. He held out his hand to help her up. She considered brushing it away, and standing on her own, but then thought better of it. He was behaving normally. She would as well, for now.

He tugged her to her feet. For a moment, Bella thought she might fall straight back down again. Her inner thighs were raw from riding the horse. She stumbled forward a few steps. Malik grabbed her by the arm as she tottered. She tried to straighten up, and each knob of her spine screamed.

"You need a dunk in the river, wake you right up."

Before she could protest, he'd picked her up in his arms and was striding across camp. Several catcalls followed them. Bella wiggled, but to no avail. Malik had her in a tight grip.

"I don't want to be dunked in the river, Malik!" She used her bossiest tone. It didn't work.

He just grinned at her. "I'll join you." And with that, he jumped into the river with Bella clasped in his arms. She screamed just as they hit, and water rushed into her mouth.

The river was icy cold, and she sputtered as they surfaced again in moments. Even Malik's warm body pressed against hers wasn't enough.

"You ass!" she yelled, and tried to push him away.

"One more dunk should do it." And he pulled them back under again. She felt the current gently tugging at her clothes and her hair, felt his arms clasped around her, holding her firm and strong against the current. She relaxed in his arms as they bobbed to the surface again. Looked up and saw his beautiful, sculpted face with his high cheekbones glistening with droplets, each catching a glint of sun. More were captured in the close dark curls of his hair. It was as if he was encrusted in diamonds.

He was looking at her as if entranced. Bella felt her heart squeeze. She longed for him, yes. But she had to know why he'd left her at the riverbank. Had to know why he'd been so angry and cold.

"Malik?" She hardly knew where to begin. She was aware that her legs throbbed in the pulse of the cold water. Any moment now, her teeth would begin to chatter.

He raised an eyebrow. "Yes, Bella?"

"Why were you so angry with me before? When you left with my parents?"

He gently kissed her on the forehead, his gaze sweeping back and forth across her face as if he were memorizing it. He took a breath.

"You quit, you almost quit in the river. It made me so angry. After all we'd done, you were about to let go." His voice was rough. "Like you didn't care after all. No one, not me, not your parents, was enough to keep you from giving up. You betrayed me in that moment, and you betrayed yourself. It made me furious with you."

Her heart sank. He was right. She'd been close to letting the river drown her, let her self-pity and misery drown her. Only her father's voice raised in song, reminding her of what she was made of, who she came from, had stopped her.

"You're right." She hated to admit it. Hated seeing the disappointment flood his face. Bella gripped him firmly by the shirt. "But I didn't quit, did I? In the end, we made it to the bank, we made it here."

"What about next time? What happens next time we are in trouble? You know we'll get in trouble again, Bella."

The wisp of a smile crossed his face as she nodded. Yes, they would. She shivered, and not just from the cold of the river. It was a premonition. She swallowed.

"Malik, what I can promise you is that I'll never quit again. Never. Even if something horrible happens, and we're parted, I won't give up. I'll come find you. I will always find you, Malik. I love you. Even when you drop me in a river to wake me up. Even when you promise me apple crisp and don't give me any.

You have my whole heart. As a friend, as my love. Is that enough?"

His smile filled her soul. He nodded slowly. "It's a start."

She splashed at him. "After all I said to you, that's all you can say to me? It's a start?"

Malik's face grew serious. "Henna said something to me when I left your parents with her. I was so angry with you, but she said that your wild nature is your own. She asked me if I would love you as much if you were not made so."

Bella closed her eyes and silently blessed her friend. She opened them to find Malik studying her. For perhaps the first time in her life, no quips popped into her head. She was content to let him speak when he was ready. She shivered in the cool of the stream, but there was nowhere she'd rather be. Malik's lips curved into a soft smile.

"I love you too, Bella. All of you, even the parts that make terrible, wild decisions."

Bella's joy soared. She raised her face. His lips met hers, softly at first, then hard and insistent. He tasted of cinnamon and need. She floated her legs around his torso, her arms around his shoulders, and clasped his body to hers, the cooling rush of the river forgotten, all the sounds in the world hushed. Only the two existed in this time, this place, this heat, this kiss.

"Practicing for a new play again?" The dry comment penetrated the beautiful bubble. Bella looked up on shore and embarrassed herself by squealing.

"Stefan!"

Her cousin grinned and shifted his weight as he crossed his arms. He put on a mock scowl. "You have to know I'm telling on you, cousin."

Bella scrambled ashore and grabbed Stefan by the shoulders. Kissed him full on the mouth. "I am so happy to see you, Stefan!"

Stefan blushed and shoved her away good-naturedly. "I can tell."

Malik stepped up beside Bella, dripping. "We've wondered where you've been." His tone was much more somber.

Stefan looked away, and when he turned back to him, his face was hard. So much older, Bella thought. She wondered then if this sort of change was what her mother had seen in her last night.

"I had things I had to take care of. I knew where you'd be." Stefan's voice seemed deeper.

Bella reached out her hand, took Stefan's in her own. "You know of your father, your mother, what happened to them?"

Pain swept across the boy's face. "Aye, I know. I was there when my father was heart shot by that filthy hangman's arrow. And also with my mother, shot through with three of them. She died to protect me." Stefan looked past them, as if he were seeing them die all over again. He trembled. "I wanted to murder the hangman's whole family in revenge. I was right outside their door."

"The wolf at the door," murmured Malik softly.

Stefan looked surprised at the comment, folded his arms tight across his chest protectively. "I didn't, though. I didn't think Mama would want me to." He looked up at Bella. "I don't know if I did right, or wrong."

Bella didn't know what to say. Her heart ached to see the joy swept away from Stefan so thoroughly. Finally, she gave his hand a squeeze.

"Your mother saved us, too. Her and your father helped us escape. Stefan... we sent them on their final journey, Ma and Da and Rose and I."

He looked at her with his brown eyes filled with gold flecks. More golden flecks than she remembered him having. He chewed the inside of his cheek and swallowed. "I would have been there if I could. But I understand you did what you needed to do."

Stefan shook himself like a dog shivering off rain. Scrubbed at his nose hard with his wrist. In that moment, he looked so like the little boy she remembered that Bella teared up for the loss of him. Grief had ripped him into becoming a man. Composing himself, Stefan gestured to them.

"Come on, the family's waiting for us. Yours too," he tossed over his shoulder at Malik as he walked away. "Everybody's pissed." Stefan stalked ahead of them through the underbrush, back towards the camp.

Bella and Malik shared a look, clasped hands, and followed him.

CHAPTER THIRTY-THREE

B ella and Malik walked into a tense scene at the campsite. Two families had already left, the absence of their painted carts leaving gaps in the circle like teeth missing from a skull. The rest of the families were stowing their gear hurriedly. Only two clans were not engaged in the packing: Bella's and Malik's. They faced each other around the campfire in front of Aisha's tent.

The air hummed with anger between the families. Bella could see it in the tense shoulders, the way Aisha paced back and forth in front of her tent, and the weary look on Ebbe's face. Even Destry had his ears pulled back, and his long black tail swished in distress.

Rose moved to Stefan, holding his arm like she'd never let him go. Vadoma had her arms crossed and was watching Aisha like she wanted to commit murder. Her mother looked up and her frown deepened when she saw Bella holding Malik's hand. She wasted no time in pleasantries.

"Aisha has informed us of the *asinine* plan you cooked up with her, poisoning yourself, Belladonna Kezia Wood!" Vadoma's voice was piercing. Bella cringed inwardly. Bella couldn't remember the last time her mother had used her entire name, but she distinctly remembered the punishment that went with it.

Bella raised her chin and adjusted forward. "No one else had a better plan. And it worked, didn't it?" She stood defiantly, mirroring her mother's stance, her arms crossed.

"It didn't work, Bella!" Rose's voice rose up next. "My parents are both dead because of you."

Malik rounded on her. "That's not fair, Rose! That was Strom's doing, not Bella's."

Stefan shoved Malik. "You weren't there. You didn't see it happen. And leave my sister alone!"

Malik shoved him back. "You weren't the one creeping around the dungeon helping those two escape!"

Bella added, "Nor were you two the ones freezing and nearly drowning in the river!"

The two boys leapt at each other, both throwing punches and landing hard in the dirt. Rose was crying again, and both Aisha and Vadoma were shouting at the boys to stop fighting. Added to the mess, the two youngest boys, Young Timbo and Pattin had crawled out of Aisha's tent and were crying too, distressed at all the commotion. Bella tried to get between the two boys, but was kicked away by Stefan after he punched her shoulder in the process of trying to rearrange Malik's face.

"You're in my way!" He roared at her, his red hair bristling all over his body. For a split second it looked to Bella like his teeth were longer in the front, and his nose seemed distended somehow. His eyes glowed golden as well. She scrabbled back, her heart racing.

A long, sharp whistle pierced the air. All the yelling stopped except for the crying of the two young boys and Rose's snuffling. Ebbe looked at them all sternly. "There's been enough sorrow and rage for a hundred years," he said quietly. "We are clan, we Travel together. We will talk this through, not beat each other over our shared grief." Then he coughed wetly, seemingly exhausted by his proclamation.

Aisha huffed and brought over a three-legged stool that stood outside her tent. She helped lower him to it as Vadoma continued to glare. Bella scooped up Pattin and dumped him into Rose's arms. "Hold your brother," she said to her abruptly.

She edged around the fire to stand next to her father, grabbing Young Timbo's hand as she did so. He bit her and ran around the other direction to cling to Stefan's knees and hide his face in them. Shaking off the bite, Bella bent down to her father.

"Da, are you all right?" He didn't look very well, his face pale under black bruises and one eye still swollen shut. He grunted. Bella crossed her arms and faced her mother. Part of her wanted to simply walk away, not confront the anger that simmered through the air. But enough was enough. She wouldn't let a geas placed over fourteen years ago continue to plague her family. Her mother's green slanted eyes sparked as they looked at her. Bella took a deep breath.

"Ma, you know as well as I do that our troubles have been pushed upon us by a curse formed of air, earth, and blood. It isn't who we were meant to be. We have to fight it." Her mother tilted her head, shook it as if she was about to argue. Bella hurried on. "I know we never, ever see eye-to-eye. But it's not our true heart. That evil man has forced it on us, Strom. We've both suffered from it, you even more than me." Bella turned to Stefan and Rose, included them with a sweeping gesture. "I know you've both suffered even more by it, and I grieve with you."

Bella reached out and took her mother's hands. She couldn't remember the touch of them, and inside her something cracked open as her mother's long brown fingers wrapped around hers. Bella fought to get her next words out. "For the record, I think you were dead wrong in keeping it a secret all these years. From now on, we are going to search together to find a way to break it." Bella saw her mother's lips clamp together and realized it was from deep emotion. She could feel it welling up in herself as well.

All or nothing, she thought to herself. Bella reached out and gathered her mother to her. It surprised her to realize they were of a height. After a moment, she felt her mother's arms wrap around her and the dam of emotion within her threatened to break open. Bella whispered into her mother's ear.

"Ma, I wouldn't let some blood curse get you killed. And if I had to pretend to die to make that happen, I was willing to do that. You should thank me, not scold me."

Vadoma nodded once and then pushed back away from Bella. She screwed her face up like she might cry. Shaking her head, she sighed. "Of course I'm grateful to you, Bella. And you're right, I shouldn't have kept it a secret. I just thought it was the right thing to do, as it was I who brought it down upon us."

Ebbe shook his head. "There is none to blame but the creator of it, my beauty."

Bella regarded her mother and felt a glint of humor rise, replacing the awful ache that and seeped down into her bones. She did love this woman, but Saints, it hurt to admit it. Was this the curse at work? Would it always be painful to love her own mother? She quirked her mouth and asked, "So Ma, which hurts more, accepting love from your daughter or admitting you were wrong?"

Vadoma sighed, then raised her shoulders and arms in a large sweep. "I've no idea." The truth of it was evident, and much of the tension eased from the group. Vadoma moved to Malik next and took his hand. "Thank you for what you did for Ebbe and I, Malik."

"You should thank Aisha too," prompted Bella.

"I can fight my own battles, girl." Aisha's slightly foreign cadence broke in. "I need no recognition for a decision I've made."

Bella nodded in her direction. "I'm sure you can fight them. Better than all of us put together, most like."

She opened up to speak to her whole clan. "I made a promise to Malik this morning that I'd never quit, no matter what the danger. That I'd always find him, always be there for him. I want to say the same to you all, and that includes making sure what I'm thinking of doing is not asinine. For I do love you. All of you." She looked directly at her mother, inhaled the sweet, damp air of the forest. Suddenly, it was easy to say. "I love you, Ma."

Her mother took in a deep shuddering breath herself. Her ears turned pink, and then she burst into tears and gathered Bella to her. In her embrace, Bella felt her heart thud and then thud again, an old, cold well of pain being overtopped with warmth. Her heart stabbed her as if it were cracking open. Then the wave of pain vanished, and only the warm remained. It was like surfacing into the sweet air after being a long time under dark waters. Bella hugged her back. She swiped back the suspicious wet stuff that seemed to leak out of her eyes.

"Now, I understand there's apple crisp?"

Many miles away in his lofty tower, Strom clutched at his heart. He was in agony, could not get any air to his lungs. A sweep of pain entered him and overpowered his body. He staggered to reach the bell that called his manservant and saw that his ruby ring now had an inclusion running into the heart of it. He knew what this was. It was the air curse rebounding on him. The gypsy witches must have cracked part of it loose. He ground his teeth. Strom forced down the pain, sucked in what air he could, and moved to the window. He looked to the east at the Darkwood. The rest of the curse still held; he could feel it. Nothing could completely break it without somehow accessing his own blood. He would win. It would just take time. "One day, you will be utterly destroyed," he vowed. "This is not done."

EPILOGUE

A month later, the clan had made good headway to the south. Their trading with the Rutgar clan had been profitable, so they wouldn't suffer by heading to the winter camp grounds early this year. Aisha had traded the last of her spices with them to procure a new cart for Rose and Stefan to use. She simply waved off their protestations by saying that she had always found their parents to be good people and not to make a fuss.

Two other families had joined their group, so they moved untroubled by brigands. They rolled along at a good pace, stopping occasionally in small villages to restock and trade. Things began to feel normal again. Bella no longer woke with her heart racing, unable to breathe, imagining she was in the house of the dead. She kept the dreams to herself, but often saw her mother looking at her with concern. Bella began to enjoy moments with her mother. It no longer bothered her that her mother wanted to braid her hair with the scarlet ribbons she loved.

Ebbe's hands continued to heal, although Bella could see that they would always be crooked and bent. He was relearning how to hold his bodhran drum and could even beat out a bit of a tune. Vadoma fussed over him and over the babies and made sure they bought a milk goat so the boys would not go without. Pattin seemed especially fond of Vadoma, while Young Timbo stuck to Stefan's side. Stefan pretended to be annoyed, but anyone with eyes could see he enjoyed being his little brother's idol.

Their journey took them to the edge of the huge Bodensee lake. Bella marveled at the size of the waters where her favorite whitefish were netted. The Travellers stayed in the last village on the lake before the mountains began for several days. The fisherfolk were not particularly welcoming, but had been glad of the little show Ebbe and Bella had put on.

Bella had tried to encourage Rose to dance with her, but the girl had shaken her head and refused. She was clearly still broken by her parent's deaths, often going for long periods of time without talking at all. Only Bella's kitten, that had grown into a fine cat with pretty orange and tan markings, Selena, seemed to draw her out of her gloom. One day, Bella simply declared that the creature was Rose's now. When the girl tried to demur, Selena ended the conversation by butting its head against Rose's arm and purring loudly. "You see?" Bella had declared. "You're her person!" It had evoked a rare smile from Rose.

Bella and Malik conspired to be together whenever they could. They were just kissing for now, after Vadoma and Aisha had ganged up on them and forced them to swear they would go no further. Bella had always thought Aisha was the most terrifying woman she'd ever met, and it was confirmed when the women had caught her and Malik in the bushes half-dressed. Bella had thought the woman would carve her into tiny pieces. Instead, the promise was extracted. In exchange, the two mothers promised the pair they could be married this winter and have a huge celebration at the winter camp. Bella had kept her fingers crossed behind her back while making the promise, however.

Climbing the mountains beyond the Bodensee had been difficult, even without the snow that capped it for most of the year. The boys had to push the carts from behind while the ponies and horses strained to pull them uphill. The women unloaded what they could from the wagons and carried their possessions on their backs in the steepest bits.

One night a bear had roared into camp, scattering campfires, terrifying everyone. Bella had been sure it was going to kill all of them out of spite, and wondered if Strom had possessed an animal. They'd been saved when a large, shaggy wolf had hurtled into its side, snarling and biting. The bear had hastened away, the wolf chasing after it. Later that night, Bella caught Ebbe muttering something to Vadoma. Her mother had looked shocked and looked over at the cart Stefan and Rose used. Bella resolved to find out what this secret might be. Maybe Malik would help her. She grinned at the thought. They'd share everything now. No secrets, no separation.

Now that they were over the mountains and in the long, wooded valley that would eventually land them in Valencia and the winter camp, Bella grew impatient to be with Malik in body, not just in kisses. She burned at the thought of him and was sure he felt the same.

The thought had grown with the passing weeks. The soft air of the surrounding countryside seemed to encourage ideas of love. Often over the campfire, she'd see Malik looking at her with intensity, and she was sure he wouldn't mind breaking that promise. Surely it wouldn't matter if they coupled a few weeks before their marriage. Besides, it might be fun to entice Malik, to feel the power of her body seduce him. For just a moment, she heard a small voice whisper that promises were made to be kept, but she brushed it aside. It was her body, her decision, after all.

That night, after the evening supper had been cleared away, Bella put on her favorite red skirt. She'd made another for Rose, and she cajoled her cousin into putting it on. Bella tied scarlet ribbons into her curly black hair, and pretty green ones into Rose's short red curls. She moved to her father, who sat contentedly looking at the stars peeking through the trees. Bella could hear the stamps and snuffles of the horses and ponies on the line, as if they were disturbed. Maybe they sensed what she was up to.

"Da, I'm in the frame of mind for a dance. And I think Rose might join me. Would you play your bodhran for us?" Bella knew her father had been practicing and was getting better all the time with his drumming, making his broken fingers move almost as well as before.

Ebbe looked up at her with a knowing glance. "You've a mind to dance, do you, daughter? And who might you be dancing for?"

Bella smiled. "Why, for everyone who watches, Da. I'd dance for the joy of it."

Ebbe chuckled. He looked over at Vadoma. "For the joy of living, for the joy of love. Good reasons." He nodded and fetched his drum.

Bella ran for Rose and took her cousin's hands in her own. Half dragging her to where the campfire had been poked bright again, Bella nodded to Ebbe. She spared a special grin for Malik, who sat on the far side of the fire. She noticed that Aisha gave her son a frown, which he ignored as Bella moved in rhythm to the beat of the drum.

Across from her, Rose slowly moved, too. Delight filled Rose's face as she remembered the steps. Vadoma clapped her hands, as did Pattin and Young Timbo, as the beat of the drum picked up the pace. Soon Bella and Rose were flying, spinning, their feet moving in complicated patterns that had been passed down for generations. Bella felt her heart beat strong and full of love as Malik watched her, his grin spreading to match her own. She felt her passion spread to include all of her family as she spun and danced. Tonight would be special. Tonight was for love.

In the bushes hidden from view, a young woodcutter watched and yearned. He paid no mind to the red-haired girl. His eyes were only for the girl with the golden eyes, the one with the black hair and the scarlet ribbons. The one that seemed to see him there and flashed smiles at him as she spun in a mad dance. He crouched low and waited. Tonight she would be his. One way or another.

This marks the end of *The Traveller's Tale.*

The stories begun here of Bella and her family, Henna, and more, continue in *The Twins of Darkwood*. That tale is set twelve years after the events in this book, and feature Bella's twins and their new stepmother. Turn the page for an excerpt.

THE TWINS OF DARKWOOD

PROLOGUE

She ran. Her long dark hair streamed behind her, catching on branches of the dark forest. Giant trees in the greying early dawn were jarring obstacles blocking her escape. Smaller ones reached out their skinny branches like skeleton hands, scraping her body. She jerked away, tripped. The smell of rotting timber and dead things beneath it engulfed her. Face down in the muck she wanted to scream, but stifled it. Wet leaves slimed her skin.

Must stay silent. He would know she was gone soon, she had to get away or he'd chain her again. She felt the blood oozing between her legs, her belly was on fire. She couldn't stop. With a groan she pushed up from the sucking soil and stumbled on, knowing this was her only chance.

Rain fell, the trees above creating huge drops that thudded onto her body like fists. The quilt she clasped to her was sodden and heavy, but she didn't dare let it go and signpost her flight from the monster behind her. Never again would she let herself be chained. She'd die first.

Driven by fear, fueled by hate and pain, she stumbled on into the rain-soaked forest, away from the woodcutter's cottage that had held her for more than a year. The Darkwood swallowed her up as if she had never been alive.

CHAPTER ONE

Once upon a time, the third daughter of a middle-class merchant who had been cursed with five daughters was promised to be wed. Her husband was to be a widower named Karl who made a living cutting wood in the forest. It was her lot, Bettina supposed. At seventeen, she was already too old to be properly married. Her two oldest sisters had each been married off when they turned fifteen to wealthy men in key port cities. Last year, after being caught half-naked in the woodshed with the hangman's son, her rebellious fourth sister had been marched off to a convent to take care of the obligation to the church and good riddance, as their great-aunt frequently said. This great-aunt was also named Bettina, but her namesake had little in common with the bossy old lady who had outlived three husbands. The elder Bettina now stayed with their family in the uppermost bedroom of the main house, complaining that her syllabub was never made correctly.

Old Bettina never minced words and was clear about Bettina's shortcomings. "That girl is like a shadow, with no substance," she'd say with regularity. "Needs to find her backbone, if you ask me."

It was true, young Bettina was a quiet girl who preferred not to be noticed. She liked to sew and mend things, and make pretty arrangements of the wildflowers she found in the meadow closest to home. She never made a fuss even if she was angry. That role had been taken by the now-nun and also by her youngest and defiant baby sister, Ally, who would live at home and take care of her parents as they aged.

Bettina felt sorry for Ally, who at nine years old was daring and inventive. She'd already run away twice to become a "pirate girl." It was a shame she'd be landlocked—house-locked—

forever until their parents died. "She'll be too old for pirating then," Bettina thought.

Bettina supposed all things considered, being wed to a man she'd met only once was not a bad thing. Karl seemed that he could be kind, although he was worn out around the edges and old, nearly thirty. He'd brought her three wooden nesting bowls he had made himself, with a pretty vine carved into the edge, so she knew he was good with his hands. He was a silent man, and the deep creases around his dark brown eyes were not created by smiles, but by concerns. He had two children already, twins who had reached their eleventh year. He admitted in his deep, slow voice that they were "a handful" as they'd sat together next to the fireplace, Bettina's mother seated in a chair a little way off to ensure propriety was upheld. Karl had paused a moment, looking into the safe flames of the little hearth, and then continued. He told Bettina that his first wife, the twin's mother, had died in a terrible accident at home, falling into their own fireplace and roasting to death before anyone could reach her.

Bettina wondered at that. It would be a difficult thing, she thought, to fall into a fireplace and not get right back out again. Perhaps, as she said to the woodcutter who might become her husband, his wife had fainted, and then was overcome by smoke. Bettina meant it kindly, to say that Karl's wife had not suffered overmuch. Karl had looked away with a frown as if contemplating a response, but then sighed and shook his head. "It is not for us to be knowing," he said gruffly. "But the twins, Gert, and Harold, they need a mother, someone who will be kind to them. You seem kind."

She smiled at him. He nodded, agreeing with himself.

"They are, as I said, a handful, but they will soon be old enough to apprentice out and away. Then we can have a peaceful home. You would like this, yes?"

Bettina turned the idea over in her head again, as she had been doing since her father had informed her he had an offer for her, and that he desired her to take it. Her thoughts wandered back to that moment when her life had taken this unexpected turn. She'd been in the garden, the sun warm on her neck, happily pruning her mother's roses back in preparation for winter. She liked the job of trimming the bushes down to the first five-leaf stem, knowing that the roses would rest, and then bloom again come spring. It was a little like magic, she'd thought as she hummed happily. The bees in the garden hummed alongside her as they filled their legs with pollen to take to their hive, and a late-season yellow butterfly flapped next to her, bringing a smile to her face.

Her peace had been broken by her mother calling from the kitchen door. "Bettina, your father wants you. In the front hall, right now, if you please." There was a worried snap to her mother's voice that Bettina knew meant she was unhappy. Bettina looked up, but her mother had already disappeared into the house.

The front hall was where her father met important clients. Bettina and her sisters were expressly forbidden to be in that section of the house. Bettina remembered how her stomach had lurched, and she worried that she'd done something wrong. With a steadying breath, she'd brushed the dirt from her hands, put her trim knife in her pocket and hurried inside the stoutly timbered house.

She'd passed through the kitchen with a smile for Cook, who had her hands full of pastry for their dinner. Bettina remembered how she'd moved quickly down the passageway that ran the length of the house, turning left into the front hall with its tapestried walls and heavy oak furniture. The fireplace burned at one end. This was always the warmest room in the house. Bettina stopped at the doorway and felt a trickle of sweat run down her back.

Her father had been standing at his desk, looking through what were sure to be important papers. Tufts of grey hair stood out just above his ears. Bettina thought privately he looked very much like a grumpy owl, with those tufts and his pointed, beaky nose, but had never said such a disrespectful thing out loud.

"Papa, you wanted to see me?" Her voice was breathy, partly from her trot through the house, but more from anxiety. Her father had continued to frown at his papers. He'd not heard her. This was a common experience for Bettina. She went unseen and unheard throughout most of her days. It was all right by her most of the time to be like a ghost in her own home, as she rarely got scolded or punished. Sometimes though, she wished for more, to have a bolder life, be a person who was seen and heard. Someone who mattered.

She cleared her throat and tried again. "I'm here, Papa."

Her father swiveled his head toward her. Just like an owl. "Ah. There you are. You are to be married. We've had a decent initial offer for your hand, and I've given my permission. He will be here next week to meet you. I expect you to accept him. We'll have the wedding here."

Bettina stood, stunned. Her jaw dropped, but no words came out. Her father had frowned and turned his whole body to face her head-on. "Now, Bettina, you should be grateful. Extremely grateful. And you will accept this man, do you hear me?"

"Who, who is it?" Bettina always stuttered when she was nervous.

"As if it matters, but he is a woodcutter named Karl. You are to be wed. You will become a proper wife and also a stepmother."

"Step, stepmother?" Bettina could barely take it in. She'd blinked rapidly, hoping she was having a dream. She pinched the top of her hand and found she was indeed awake.

"Stop repeating what I say, Bettina. And why are you shaking your hand like that? You've been taught to be a proper lady, I'm sure you'll do very well." Her father had turned back to his papers at that. Bettina was dismissed.

She'd blindly stumbled up the back stairs to the room she shared with her sister Ally and laid down on her cot to try to stop her head from spinning. She hadn't known what to feel. Not gratitude, even though she'd been sure gratitude was what she was supposed to be filled with. Not fear either. It was an odd, prickly feeling. She'd trembled all over and felt bile rise in her throat. What would it be like to leave this room, with its sloping ceiling, high on her side, low on Ally's, with its peeling bit of plaster which looked like three little bears sitting in a row? Her thoughts had bounced back and forth. Maybe it would be wonderful to live in a new place, to see different things and meet new people. But if she left this place she'd always known to go somewhere entirely new, would she know how to behave? And how did one "stepmother?"

Later that night, she'd whispered to Ally about her possible impending marriage to a woodcutter. Ally had frowned and cried a little and begged her to run away with her that night. "We could pack up a loaf of bread and some cheese, and go north to the sea, and find a ship and be pirate girls, together!"

Bettina smiled at the memory. She was brought abruptly back to the present by her mother, who cleared her throat loudly and cracked a single word at her. "Bettina!"

Startled, Bettina looked to her mother, who widened her eyes and shifted them to bring her attention back to her suitor. Bettina wished that her mother would've given her some sort of advice before this meeting. She felt her body tense as she looked up at the woodcutter, whose face had moved from kind query to frowning. How long had she been lost in memory?

Bettina twisted her fingers together. It was now or never. She had a choice to make. She wasn't used to having those. It would upset her father if she refused this husband and his mysterious, difficult children. To her parents, she was simply an extra mouth to feed. Someone to be ordered to mend or tend something. She'd become accustomed to keeping her eyes downcast and being as small and meek as possible. Was it easier to be overlooked than to be a stepmother? But if she didn't take this offer, she'd be forever the girl who couldn't find a husband. A useless burden. Her stomach flipped at the thought. She hunched her shoulders up and the wild idea occurred to her that running away with Ally to be pirate girls was not such a bad idea after all.

Karl fisted his hands on his knees. "Was I not clear in my asking you to wed just now?" He looked displeased with her. Fear struck deeply in Bettina. She hated disappointing people; it made her heart ache and colored all of her tasks with sadness for days afterwards. She must speak up and answer, but her throat was so dry. Hollowness in her gut thrummed in warning. If she didn't reply immediately, her final opportunity to try out a new life would be lost to her. Karl might be old and rather odd, frightening even, but better that than living her life out as a useless burden. It was time to prune her old life away with the snip of a decision.

She forced herself to look him in the eyes. After a deep breath, she managed, "Yes, Karl I will come and be your wife, and a stepmother to your children." Out of the corner of her eye, Bettina thought she saw her mother twitch as if she wanted to stand up or speak. Turning toward her mother, Bettina could tell something was distressing her. Bettina had gotten particularly good at reading people in her efforts to be as unobtrusive as possible. But then her mother gathered herself, and nodded once, lips pressed together as if holding in a secret.

Karl grunted. "It is done then." His hands relaxed on his knees, the knuckles holding white for a moment, betraying how tightly they had been fisted.

With a gesture that was bold for her, Bettina reached out and covered that large, work scarred hand with her own. She liked the hardness of his hand, the way his fingers eventually curled gently around her own tiny soft one. They sat just like that for a long while and during the not-uncomfortable silence Bettina made up her mind to make this man's later years as happy as she could, and make the children that were not her own behave. Perhaps—and the very thought made her cheeks flush bright red —they would make a baby of their own, too.

CHAPTER TWO

Her father was satisfied with the match, or perhaps he was simply happy to get his roof and barn re-roofed for free by the woodcutter. Bettina wasn't supposed to know the particulars, but she and Ally had peeped through the crack in the door and listened as the final deal was struck. Her hand in marriage was traded for wooden shingles and the labor to place them on both house and barn within the next two years.

Ally turned to her and whispered, "At least you'll come back for a visit when he comes to do the roof." Her eyes were so sad, it made Bettina sad too, and her stomach lurched. To shake off her uneasiness and make her little sister smile again, Bettina reached out and tickled Ally, who clapped her hand over her mouth to stifle her giggles as she raced away. Bettina grinned and ran after her.

Later, when Bettina packed her small trunk, she paused for a moment, holding her favorite yellow ribbons with the green shamrocks stitched in them for luck before she placed them inside. She'd had them for as long as she could remember, purchased at the annual Saint's Day fair from some Travellers. Cook had said they looked pretty in her curling brown hair.

Bettina was worried she'd never see Cook or Ally again. Perhaps Karl was the sort of man who didn't allow his wife to travel. After all, they never saw her oldest sister Carlotta anymore, as her husband believed wives should remain in the house, tending to it and the children. Bettina missed Carlotta and the marvelous stories she used to tell, filled with pirates and treasure and quests, and bears in the woods. In Carlotta's stories, it was the girls who won at the end of the day, not like real life at all.

The next morning, Cook helped her put on her best blue dress and lace up her good boots. Cook held Bettina's hands for a long time, clearing her throat, her eyes welling with unshed tears. She gave Bettina a quick kiss on the cheek, handed her some late-blooming flowers to hold, and hurried away. Bettina's father was standing just outside the kitchen door, rocking back and forth from heel to toe as if he'd rather the event was already over.

"Cleaned up well, so you did, Bettina. You look very pretty." He offered his arm. After a startled beat, she took it awkwardly. They started walking down the long hall. Bettina felt she should say something during this rare moment, but her thoughts had flown away. Step by step, the hallway pulled them to the front hall.

Her father leaned over to her and whispered, "Burgermeister Strom himself has graced us with his presence for your wedding. Your mother used to work for him, you know, as a maid. It was Strom who arranged my marriage to her. Your sister Carlotta was born eight months later, strong, and healthy. Blessed, we were."

Bettina hadn't known. Indeed, this was the most personal information her father had ever imparted. She looked up at him, but he was already peering forward into the front hall. He jerked his chin up as they walked forward, making his beaky nose even more prominent. She looked towards the fireplace and saw Karl. He looked just as uncomfortable as she felt in a too-tight jacket, his work-torn hands twisting in front of him. It made her feel a little better to know she wasn't the only one feeling nervous.

Her mother was there too, her lips pinched together and her face white. Strom, the town's mayor, looked young, handsome, and stern with his thick black hair with a single streak of white in it. Bettina had never seen him up close, even though he'd been

the Burgermeister since before she'd been born. He gave her a
smile as she approached. Surely it was meant to be kind, but
Bettina clutched her father's arm a little harder and wished he'd
look elsewhere.

Her father bustled them forward and put her small white hand
into Karl's giant one. Bettina swallowed hard as she felt her
father move away to join her mother. She felt like she was
spinning adrift in a vast ocean. She dipped her nose into the
sweet flowers Cook had given her, glad of their familiar
fragrance. Bettina spoke the appropriate words about vows and
obedience when prompted by the clergyman. Bettina felt that she
was outside of herself, watching the quick ceremony from a
distance. How odd, she thought as the clergyman pronounced
them husband and wife, that such a change in her life would be
over and done so quickly.

After being served a slice of wedding cake and having a few
sips of father's best brandy, the Burgermeister took his leave
along with the clergyman. He had a word with her father at the
door, shaking his hand as if a deal had been struck between
them. Once he was gone, the air seemed lighter. Her mother
heaved in a deep breath as if she'd been holding it for a long
time. Her father clapped his hands together, well-satisfied, and
called for the servants to put her trunk in Karl's cart.

Bettina climbed the wooden stairs to bid goodbye to her great-
aunt Bettina, but the old woman turned her head away, muttering
something about how marrying in haste never came to any good
whatsoever. Bettina tucked her head one last time into her old
bedroom, which already seemed empty and unloved, the
mattress stripped and rolled up against dust. With a sigh, Bettina
made her way out of the house. Karl was already up in his cart
and ready to leave. His gaze was fixed on the road ahead.

Bettina climbed up into the cart with the help of one of the
servants. Her father and mother stood at the door to watch her
go. At the last minute, Ally, who had pouted in the barn and

refused to come to the wedding at all, ran up and thrust a tiny kitten at Bettina. "There, now you have something that will love you and won't leave." Ally burst into tears and fled into the house.

Bettina felt her heart tear. She was going to miss Ally, she realized, and the comfortable home where she'd lived all of her seventeen years. "Goodbye," she called to her parents. They both raised their hands in farewell, turned back into the house, and shut the door firmly.

Feeling shunned and alone, she looked to her husband. Karl looked at her and then at the kitten. He cleared his throat as if to say something, but instead picked up the reins and clucked to his mare. Bettina felt her heart thudding. She was glad he'd not forbidden her the kitten, glad of its warmth and its little beating heart as they started their two-day journey to the Darkwood where Karl lived.

They left the town over the stone bridge that crossed the sparkling river she'd known for her entire seventeen years and proceeded to drive through outliers of thin woods and wide meadows. They drove southeast, headed to where the forests grew tall and dark and then taller and darker still. The far-away mountains grew steadily closer. They were tipped with snow as winter was already starting in the high places. Bettina watched the side of the road and saw the familiar grasses and wildflowers she loved dwindle in numbers and then disappear altogether. They gave way to brambles of underbrush and stinging nettles. Thick ivy twined along limestone fenceposts that marked the road at intervals, with narrow tracks indicating that other villages and towns were scattered somewhere over the horizon to the right or left of them. They drove on for most of the day at a steady pace, so as to reach the village where they would pause their journey by nightfall. The kitten slumbered in her lap. It seemed like the only sound in the world was the steady clop, clop, clop of the mare.

Bettina racked her brain to think of something to say to her husband. It seemed too forward to ask him any questions, and she had the suspicion that her life up to this point had nothing of real interest in it. She'd been an unobtrusive, dutiful daughter, that was all. Bettina watched the horse, black with a scattering of white splotches on the backside and a K branded on the right back haunch, the skin puckered and pink where no hair would ever grow again. She flinched at the thought of the brand burning the creature's skin. How frightening that must have been.

She must have made some sort of noise, because Karl looked at her. His face seemed hooded, and his eyes didn't seem to see her. Rather, they measured her. He turned away as if disappointed at what he was seeing. She spoke up, desperate to keep his attention.

"The horse's backside looks like the night sky with white stars scattered on it," she said in her brightest tone of voice. The one she used when it seemed her great aunt was about to complain about something.

Karl was silent for a long while, and then grunted and moved his chin upward in assent. Nothing else. The horse kept clip clopping along the dirt road.

Bettina was further from home than she had ever been in her life.

As the sky began to turn from bright blue to pink and then deepened to purple, Bettina worried about the night to come, her honeymoon night. She didn't know what to do. Years ago she'd carefully sewn a nightgown for her trousseau. When Bettina had asked her mother about her wedding night, her mother had said, "You will become a woman," then buttoned her lips tightly together, only opening them to criticize Bettina's stitching. Bettina had wondered how such a shy woman had birthed five children.

"Karl," she began tentatively and stopped, twisting her fingers together.

"We are almost to Hamsdorf, where we will stay tonight with the Smith who buys my wood." Karl looked at over at her. "Are you tired?"

"No, not really." She couldn't bring herself to ask him what he expected of her. They hadn't even kissed at the wedding. Would they start with that?

Silence fell between them for the next few miles, and the sky continued to darken. Bettina fought back tears. There was no good reason for her to cry, she thought. This was, after all, what men and women did, just like all the other animals. The cats never seemed to enjoy it, though. She snuggled the tiny kitten her sister had given her to her cheek.

A cluster of cottages appeared on the horizon. Bettina could see a fire pit in the front of what she guessed was the smithy. It glowed a dull orange, making everything else look grey. She looked for an inn sign as they rolled up to the building and stopped. The cottages nearby were empty and in disrepair or dark, their shutters closed against the night. Even the smithy was dark except for a small lantern in the window. No inn signs at all. The place had a haunted feel to it, as if any life had been sucked from the village long ago.

"Hallo the house," called Karl in a deep, loud voice.

After a long moment, the wooden door opened, and a burly man stepped out, wiping his mouth with his hand. "Later than we expected, Woodcutter."

"Aye."

Bettina waited for Karl to introduce her, but he said nothing. The burly man waved his hand to a decrepit structure beyond his cottage.

"Well, you're welcome to the barn for yourselves and the horse. I suppose you'll want supper."

"As we arranged." Karl got down from the wagon and unhitched the horse as if nothing at all was wrong. Bettina sat frozen on the wagon. She was to honeymoon in a barn?

The burly man squinted up at her. "The privy is out the back if you need it."

Bettina was glad the night covered up her flush of embarrassment. Tucking the kitten into her shawl, she gathered her skirts and clambered down from the wagon. The privy turned out to be a half stone wall behind which a hole in the ground yawned with two planks stretched across it. Bettina was repulsed but having no other option, she planted her feet, hiked up her skirts and let her bladder release in a steady warm stream. She let out a sigh of pure relief.

"Held that for a while," a sly voice whispered from the dark. Bettina startled, nearly losing her footing on the planks as she turned wildly around. The smith grinned at her, leaning on the stone wall. He was close enough that she could see he was missing several teeth. Shaking her skirts down, she ignored his coarse chuckle, tucked her chin, and scurried as fast as she could towards the barn. Yanking open the doors, she moved quickly to Karl.

"That man," she began. "He was staring at me, he watched me…"

Karl held up a hand and gave her a hard look. "He is a good customer and has no need to put us up for the night. I'll brook no complaints, wife."

Bettina sucked in air. Where was the gentle man she'd spoken with by the fire? She felt her stomach quiver as she clenched every muscle to stand still and not flee. She stared at the ground where dirty bits of straw mixed with the mud floor. In all her years of dreaming of boys and marriage, never had she imagined this as her wedding night.

The barn door creaked. A bone-thin elderly woman entered carrying two pails. She placed them inside next to the door, then stood, hands on the small of her back. "There be stew and water for ye both. The horse blankets will have to do you, we've no extra bedding."

"Thanks to you, mistress." Karl nodded. "We're grateful for the shelter."

"As ye should be. The wolves have come ravening from the mountains and they have no care if ye be two-legged or four if they eye you for their meal. We lost a cow to them not two days past."

With a squinted eye, she regarded Bettina, then snorted. "Ye'll not last the winter. I'd bet our best bed on it." Her lips snapped shut as she nodded firmly.

Karl frowned. Bettina couldn't tell if he was angry at the woman's words or if he was considering if they were true.

"Are there bowls to go with that stew?" Bettina couldn't help herself, the words just popped out. "Please?" she added as an afterthought.

"You didn't pack any for travel?" The woman was astonished.

"You have the ones I made for you. Fetch them from the trunk." Karl's tone was annoyed. Bettina felt chastened that she'd forgotten about his engagement gift to her.

"Of, of course," she stuttered, and headed for the cart where her dowry trunk lay. She heard Karl behind her.

"We'd be grateful for spoons, however."

"I suppose I can fetch some." The woman gave Bettina another disparaging look as she left.

Bettina found the bowls and mutely held them out to Karl. He took them from her. "We cannot afford to anger these people," he explained in a gentler tone. "I trade with them for my knives and my axes."

Bettina nodded. "I'm sorry, husband." Her voice cracked on the last odd word. *Husband.* She was suddenly terrified of what might come next, what being a wife to a husband such as this might mean. But if she ran away, the ravening wolves might be waiting for her, their mouths full of sharp teeth, claws ready to rend the flesh from her bones.

He shook his head dismissively. "You'll learn. Now, make up a bed with the hay and these blankets." He passed her two heavy horsehair blankets. They were prickly and smelled of animals and rot. Bettina struggled not to show how heavy they were. She didn't want to make any more mistakes.

She also didn't want to spend her wedding night in a barn. She had no idea how to make a bed of straw, but she was determined to take some charge over what might happen in the night. Piling up some straw, she made two mounds a little distance from each other, rather than one larger one. She placed a blanket upon each.

"Is that right?" she asked.

He looked at her for a long moment, then stared off into the distance. With a sigh, he nodded. "They will do, wife."

CHAPTER THREE

It was a long, cold night. Bettina lay on the uncomfortable blanket. She listened to Karl's snores, stared at his large back. Little noises in the barn spoke of mice and bugs squirming through the prickly straw. Thankfully, Karl had kept all his clothes on, as had she. Bettina worried that perhaps she'd been wrong, making up two beds. Now that she was a properly married woman she knew she should want to lay with her husband. Truth be told, she was curious as to what lying with a husband might be like. Rolling to her other side, she hoped that it would be dawn soon. Cracks in the wood let in small beams of light, but it was just the moon rising. A distant flurry of howls sent shivers up her spine. The woman had not been lying about the wolves. Bettina tried to imagine the moonbeams as little rays of hope, but failed miserably.

She wouldn't cry. This was nothing to cry over. This was just a night in a barn and on the morrow they'd get to Karl's house and start their life together there. She'd block this out and pretend it never happened. Bettina rolled back over to look at

Karl. She resolved to think nothing but good thoughts about him. Look at his strong arms, she told herself. That broad back. Feeling bolder, she reached out and held her hand just inches from him, feeling the heat rise off of his flesh. She shivered, wondering how his skin would feel, all that heat pressed up against her. What would kissing him be like? His lips didn't look soft, just two hard slashes pressed together. She'd kissed her cousin Johann once when they were twelve, just to practice. It had been wet and blubbery. Slippery, like eel pie. She didn't think kissing Karl would be like that. Not at all.

They rose early in the morning. Bettina scurried one more time out to the privy, making sure to look around for the smith before lifting her skirts. She did her business quickly, then joined Karl on the wagon. Neither the smith nor his skeletal wife came out to say goodbye. Karl didn't speak to her either. They started back on the road, leaving the decaying little village behind them, headed for the dark woods that loomed on the horizon.

The wind blew cold. Bettina hunched as far down as she could and snuggled her kitten close to her. She wished it could be a fine summer day, but the year was fast rolling around to winter. What would it be like in the deep woods in winter? Perhaps it would be warmer with all those trees blocking the wind. She wondered how big Karl's house was. Her house. *Home*, Bettina thought. *I must think of it as home now.*

She started to ask Karl about it, but changed her mind when she looked at him. He seemed angry this morning, broody. His eyes were fixed on the woods ahead. He gripped the reins like he wanted to snap them in half. The tendons in his hands stood out, white and gnarled. The horse had stopped her clip clopping pace, and seemed to drag her steps as if she also dreaded entering the forest.

They passed only one other cart that day. It came from the direction they were headed. Bettina sat up straight, eager to see who might be travelling from the woods. Maybe it was a neighbor she could meet. The cart, drawn by a single dray horse, held a tanned woman with multicolored ribbons in her curly red hair and a baby on her lap. A burly young man walked ahead, leading the dray. When they drew close, the young man doffed his cap, revealing shaggy red hair. He pulled their brown and green wagon off the road into the tall grasses so Karl could pass.

Bettina started to smile and wave in thanks for the politeness, but Karl pushed her hand down. Then he hacked and spit. The globule hit the young man's feet, but he didn't move. The woman raised her chin, but turned her head to look away from them, her ribbons fluttering in the breeze. Karl clicked his tongue at their own horse and slapped the reins to speed them past.

Bettina turned around to see the cart pull back onto the track. The woman glared at her with pure hatred. Stunned by the whole exchange, Bettina looked at Karl. He returned her look. "You've never seen Travellers before?" asked Karl. "Well, pay them no mind. They are the lowest of the low. If you'd been on your own, they'd have killed you and taken all you had. We've no business with them, ever. They're vermin, Travellers." He spat again, as if to rid his mouth of the name.

It was more words in a row than Bettina had ever heard him speak. She risked a sideways glance at him from beneath her eyelashes. He looked angry, with a raw edge to it. Her father had often looked like that, right before he beat one of the servants. Bettina made herself become small and still in her seat. When men looked like that, being invisible was best.

Travellers, she mused. Bettina knew of them, of course she did. One band or another always showed up at the yearly Saints Day festival in town. They'd worn colored ribbons in their hair like the woman on the cart and had sung and danced. Bettina had thought them charming. So alive. So free. She'd gotten the yellow ribbons with the green shamrocks she had in her dower chest from them. Bettina decided some things were better left unsaid and that Karl never had to know where her ribbons came from.

Later, as the cart rumbled on, the road became a barely visible path that the outliers of the Darkwood was trying its best to erase. The wind blew straight at them as if trying to push them away, cold and unwelcoming. Bettina drew her cloak around her more closely and wished her dowry had included a few more woolen things.

Karl noticed her discomfort. He pulled the battered green scarf he'd been wearing and placed it around her neck. It was a tender gesture and Bettina smiled at him warmly. He can be a good man, she thought. Here was proof. Everything will be all right. She scooted a few inches closer to him on the bench.

They entered the woods proper. Silver birch lined the track, their leaves just starting to yellow. Taller beech trees were behind them, as well as oak tinged with red and orange. Towering over all the pine and fir trees growing so tall they created their own type of night just a few hundred strides to either side of them. The smell of the air changed as well, becoming richer, full of the scent of pine and moldering leaves, and the musk of animals hiding just beyond their sight. Bettina knew all sorts of predators lived in the woods besides wolves. There were brown bears, lynx, and wild boar as well as poisonous snakes like adders and the asp viper. She kept her eyes open as they continued to move through the forest. Karl was also mindful of the edges of the path, his axe ready at their feet.

Karl seemed to read her mind. "The wild things will not bother us in the daylight."

Bettina nodded, grateful for his reassurance. "I've heard tales of these woods, that wild creatures make it a dangerous place." She paused, then added, "And that bands of Travellers make it dangerous too."

He squinted at her. "No doubt for the unprepared. But the Travellers no longer have a home here. The Rutgar clan and the village chased them out two years ago."

"There's a village?" Bettina perked up, imagining shops where she could trade for pretty things, and an inn with an eating house. Perhaps she could meet people there. She'd enjoyed the weekly market day outings in her old town. Greeting people, sharing pleasantries or small complaints with familiar faces, exchanging nods and smiles with new folk.

"It is small and a long way from my steading," he replied. "Over a half day's walk, all told, for those used to walking." He gave her a sidelong glance. Bettina felt slighted. She walked all the time. She covered her irritation and nodded at him politely to continue. "I trade for supplies there perhaps twice a year if I must."

"Are there people near your house?" Bettina asked, her hopes for company fading.

"Some. Old Matilda who bakes bread and sweets is an hour's walk further up this trail at the intersection of the south road. The Rutgar clan who are hunters and trappers are another hour past that. Tinkers make their way past the house at times. The Travellers used to have their summer camp past Matilda's, but as I said, we drove the thieving bunch from it."

His lips clamped shut, and while Bettina could tell there was more he might say about the Travellers, she couldn't think of a way to draw it out of him. She wondered why he'd made his home so far away from other people. She supposed for a moment he needed to be nearer the trees where he made his living, but then realized what a silly thought that was. Trees were everywhere here. He could've put his house anywhere he liked.

Many hours later, as the shadows fell long behind them and the light was nearly gone, they pulled up to a small, but well-made faded wooden cottage. Bettina took in the sturdy door with iron hasps and the scraped skin window beside it. A large stone chimney rose on the left side of the house, with lapped wooden shingles slanting down from the chimney halfway to the ground on the other side. It shared a dirt clearing with a small barn and pen that contained a pair of brown and white goats. A water well with a cover stood by the track, evidence that perhaps travelers would be given water and exchange a word or two. It was a lonely place, thought Bettina. She cast about for something kind to say.

"It is so—quiet here. Where are the children?" Bettina asked, her throat tightening in spite of her resolve to remain sunny and positive. She was nervous about meeting them. Bettina had saved them each a slice of wedding cake, hoping that the sweets would make her introduction go more smoothly.

"Old Matilda watches them when I cannot." Karl went behind the cart and lifted out her trunk. She turned to watch him. "I'll fetch them tomorrow."

Bettina's throat tightened even more, and her mind raced. They were to be alone tonight. The formal wedding night. She knew this was what was right and proper. After her mother had refused to speak of it, she'd gone to Cook and asked her what she should do. Cook had given her a few short words of advice. That it would hurt for a moment but that she was to be quiet about that, and be sure to wash the blood with salt from the sheets with salt the next morning so they didn't hold a stain. Bettina worried about this part, of cleaving to her husband. She'd always thought that was a violent word, cleaving, as if axes were involved, a severing of limbs or spirit. Bettina made herself look up and smile in spite of her misgivings and was rewarded by a gentle smile back. Bettina was relieved. There was the man she had met at her parent's house. Perhaps Karl didn't like travel and that would account for his cold behavior for most of the trip.

Karl carried her trunk into the house. Bettina waited, not sure if she should follow. Karl came back out and seeing her seated, gave her a wry look. "Go in and start the fire, while I tend to the mare." He lifted her down out of the cart easily, as if she weighed nothing at all. Bettina shivered at his strength. He handed her the basket of food they'd brought from her old home. He led the mare toward the barn. Bettina saw some chickens wandering in the pen and their henhouse in the near corner. Good, she thought, we have goat's milk and eggs, we will not starve. She mustered her spirits. It was time to be a good wife.

Clutching the kitten to her chest with one hand, the basket in the other, Bettina walked into her new home. It was dark inside the single room which smelled of dust and cold ashes. Two rag rugs that needed mending lay on the wooden floor. A sturdy table with four well-made wooden chairs stood nearest the door, a black oak food cupboard and two small bed pallets on the other side of the fireplace at the back of the room. A stepladder in the back climbed steeply to an open half loft where Bettina could see a larger bed. Everything was cold and still. There was no feeling of welcome or warmth here. Bettina swallowed. She thought of Old Bettina and her ongoing proclamation that her namesake should find her backbone. Well she would, Bettina thought, surprising herself.

She moved to the fireplace and found the striker stones. The smell of charred meat wafted into her face as she bent to the task, and Bettina saw in her mind the horror of a woman screaming, dying in the flames. Bettina gasped and pulled herself away from the fireplace, shaking. At her feet, the kitten mewed and wound around her ankles. Taking a deep breath, Bettina bent again to fireplace, and as the flames caught, backed away. She took a taper, and lit the lantern that stood on the table. Something metal gleamed in the extra light. Bettina kneeled down and saw that a thick iron ring had been driven into the stone of the fireplace. Solid and hard, it looked like it had grown from the stone itself. She wondered what it would be used for, but couldn't come up with an answer. A large dog perhaps? Shrugging, she stood to explore the food cupboard.

Inside the cupboard she found a small sack of pease for porridge and a round cheese. There were some pretty plates and intricately carved cups as well. Bettina wondered if they were part of the dowry that Karl's first wife had brought with her. Touching the other woman's things made her wonder what she'd been like, if she'd been happy with her twins and her husband here in the lonely woods. With a shake of her head, Bettina moved to the ladder, determined that she would make this place her own.

She climbed the eight steep rungs and stopped. Instead of a proper quilt, there was a large fur covering the bedframe. Bettina touched it and saw that it was stitched together beautifully. Multiple rabbit furs had been matched precisely, with a trim of red fox on the edging. Bettina was adept at stitching herself and knew the time and craft that had gone into it.

Finely made or not, it was not hers. She folded the fur and put it on top of the wardrobe. She placed the quilt with squares of blue and gray she'd made years ago for her dowry chest, and spread it on the bed—the marriage bed. She shuddered at what might be expected of her there. Bettina couldn't tell if the shudder was excitement or dread. Pushing the thought away, she went back downstairs and pulled out the pretty green tablecloth she'd embroidered. She draped the table with it and placed her aunt's wedding gift of candlesticks and good candles on top. After lighting them, She pulled out the food from her basket, a meat pie to add to the cheese and a stoppered flask of ale. After hesitating a moment she set out the first wife's plates and cups.

Bettina sliced off a piece of the cheese and kneeled down to offer it to the kitten. It pounced on the treat, making her laugh. The dark in the cottage fought back against the laugh, against the light and the pretty tablecloth. Bettina's courage faltered, but she squeezed her fingers together and clenched her toes up tight. She would be brave; she'd find her backbone. The little kitten arched its back and hissed as the door opened. Karl filled the doorway.

The flickering firelight caught on the crags of his face, shifting them to demon form. Bettina swallowed hard, then stood even though her knees threatened to give way and looked up at her husband.

CHAPTER FOUR

Karl faced his new, delicate, dove-like wife. She trembled, her fingers twisted together, but her chin was up and her deep brown eyes were steady. He made himself smile at her even though his skin felt oddly stretched when he did so. "I will get some water, so we can wash."

Karl picked up the bucket by the door and walked out to the well. His gut clenched as he set the pail to the hook and lowered it to let it fill. He pulled the water up and wondered what he'd been thinking, bringing such a girl to the woods. A plain girl with soft hands and a sweet smile, but little else to recommend her. The water sloshed as he unhooked the bucket, and he stifled a curse. He'd been thinking of the children. They needed a mother, one that was kind, and that was all there was to it. He couldn't make his livelihood and watch over the twins. He could hardly believe they were his, sometimes. On his darkest nights, he wondered if their real mother had mated with wolves in the forest.

Karl let the bucket rest on the edge of the well and wondered if he should tell Bettina the truth; that she was not his second wife, but his third. That his first wife, Belladonna, had disappeared the night the children were born. He frowned, remembering that wild, horrible night. The rain pouring down, the door ajar, the empty birthing bed. He'd searched for her all night and for days after, alternating between rage and despair. He'd only found some of her dark hair clinging to the branches of the forest and the place she'd fallen, but had never found her. Even the Rutgar clan far out at the croft hadn't seen her, or so they claimed. There'd been a wariness in their eyes though, as if they were only partially telling the truth. Untrustworthy, the lot of them. Even now, as he thought of the children's mother, he burned inside. He clenched his fists in an effort to shove away the feelings. He didn't know if it was passion or fury that raged inside him. That red heat would do him no good with this soft, sweet girl he'd brought home, so he relentlessly pushed those thoughts away into the dark places of his soul.

Karl thought about the coldness of his second wife. He'd had no desire to tell her about Belladonna. He had found that wife with the help of Old Matilda the baker, who knew how to keep secrets. She'd written to a widow she knew. She'd been a dutiful if dour wife to him and had fed and clothed the children. She'd not loved them though, that was always clear, and she had certainly not loved nor desired him, although she'd submit to him if he demanded it, laying still and silent until he finished. The children had hated her, their faces growing hard and still when she was near.

The children. The twins. Karl looked down the path where they were staying, just an hour's walk away. He wished he were not obliged to bring them back under his roof. His jaw clenched, and for a moment he hated himself. They were just children, even if they were spiteful and hard to control. Whip-thin Gert with her sharp tongue and sly looks dressed in innocence when she was caught out. She made him lose sleep at night, wondering what evil thing she'd think up next. And then there was Harold, twice the size of his twin. Rarely speaking, content to stand like a rooted tree and stare at nothing for hours, his head listing slightly as if too heavy for his neck. *Something's wrong with the inside of that boy's head,* thought Karl for the thousandth time, his frown lines deepening. Harold wasn't mean like Gert was, but he didn't seem to comprehend right from wrong. Last summer, one of the chickens had pecked Gert. She'd flown into a rage, demanding her twin enact revenge. It had taken two nights without food locked into the barn, but the children had at last relented, and Gert told him the truth of it. Harold hadn't thought twice, he'd just done as she demanded, solemnly twisting off the heads of all the chickens as Gert caught them.

Karl winced as he remembered the beating he had given them after the confession. He could tell Harold didn't know why he'd been beaten. He'd just taken it silently, as Gert had done, but Gert had smiled afterwards as if she'd earned a victory. But how else would they learn right from wrong, except by beatings? It was how he had been taught after all, by his father. *Spare the rod and spoil the child.*

Karl shook himself from the memory. It would get better now that they had a stepmother again. In a year or so, Harold would come with him into the forest to cut the wood. The boy was already showing an interest in carving wood, or mayhap it was just cutting things with knives that he liked. No matter. Perhaps Gert could be sent to town to earn her keep as a maid, or a seamstress. Bettina could teach her how to mend for a start. Perhaps the simple task of teaching and learning would bond them. Karl frowned and felt the hardship of children who lacked the ability to love. Maybe it would be best if he told Bettina everything, start anew with her. Perhaps find forgiveness for his sins.

He turned to face the house with his bucket of cold, sweet water. Karl relaxed, taking in the hominess of the cottage with its good walls and sturdy chimney, the smoke curling gently out of it speaking of a welcoming hearth. Then another vision removed all sense of comfort from him. The image of the curled and blackened corpse of his second wife, her fingers clutched around the edges of the fireplace, pointed nails and bones with shreds of blackened flesh clinging to them, as if in her last moments she had tried to claw her way out of the fire. Her eyes and nose gone, melted off, but her mouth opened in an unending scream.

Shaking his head like he did when the blackflies rose from swampy ground to torture his horse and himself, Karl tightened his grip on the bucket and strode back to the house. He'd make a home with this new wife, Bettina. Her gentle ways would tame the children, and maybe at long last he could find the peace he craved, the red fire of longing for Belladonna, his first wife, extinguished. There was no need to sully this relationship with that one. Bettina need not know anything about it.

AFTERWORD

Thank you for reading my book! If you liked it, please write a review for Amazon, it would mean a lot to me. Here's the link to get the free companion novella to this book, "The Witch of Darkwood," Henna's origin story. Grab yours, and join my Newsletter.https://www.subscribepage.com/m2f4a3

I love connecting with readers. You can join me and other readers of the series (who help me name characters and are able to join my ARC team for free first looks at books): https://www.facebook.com/groups/874094903257492

I also have a weekly blog about eating, playing and writing. Good recipes, too. Go to https://www.eatwriteplay.com

ACKNOWLEDGMENTS

Thank you to the wonderful people who helped make this book possible:

My family: For your sustaining belief in me, and not coming into the writing area when the door was closed.

My amazing Beta Readers, Jasmin Zamora, Grace Reed, and Paola Turner: For all the catches, and suggestions, and liking what you were reading. Yes, Paola, the city *is* on the left side of the river...

The sharp-eyed Julie Kramer for proofreading, and telling me that people are *always* aware of the breath they are holding.

Cover Artist Lauren Johnson from allaboutbookcovers for her patience and artistry.

And thank you dear reader, the most important of all.

ABOUT AUTHOR

Stacey is a produced writer of screenplays and plays. She and her husband have raised three lovely people and have a beloved rescue dog who saved them from a house fire. When she is not reading or writing, Stacey goes for walks, long swims, and bakes. She gets nearly all of her ideas doing one of those three things.

Made in United States
Orlando, FL
12 March 2022

15691109R00161